CRITICAL ACCLAIM FOR *THE WHITE BOY SHUFFLE*

"*The White Boy Shuffle* is one of those novels of enormous energy and verbal dazzle. . . . Mr. Beatty is a fertile and original writer, one to watch."
—*The New York Times*

"A bombastic coming-of-age novel set in L.A. . . . *The White Boy Shuffle* has the uncanny ability to make readers want to laugh and cry at the same time. Beatty mingles horrific reality with wild fancy without ever losing a grip on his story."
—*Los Angeles Times*

"Laugh-out-loud funny and weep-in-silence sad. . . . The language is always vibrant and alluring."
—*The Nation*

"Ferocious and funny, literate and also streetwise, *The White Boy Shuffle* celebrates exuberantly its own virtuoso range while dishing out merciless social satire."
—*The Boston Sunday Globe*

"An achingly funny first novel. . . . Beatty is an acute observer of stereotypes and delights in examining them and then twisting them around. . . . Captures the problems and challenges of young blacks with a precision that ought to put most sociologists to shame."
—*The Denver Post*

"*The White Boy Shuffle* is farcical, topical, and fueled by a profoundly zany imagination. . . . Beatty's satire is deadly. . . . No stereotype goes unexamined."
—*Newsday*

D0201824

"This poet's hip-hop epic never misses a beat. . . . Simultaneously hilarious . . . and immensely moving, Beatty's Pynchonesque non sequiturs cascade with the seeming ease of an Armstrong trill."

—*The New Yorker*

"From that first page to the epilogue . . . it's a hell of a ride."

—*Newsweek*

"*The White Boy Shuffle* is an eloquent, intelligent work of fiction that cross-references cartoons, Roller Derby, and Spike Lee."

—*The Village Voice*

"*The White Boy Shuffle* is not only a funny and engaging novel, it is an intelligent story about race and class in America. Reading it is like taking a long ride with a lunatic. You will hear things you probably never heard before and you'll be taken places you never thought you'd go."

—*The Philadelphia City Paper*

"Beatty drags you by the ear through a hilarious, no-holds-barred, tragically gut-wrenching ride. His syncopative, intravenous linguistic groove is a deceptive foil to his crisp sociological cynicism and nonstop nihilism. Chuckles and tears are no longer mutually exclusive as Beatty, pen poised, lets the hot air out of any self-aggrandizing movement, personage, belief, institution, or sect, from Afrocentrism and white PC liberalism to academics and athletics."

—*The San Francisco Review*

"Beatty . . . shows himself as an astute observer of the ubiquitous power of cultural stereotype and of the elasticity of identity and community. . . . Beatty has a gift for hyperbolic cartoon-like characterizations and poetic parody and a sharp ear for the vivid spoken-word poetry of hip-hop and urban black slang. . . . His language and outlandish characters combine to produce an extravagantly comic vision of the American cultural moment."

—*Publishers Weekly*

the white boy shuffle

the white boy shuffle
Paul Beatty

An Owl Book

Henry Holt and Company
New York

Pam Spritzer, thank you

Henry Holt and Company, Inc.
Publishers since 1866
115 West 18th Street
New York, New York 10011

Henry Holt® is a registered
trademark of Henry Holt and Company, Inc.

Published in Canada by Fitzhenry & Whiteside Ltd.,
195 Allstate Parkway, Markham, Ontario L3R 4T8.

Library of Congress Cataloging-in-Publication Data
Beatty, Paul.
The white boy shuffle / Paul Beatty.—1st Owl book ed.
p.   cm.
"An Owl book."
ISBN 0-8050-5351-4 (alk. paper)
1. Afro-American men—Fiction.   I. Title.
PS3552.E19W45   1997   97-9991
813'.54—dc21   CIP

Henry Holt books are available for special promotions and
premiums. For details contact: Director, Special Markets.

First published in hardcover in 1996 by
Houghton Mifflin Company.

Designed by Melodie Wertelet

First Owl Book Edition—1997

Printed in the United States of America
All first editions are printed on acid-free paper.∞

5   7   9   10   8   6   4

For Yvonne Beatty,
my mother

the white boy shuffle

prologue

ON ONE HAND this messiah gig is a bitch. On the other I've managed to fill the perennial void in African-American leadership. There is no longer a need for fed-up second-class citizens to place a want ad in the Sunday classifieds reading:

> Negro Demagogue
> Must have ability to lead a divided, downtrodden, and alien-ated people to the Promised Land. Good communication skills required. Pay commensurate with ability. No experience necessary.

Being a poet, and thus expert in the ways of soulful coercion, I am eminently qualified. My book, *Watermelanin,* has sold 126 million copies. I have the ear of the academics, the street denizens, and the political cabalists. Leader of the Black Community? There is no better job fit.

I didn't interview for the job. I was drafted by 22 million hitherto unaffiliated souls into serving as full-time Svengali and foster parent to an abandoned people. I spoon-feed them grueled futility, unveil the oblivion that is black America's existence and the hopelessness of the struggle. In return I receive fanatical avian obedience. Wherever I travel, a long queue of baby black goslings files behind a plastic wind-up bard spring-driven toward self-destruction, crossing the information superhighway and refusing to look both ways. If a movie mogul buys the film rights to my life, the *TV Guide* synopsis will read:

> In the struggle for freedom, a reluctant young poet convinces black Americans to give up hope and kill themselves in a climactic crash 'n' burn finale. Full of laughs and high jinks. Some violence and adult language.

In the quest for equality, black folks have tried everything. We've begged, revolted, entertained, intermarried, and are still treated like shit. Nothing works, so why suffer the slow deaths of toxic addiction and the American work ethic when the immediate gratification of suicide awaits? In glorious defiance of the survival instinct, Negroes stream into Hillside, California, like lemmings. Every day they wishfully look heavenward, peering into the California smog for a metallic gray atomic dot that will gradually expand until it explodes some one thousand feet over our natural and processed heads. It will be the Emancipation Disintegration. Lunch counters, bus seats, and executive washrooms be damned; our mass suicide will be the ultimate sit-in.

They're all here, the black American iconographic array, making final preparations for Elysium approximately five hundred years after our arrival in this purgatory. The well-dressed guy who worked in the corporate mailroom and malapropped his way through your patronizing efforts to engage him in small talk wonders if he left the stove on, then laughs aloud at the absurdity of it all. The innocuous Democratic ex-mayor of your city writes mediocre elegiac verse without a nod to the absurdity of it all. That fine young black thing you drooled over in eighth-grade gym class struts up and down the block looking for one last world to rock. The woman who sat next to you clutching her handbag while you waited for the morning bus and then elbowed you in the solar plexus fighting for a seat plans to call her boss and talk shit until the last minute, then put the receiver to the explosion, saying, "I won't be in to work tomorrow. I'll be a fuckin' evaporated carbon dustball. You slave-drivin' fuck."

Last week's issue of *Time* magazine identified me as the "Ebon Pied Piper." In *U.S. News & World Report* I was "the bellwether to ethnic hara-kiri." History will add my name to the list of maniacal messiahs who sit in Hell's homeroom answering the Devil's roll call: Jim Jones, David Koresh, whoever led the charge of the Light Brigade, Charles Manson, General Westmoreland, and me. These pages are my memoirs, the battlefield remains of a frightened deserter in the eternal war for civility.

Paul Beatty

"mama baby, papa maybe"

one

UNLIKE THE TYPICAL bluesy earthy folksy denim-overalls noble-in-the-face-of-cracker-racism aw shucks Pulitzer-Prize-winning protagonist mojo magic black man, I am not the seventh son of a seventh son of a seventh son. I wish I were, but fate shorted me by six brothers and three uncles. The chieftains and queens who sit on top of old Mount Kilimanjaro left me out of the will. They bequeathed me nothing, stingy bastards. Cruelly cheating me of my mythological inheritance, my aboriginal superpowers. I never possessed the god-given ability to strike down race politic evildoers with a tribal chant, the wave of a beaded whammy stick, and a mean glance. Maybe some family fool fucked up and slighted the ancients. Pissed off the gods, too much mumbo in the jumbo perhaps, and so the sons must suffer the sins of the father.

My name is Kaufman, Gunnar Kaufman. I'm black Orestes in the cursed House of Atreus. Preordained by a set of weak-kneed DNA to shuffle in the footsteps of a long cowardly queue of coons, Uncle Toms, and faithful boogedy-boogedy retainers. I am the number-one son of a spineless colorstruck son of a bitch who was the third son of an ass-kissing sell-out house Negro who was indeed a seventh son but only by default. (Grandpa Giuseppi Kaufman rolled over his older twin brother Johann in his sleep, smothering him and staking claim to the cherished seventh sonship.) From birth my parents indoctrinated me with the idea that the surreal escapades and "I's a-comin'" watermelon chicanery of my forefathers was the stuff a hero worship. Their resolute deeds and Uncle Tom exploits were passed down by my mother's dinner table macaroni-and-cheese oral history lessons. There is nothing worse than a loud griot, and my mother was the loudest.

Mom raised my sisters and me as the hard-won spoils of a vicious custody battle that left the porcelain shrapnel of supper-dish grenades embedded in my father's neck. The divorce made Mama, Ms. Brenda W. Kaufman, determined to make sure that her children knew their forebears. As a Brooklyn orphan who had never seen her parents or her birth certificate, Mom adopted my father's patriarchal family history for her misbegotten origins.

On summer afternoons Nicole, Christina, and I sat at my mother's feet, tracing our bloodlines by running our fingers over the bulging veins that tunneled in her ashy legs. She'd place her hideous pedal extremities on a throw pillow and we would conduct our ancestral investigation while filing down the rock-hard bunions and other dermal crustaceans on her feet.

We started with the basics. Danger, Kids at Work. Nicole, my youngest sister, whom I nicknamed the Incredible Eternal Wailing Baby, would open up the questioning in her self-centered style, all the while scraping the mound of dead skin that was my mother's left heel.

"Maw, am I adopted?"

"No, you are not adopted. I showed you the stretch marks last week. Put some elbow grease into it, goddammit. Pull the skin off with your fingers if you have to, shit."

Then Christina, middle child, whom I lovingly rechristened with the Native American appellation Fingers-in-Both-Nostrils-Thumb-in-Mouth-and-Snot-All-Over-the-Fucking-Place, would pull on the heartstrings to tighten the filial ties.

"What about me and Gunnar?"

"No."

"Can you prove it?" Christina would ask, anxious and unconvinced, her heavy breathing blowing mucus bubbles from her nose.

"Which ones those crinkly lines on your stomach is mines?"

"Chrissy, if anyone is fool enough to tell you that they your parents, believe them. Okay?"

"Maw."

"What, Gunnar?"

"Your feet stank."

"Shut up before I make you fill out that application to military school."

The advanced course in Kaufman genealogy didn't start until Mom returned home from earning our livings by testing the unlucky poor for VD at a free clinic in East Los Angeles. I remember she enjoyed bringing the sharp stainless-steel tools of her trade and glossy Polaroids of the most advanced cases to the dinner table. Spit-shining the speculums and catheters, she'd tell her awful jokes about "pricking the pricks and hunting the cunts." I swear somewhere in her unknown past traveling minstrels cakewalked across candlelit theater stages.

The seven o'clock suppers were carnival sideshows, featuring Mom the Amazing Crazy Lady. She'd wipe our greasy lips, lecturing us about the horrors of sexually transmitted disease while passing mashed potatoes and photos of pussy lesions around the table. For the coup de grâce she'd open a prophylactic package, remove and unroll a blue sheath, and stuff the receptacle end into a nostril. Then she'd sit there lecturing us about the joys of safe sex with a crumpled condom swinging from her nose and bouncing off her chin with each syllable. Suddenly she'd press the open nostril closed with her finger and with a snort snake the unlubricated rubber up her nose. She'd open her mouth and produce a soggy piece of latex, holding it up for all to see with a gloating "Ta-dah. Let's eat."

The festivities continued throughout the meal. Though her designation as world's loudest griot cannot be substantiated, the *Guinness Book of World Records* lists her as having the world's loudest swallow.

SWALLOW. Ms. Brenda W. Kaufman (b. 1955) of Los Angeles recorded unamplified swallows at 47 db (busy street = 70 db, jet engine = 130) while guesting on the David Letterman show drinking New York City tap water on May 3, 1985.

On her birthdays I watch the videotape of her performance. A man with an English accent holds a microphone to her throat while she enthusiastically drinks a clear glass of water. In the bottom righthand corner of the screen is a VU meter with a needle that jumps wildly with every booming swallow. My sisters and I yelled our heads off every time the needle moved into the red zone.

When she returned, we proudly took turns placing our fingers on her bobbing Adam's apple as she drank her milk. Between swallows Mom would ask about our schoolwork and bemoan our miseducations. Slamming down an empty glass of milk, she'd run her tongue over her top lip and bellow, "See, there isn't anything a Kaufman can't do. Those history books say anything about your great-great-great-great-great-great-great-grandfather on your father's side, Euripides Kaufman? Betcha they don't. Pass the fucking dinner buns and let Mama tell you about a colonial Negro who would've pulled himself up by the bootstraps had he had boots. The first of a legacy of colored men who forged their own way in the world. Gunnar, you listenin'?"

"Uh-huh."

"What?"

"Yes, ma'am."

Mom could tell a motherfucking story. She'd start in with Euripides Kaufman, the youngest slave in history to buy his freedom. I heard the chains shackled to the spirits of Kaufman Negroes past slink and rattle up to the dining room windows. Dead niggers who smacked their arid lips and held their rumbling vacuous stomachs while they stared at the fried chicken, waiting for Mom to tell their tales.

Too small to smelt and work iron in his master's Boston blacksmith shop, Euripides spent his bondage doing donkey work. After running barefoot errands over the downtown cobblestones, he'd look for ways to fill his idle time. Sitting on the grassy banks of the Charles River, he'd watch the jongleurs woo money from the pockets of sentimental passersby. At age seven Euripides saw a means of income. The baby entrepreneur ran home, spread globs of lamp oil over sooty black skin, and parked himself outside the busiest entrance to the Boston Common. Every promenading Bostonian who passed him by answered Euripides's toothy obsequious grin and gleaming complexion with a concerned "Can I help you, son?" To which Euripides replied, "Would you like to rub me head for good luck? Cost a sixpence."

Soon Euripides had a steady clientele of Brahmins and Tories, redcoats and militiamen paying to pass their palms over his bristly head for luck and a guaranteed afterlife. Six months later he decided to shave his skull to heighten the tactile pleasure, and business boomed. Word quickly got back to his owner and eponym Chauncy Kaufman about the little tar baby's ingenuity in bringing a small measure of fame to his shop. Soon customers came into the shop to have their horses shod and to pat the "l'il black bastard's" head. Customers rode up, tied their horses to the hitching post, and proclaimed, "Four new shoes, Chauncy. Where's Euripides? Last week I forgot to palm his stubbly skull and the missus caught me buggering the Negro lass in the attic. Come 'ere, you baldheaded good-luck charm, you."

One mild spring day the nine-year-old Euripides puzzled out how much to charge for a "He's so cute" grab 'n' twist of the cheek. He looked up to see a black boy about his age auctioned off next to a fruit stand for fifteen pounds. "Snookums, on your way back from getting the wig powdered at the coiffeur's, would you please pick up some tomatoes, a head of lettuce, and a little nigger child?" Ever the shrewd businesskid and eager to appraise his own worth, Euripides asked his sweaty coal-faced owner if he was worth fifteen pounds on the open market. Master Kaufman assured Euripides that a clever pickaninny such as himself was worth twice that amount. Euripides then reached into his satchel and plonked down thirty pounds in savings from his head-rubbing business on the anvil. Euripides Kaufman walked out of the shop a nine-year-old freeman, never giving a second thought to buying a hat. He went on to become a merchant sailor who attained unheralded fame for being, in Mama's words, "the brains behind the Boston Massacre."

Familial legend has it that on March 5, 1770, Euripides Kaufman artfully dodged a redcoat's musket shot with his name on it and Crispus Attucks woke up in nigger heaven a martyr. That historic afternoon Euripides and Crispus, his ace boon coon since childhood, sat in a Boston pub drinking drafts of Samuel Adam's pale ale. Oh to be free, black, and twenty-one, drunk on home-brewed hops and the mascot-like acceptance of his fellow white merchant seafarers. The only drawback to Euripides's freedom was that he couldn't charge when the locals rubbed his head with vigorous patronization. "Euripides, you dusky halyard-knot–headed black bloke, how old were you when you started to shed your monkey fur? Maybe you still sleep in it to keep warm at night?"

What're a few nigger jokes among friends? We Kaufmans have always been the type of niggers who can take a joke. I used to visit my father, the sketch artist at the Wilshire LAPD precinct. His fellow officers would stand around cluttered desks breaking themselves up by telling how-many-niggers-does-it-take jokes, pounding each other on the back and looking over their broad shoulders to see if me and Daddy were laughing. Dad always was. The epaulets on his shoulders raising up like inchworms as he giggled. I never laughed until my father slapped me hard between the shoulder blades. The heavy-handed blow bringing my weight to my tiptoes, raising my chin from my chest, and I'd burp out a couple of titters of self-defilement. Even if I didn't get the joke. "What they mean, 'Lick their lips and stick 'em to the wall'?" Later I'd watch my father draw composite sketches for victimized citizens who used his face as reference point. "He was thick-lipped, nose a tad bigger than yours, with your nostril flare though." Daddy would bring some felon to still life and without looking up from his measured strokes admonish me that my face better not appear on any police officer's sketchpad. He'd send me home in a patrol car, black charcoal smudged all over my face and his patriotic wisdom ringing in my ears: "Remember, Gunnar, God, country, and laughter, the world's best medicine. Did your mother get the check?"

It figures a sell-out Kaufman helped jump-start the American Revolution.

Liver-lipped Euripides Kaufman, pint full, whistle and lips wet, deftly redirected the scorn of his colonial rabble-rousing shipmates from him onto a lone adolescent redcoat sentinel stationed in front of the House of Commons just outside the tavern. "Hey, blokes. Isn't that lobster-backed scoundrel the Brit scalawag who cheated the barber Jack Milton out of the coinage for a fair-priced trimming 'n' shave yesterday past?" With Euripides and Crispus leading the way, the drunken mob scampered outside for a closer look. Mugs in hand, they surrounded the nervous guard and peppered him with insults. Euripides stood about a yard away from the redcoat, looked him up and down, turned to his mates, and said, "Verily, that's the tea-and-crumpet-eating-scofflaw. Crispus will support me claim, won't you, big boy?"

Crispus's eyes, like my father's, like Euripides's, were eager to please, but his mouth was empty of revolutionary dozens. Pining for white America's affection, Crispus Attucks looked toward my great-great-great-great-great-great-great-grandad for guidance. Then he parroted Euripides Kaufman's caustic sentiments into the face of the lone attaché of England's New World venture capitalism. "Aye, a Cockney chimpanzee with his sparkling flushed pink arse a bit distant from the rest of the pack. Where's your scone-colored missus? Snuggling up to King George, rubbing his pasty paunch and counting our taxes? Squawk! Crispus Attucks wants a cracker! Squawk!"

How could two nominally free niggers be more libertine? Inciting the colony's whine for independence, black booster engines to the forthcoming rocket's red glare. At some point during the famous imbroglio, Euripides, emboldened and bloated with beer, took out his penis and produced a pool of piss in front of the brigade of British reinforcements. Sensing that the armed platoon had reached its saturation point, he shouted, "Tax this!" and smartly marched to the rear of the now uproarious crowd. Leaving an inky, drunken Crispus Attucks fronting the overwhelmingly white mob, blathering unintelligible insults to the throne, threatening the entire British empire with his wooden nigger-beater. Then the now famous volley of shoots and thud of bodies flopping onto the dusty cobblestones.

American history found Crispus Attucks dead on a Boston street, but has yet to find Euripides Kaufman's contribution. At the subsequent trial a witness for the prosecution recounted that he heard the soldier who deposited the ball of lead in Crispus's heart regretfully say, "Damn, I shot the wrong bloody nigger." Good thing too, because had that British soldier shot the right nigger, my seventh-grade class at Manischewitz Junior High would never have gotten to laugh at the ridiculous sons and daughters of the confederacy's servant class. All fathered by my great-to-the-seventh-power granddad Euripides Kaufman.

It was in Ms. Murphy's class that for the first time anyone outside my immediate family heard the tales of the groveling Kaufman male birthright. During Black History Month, to put a class of rootless urchins in touch with our disparate niggerhoods, Ms. Murphy assigned us to make family trees. Although most kids could only go back as far as their grandparents, it was with unabashed pride that we gave oral encapsulations of our caricature American ancestries. No one knew enough to be embarrassed at not knowing our own histories, much less those of any of the posterboard Negro heroes on the walls.

I sat midway up the first row of seats in from the door, bored with kids holding up their family trees and giving the same speech: "Ummmmm, the boys are the circles and the girls have the triangle heads. This is me. My six sisters. My brother, he dead. My other brother, he dead too. My mom. My dad. And here go my grandparents. My grandfather was in Vietnam and he crazy. Any questions? Where was my mother born? She was born in Arkansas and she met my father on the Greyhound bus. They fell in love in San Antonio and he touched her in the restrooms in Tucumcari, New Mexico. Then I came. Fuck you, Denise, I wasn't born in no nickel pay toilet."

Finally Ms. Murphy called my name. I tucked my family tree under my arm and made my way to the front of the classroom, slapping my boy Jimmy Lopez upside his noggin for good measure. Lifting one hand high above my head, I unfurled my gigantic family tree. It rolled well past my knees and the class ooohed the generations of crinkled stick nigger couples holding stick hands.

I started at the top, with Euripides Kaufman, and went from there. With my mother's hand in my back, her words pouring from my mouth, I stiffly yapped on like a skinny ventriloquist's dummy. I told the class how the Kaufmans migrated south when Swen Kaufman, Euripides's well-traveled grandson, left Boston, unintentionally becoming the only person ever to run away into slavery. Being persona non anglo-saxon, Swen was unable to fulfill his uppity dreams of becoming a serious dancer. He was unwelcome in serious dance circles, and the local variety shows couldn't use his "Frenchified royal court body syncopations" in their coony-coony minstrel productions. "Take the crown off your head, jigaboo. Show some teeth," they said. Swen would stoop and bow under any other circumstances, but when it came to dance he refused to compromise. So on a windy night he packed his ballet slippers and stowed away on a merchant ship bound for the Cotton Belt.

Debarking in coastal North Carolina, Swen set out on a sojourn, seeking artistic freedom. He traipsed the tobacco roads, using his New England blue-blood diction to put off the curiosities of those concerned with his freeman status. When he ran across lynch mobs, hound dogs, and defenseless parasol-toting Southern belles, he'd simultaneously gaze at their feet and hold his nose just high enough to suggest a hint of breeding. Answering their inquiries, Swen rolled his r's in polite deference.

"You ain't from 'round here, is you, bwoy?"

"No sir. Do the leotards give me away, sir?"

"Mind if we ask you in a few questions?"

"Why no, I fully understand your rrrreasons for rrrrrousting me under suspicion of my being a rrrrrunaway Negrrrrrro. Please rrrrrrresume your interrogation forrrthwith."

"You ain't Scottish, iz ya, bwoy?"

After three days on the road, Swen found himself on the outskirts of a small farming town called Mercy, North Carolina. There he came upon the fields of the Tannenberry plantation, where some slave hands were turning up rows of tobacco. The rise-and-fall rhythm of the hoes and pickaxes and the austere urgency of the work songs gave him an idea for a "groundbreaking" dance opera. A renegade piece that intertwined the stoic movement of forced labor with the casual assuredness of the aristocratic lyric. Entranced with the possibilities, Swen impetuously hopped the wooden fence that separated the slave from the free. Picking up a tool, he smiled at the bewildered nigger next to him and churned feudal earth until sundown, determined to learn the ways of the field slaves. I suppose the niggers warned him, but Swen wouldn't have understood their pidgin drawl. "Fool, I don't know who you is, but whoebba you is, if you gwine slave in this heah tobacky row, you bettuh stop scatterin' the top serl in the wind. 'Cuz if de Tannenberrys don't eat, den you knows the pigs and chickens gwine watch the niggers die." Swen headed back to Marse Tom Tannenberry's sleeping quarters happy with his first day of slavery. He went to bed that night on a stomach full of pig ears and corn leaves, and from every daybreak until his death he woke up an unindentured servant.

Initially, upon seeing a free extra hand in the cabins, Marse Tom Tannenberry smiled at his good fortune, recalling poorer days when family members outnumbered the slaves. A precocious Confederate tyke, he'd pulled on Grandma Verona's billowing yellow whalebone dress, pleading and pouting for a nigger of his own. Marse Tom recalled the spittle and scorn in her voice when she replied with something about darkies not growing on trees.

In the chill of a just-breaking morning, Swen Kaufman danced to work. Giddily in rehearsal for his magnum opus, his lanky frame spun "jump, ball, change" in the lifting dark North Carolinian mist. The slaves hated him. Marse Tom grew to hate him. Swen returned from the fields happier than he'd ever been in Boston. He considered himself dancer-in-residence at the Tannenberry plantation, free room and board and plenty of rehearsal space. Come sundown the dirty energetic primo cotton picker pranced home, back straight, chin up, a Yankee clipper lost at sea, pointing his toes in the wind.

Marse Tom decided Swen's cultured Boston manners and skip-to-my-lou verve were bad for morale. Worse yet was the fascination in Missus Courtney Tannenberry's lit-up cheeky countenance as she sat around listening to Swen's stories of his carefree European escapades as a fashionable *valet noir* for a French choreographer. Raised in northern Virginia, Missus Tannenberry considered herself a balletomane and aficionado of high art. She'd sit under the bighouse portico fanning herself and aching for culture not based on agrarian harvest cycles. Swen was eager to play raconteur. Excused by the missus from fieldwork, he'd fill her swooning head with stories of dining in seaport bistros in Marseilles and witnessing the exquisite nascence of modern dance at the Paris Opera, the Royal Theater in Copenhagen, and London's renowned King Theater. They discussed Swen's theories on how the rigid daring obstinate Russian psyche would push ballet to the heights of expressionistic art. Punctuating his points with leaps and sashays around the gazebo, Swen conducted ironic lectures on how the tradition of European patrician gloating and African tribal rituals influenced the Southern cotillions. In wishful reenactments of performances staged hundreds of times in his head, he'd spin and lift Missus Tannenberry's toddling daughters to the clouds. Marse Tom wasn't havin' it and demanded that Swen leave the grounds. Swen refused. How could he leave midway through choreographing a hand dance based on the dexterity needed to remove cotton balls cleanly from the stem and the intricacies of the Missus's crocheting techniques?

Didn't a whole lot of niggers get whipped on Tom Tannenberry's plantation, but Marse Tom whipped Swen Kaufman. Demi-plié — five lashes. Second position — ten lashes. Pirouette over the cotton seedlings — fifteen lashes; rock salt and scotch in the wounds. A performance of Swen's "Dance of the Discreet Glance" behind the stables merited a beating that started the dogs barking and kept slaves and masters up through the night listening to Swen's skin sizzle. Eventually the slaves came to admire Swen's persistence and to appreciate his art, but not before Tom Tannenberry beat the classic romanticism out of Swen's feet and slapped the worldly effluvium from his mouth. Crumpled and broken on the ground, lips painted with blood, face powdered with red clay dust, Swen was told he could nigger jig to his heart's content.

He healed and did, soon falling in love with his favorite partner, Clocinda Didion. Swen and Clocinda's wedding was his final performance. Under the guise of rehearsing an elaborate wedding ceremony, he used every slave on the plantation in a glorious swirling production. On the wedding day they danced. To the accompaniment of body drums and fiddles, maids of honor, bridegroom, and guests swooped across the fields. They tightroped the tops of fences many had never even dared look at, much less touch. For most it was the first time they'd been within twenty yards of the fences. The audience consisted of the pregnant Missus Tannenberry and her four daughters, trailing the action as it traversed the grounds, applauding at the appropriate intervals. In the middle of the ceremony the Tannenberry women held the broom, cheering as the happy helot couple jumped over it, kissing in midair, landing in matrimony. In the last movement the adults passed unlit torches to the children, then lay in the slaves' graveyard next to the mounds of earth and rotted tombstones. The children peered into the windows of the bighouse, the still unlit torches resting on their bony shoulders. Then they too went to the graveyard and lay down next to their parents. Missus Tannenberry cried for a month afterward and on every anniversary of Clocinda and Swen's regal wedding visited the graveyard.

All this before recess. Over coffeecake and chocolate milk, kids who normally spent the respite from math teasing me about the length of my pants and placing bets on which of two shirts I would wear tomorrow begged me to continue my story.

"What happened next?"

"Why didn't they light the torches?"

"How much is a sixpence in American money?"

"Did Euripides Kaufman know George Washington?"

"What happened next, motherfucker?"

The bell rang and they rushed back to the classroom to find Ms. Murphy sitting on the edge of her desk. The students sat in little plastic orange chairs and leaned over the tabletops. All ears and big eyes. I continued my presentation, swelling with a strange pride.

Swen and Clocinda Kaufman begat some astoundingly servile niggers. One of whom, Franz von Kaufman, was exceedingly bootlicking even for a slave. Franz von Kaufman was born looking like the quintessential Mathew Brady 1857 nigger daguerreotype. Though fresh out of Clocinda's womb, Franz von's glossy dark black skin was fissured by creased and starched wrinkles. A shock of wispy gray hair capped a sunken face, tight lips, and sullen yellow watery suffering eyes. Everyone called him "Old Franz von." Missus Tannenberry delivered Compton Benjamin Quentin, the Tannenberry's youngest and only male child, within days of Franz von. The two boys shared the same crib and nipples. Even in infancy Franz von's subservience was evident. If baby Marse Compton wanted the nipple Franz von suckled, he'd nudge Franz von, whine, and drool in his ear, and Franz von would move without complaint. No whining, no whimpering. Clocinda soon figured out that the little Tannenberry devil was born greedy and nearly blind.

The stubborn Compton fancied himself a brave explorer and refused to let his poor sight handicap him. One nose-to-nose close-up look at his dusky running buddy Old Franz von and young Marse Compton knew intuitively that to realize his lofty goals, he'd need a loyal manservant. He asked his father that Franz von be given to him, and Tom Tannenberry, remembering his longing for a "nigger of his own," quickly agreed. While Franz von was still a pup, Marse Tom handed his leash over to Compton Tannenberry. "Remember, son, you promised to take care of it."

In years to come Old Franz von served as Compton's Seeing Eye dog, constant companion, and best friend. Franz von and Compton could be found playing Inquisition in the walnut groves. This game was a degenerate version of hide-and-seek where Franz von would roll in a honeysuckle patch and then play the heathen. Bathed in young Marse Compton's favorite smell, Franz von would hide among the walnut trees, awaiting discovery and salvation. The sightless erstwhile Torquemada would seek Franz von out, nose open for the unique scent of honeysuckle and unwashed infidel. His ears honing in on Franz von's faux heretic war cries and blasphemes. "The creek's burble 'n' gurgle, the rustle in the leaves, are the boogers, sniffles, and breeze of the sneezing gods of Dixie." Compton would find Franz von, tie him to a tree, trade his spit for Franz von's land and soul, pelt him with walnuts, and convert the swarthy pagan by reciting biblical verse.

Time aged Marse Compton more than it did Franz von. At twenty-five Old Franz von remained a taller version of the tame Negro he'd always been; only the wrinkles circling his eyes and lips had deepened. He hadn't grown wiser, more worldly, or even bitter about his servitude. Newfangled ideas confused him. Franz von the young adult didn't understand the nigger talk about abolition, or the white folks'

Paul Beatty

pride in their metal gunboats. Those Braille books Marse Compton got with increasing frequency in the mail frightened him. How could he read Marse Compton the poems of Ovid and Homer if the great myths were transformed to raised dots? "Can't teach an old nigger new tricks," the Tannenberrys teased him. Old Franz von laughed at their perceptiveness and stayed by Compton's side, safely leading him past the few pitfalls faced by a spoiled Southern aristocrat.

Compton Tannenberry slipped just as easily into his destined adulthood. The denizens of Mercy marveled at the contrast of his princely smooth upright blind gait to Franz von's sighted slumped-over shuffle. In Compton's presence the white folks could often be heard saying how he'd aged gracefully, gone from barley malt to fine scotch whisky. When Marse Compton wasn't around, the niggers who toiled under the sun and his Confederate shogunate would say that Marse Compton hadn't aged but curdled like stagnant milk. His white arrogance had piled and thickened, casting its sour odor wherever he went.

Sundays were for church 'n' cards. In the afternoon Franz von sat in an unvarnished pew in the farthest corner of the Anglican Saxon Triple Baptist Church. From there he watched the good Reverend William Dern deliver sermons that alternated between damnation and salvation. Compton Tannenberry allowed no one but Franz von to shepherd him down the aisle to partake in the communion. He held Franz von tightly at the elbow while receiving the vintage spirit and the cracker body of Christ. Nights were spent in the sacrosanct parlors of the Mercy Socialite Club for Genteel Gentlemen. During the high-stakes poker games Franz von sat at Compton's side, placing Compton's bets for him, tapping out their secret code on Compton's arm to let him know the cards in his hand. Compton quickly calculated his odds, and Franz von humbly reeled in the winnings from the astonished stately Tar Heel gentry. Once safely away from the gaming tables, Franz von and Compton would tell their running joke that they had the advantage because no one could read a blind man's eyes and no one could read a nigger's mind.

When the Civil War broke out, Compton enthusiastically went to enlist, knowing that he'd be turned away but hoping to serve the South in some capacity. As expected, the draft board told Compton he was unfit for combat, though his breeding, poker face, and guile could be used in other ways. The Confederacy asked him to be the chief negotiator in the top-secret trading of surplus bales of Southern cotton for the Union opium the Rebels desperately needed to treat their wounded. This job required Compton to take a train from Durham to Washington, D.C., every two weeks to meet with the penny-pinching Yankees. The catch was that Franz von couldn't accompany his master on these missions, since a crafty nigra, even one as outwardly dutiful as Franz von, would be an unnecessary breach of security.

Franz von spent the first two years of his war fighting separation anxiety and faithfully awaiting the 6:15 P.M. arrival of the Hootenanny Choo-Choo from Washington, D.C. Franz von was never happier than serving as his friend's footstool into the carriage that carried them back to the Tannenberry plantation.

Sunday, March 27, 1864. The 6:15 pulled in and Marse Compton Tannenberry's cane never made its exploratory pokes from the first-class car. Compton's whiny yell of "Where's my nigger?" failed to travel down the length of the platform. Franz von waited for hours, then drove the empty buggy back to the plantation. Why won't the Tannenberrys look him in the eye when he tells them Marse Tom wasn't on the train? Franz von returns to the station at 6:15 the next night and every night for the rest of his life, looking every passenger that gets off the train dead in the face. No one ever had the nerve to tell Franz von that his comrade and owner died when he accidentally swallowed a piece of opium he was transporting, mistaking it for one of the sugar cubes he brought back for Old Franz von and the unrequisitioned horses.

I wish that my shameful history had stopped with pitiful Franz von, that I could say that after years of obedience my forefathers embraced the twentieth century's waves of black pride. The seventh-graders ate quiet lunches in the school cafeteria. I told the story of Wolfgang Kaufman to the rustle of brown paper bags and the muffled crunches of mouthfuls of potato chips. Wolfgang Kaufman was my great-great-uncle who once held the highest appointed municipal position a Negro in Nashville, Tennessee, could aspire to in the 1920s, chief of the Department of Visual Segregation. With Jim Crow as his muse, he spent muggy afternoons under a splotchy painter's cap, painting and hanging the FOR WHITES ONLY and FOR COLORED ONLY signs that hung over quasi-public places throughout Nashville. At five dollars an hour, not many Nashville blacks were doing much better, and Wolfgang took pride in his stenciled artistry. A fit of absentmindedness caused him to lose the precious contract when he was spotted exiting from the men's room after taking a satisfying early-morning number two in the whites-only toilet. The sight of a dark black man zipping up his fly and pulling underwear from the crack of his ass was too much for any virtuous white woman, especially the one passed out in horror at his feet. Ms. O'Dwyer came to with Wolfgang hovering over her face, apologetically jabbering something about there being no toilet paper in the colored washroom. Quickly regaining her faculties and privileged sensibilities, Ms. O'Dwyer slapped Wolfgang across his pleading lips and reported him to the mayor's office. Some benevolent civic official commuted his lynching, and soon after the nigger moved to Chicago and was polishing floors at WGN radio with a huge "Thank ya, Lawd" smile on his face.

One sunny Tuesday morning a tacky fat-and-skinny twosome barreled into the station to rehearse scenarios for a new radio show. Wolfgang briefly stopped squeegeeing the soundstage windows to listen to the duo, Freeman F. Gosden and Charles J. Correll, run through their stale repertoire. "Funny thing happened to me on the way to the station today." Along with the station managers, Wolfgang groaned and covered his ears, remembering hearing their baritone voices when he was hightailing through New Orleans. They were good mimics, but their material was awful. Wolfgang decided to help the boys out. During a break in rehearsal, he popped his derby-topped head into the studio, removed the stubby cigar from his mouth, and suggested to the worried-looking Gosden and Correll that they join him for lunch. "Y'all gonna hear some real comedic genius." Having nothing to lose, the white boys followed Wolfgang to the Chicago Circle Cab Company, where a group of cabbies on their lunch breaks sat inside the dispatch booth talking about each other's shortcomings and women and telling hilarious, if only slightly exaggerated, stories of black life in a big city. The bashful peckerwoods sat dumbfounded on the fender of a broken-down cab. Neither man had ever contemplated the existence of a black society beyond elevator operators and occasional snapshots of well-to-do Negroes in the *Sun-Times*. Here were men talking in a myriad of dialects about a vivacious life which to most of America was invisible. The butt of most of the jokes was an understated college-educated cabdriver named Enos. The loudest and most rambunctious of the Negro storytellers was a plump unemployed dandy named Sandy. Wolfgang smiled as the similarities in physique and personality dawned on the struggling radio personalities. Wolfgang stood up and sang a slow rendition of "Carry Me Back to Ol' Virginny," and Gosden and Correll raced back to the station, their heads buzzing with ideas for a weekly show called *Amos 'n' Andy*. Soulless white American radio was destined for droll hours of Fibber McGee and Molly till Wolfgang Kaufman shucked 'n' jived to its rescue. America got a pair of stumbling jitterbugging icons; Wolfgang Kaufman got a ten-cent raise.

Ms. Murphy's seventh-grade history class, still in rapt attention, unanimously voted to skip watching *Eyes on the Prize* so they could hear the tale of Ludwig Kaufman. Son of Wolfgang, Cousin Ludwig used his father's tenuous mop-bucket industry connections to become a manager of white acts that ripped off the Motown rhythm-and-blues hysteria. Some of his more popular acts were Gladys White and the Waitress Tips and the Stevedores, whose melodic hit, "Three Times a Longshoreman," made a little noise on the eastern seaboard. Ludwig was proudest of his project the Four Cops, a Los Angeles–based quartet who charted with a ballad entitled "Reach Out and I'll Be There Hittin' You Upside the Head with a Nightstick."

Lost in Chicago's South Side, the dapper Ludwig Kaufman stumbled into Mosque 27 looking for directions to a club that had booked his sequined law enforcement officers. Playing the rear in a metal folding chair, Uncle Kaufman was fascinated with the temple's rhythmical rhetoric and style, and the potential in a group called the Blond Muhammadettes intrigued him. He quickly asked how he could join and where he could get some of those bow ties and shiny shoes. Knowing a mark when they saw one, the Black Muslims and the FBI trained Ludwig to be the Judas to black nationalism's Jesus. It was Cousin Ludwig who on February 21, 1965, stood up in the middle of the Audubon Ballroom moments before Malcolm X was to give his last speech and shouted, "Hey man! Get your hands out of my pocket." Eight months later the police found him in Tin Pan Alley, dead and sans shiny shoes.

After school I held court near the kickball diamond, leaning against the metal backstop, rambling on about my cousin Solveig Kaufman. *Newsweek* magazine assigned Cousin Solveig to report on the press conference announcing the results of the reinvestigation of Martin Luther King's assassination. The panel opened up the questioning by choosing an affirmative action baby who'd benefited from King's movement. On national television Solveig repaid the civil rights movement. He stood up, pen and pad in hand, and said, "Never mind James Earl Ray and FBI intervention, inquiring minds want to know who's fucking Coretta Scott King?" The aging eternal widow's next public appearance was her funeral four months later. Some say natural causes, some say suicide, some death by public embarrassment.

These schoolyard chronicles never included my father's misdeeds. I could distance myself from the fuckups of the previous generations, but his weakness shadowed my shame from sun to sun. His history was my history. A reprobate ancestry that snuggled up to me and tucked me in at night. In the morning it kissed me on the back of the neck, plopped its dick in my hands, and asked me to blow reveille. Front and center, nigger.

The racist campestral doctrine of Yeehaw, Mississippi, raised Mr. Rölf Kaufman, a.k.a. Daddy. Instead of pumping property taxes into neighborhood schools, the town stuck its tongue out at *Brown v. Board of Education* and satisfied the Supreme Court's integrationist stipulations by busing the dark-skinned niggers and the light-skinned niggers to Dred Scott High. Living in the only black household within walking distance of exclusively white and predominantly redneck Jefferson Davis High, my father didn't even know about the colored bus. He showed up for the first day of high school dressed in cuffed Levis, a flannel shirt, a Daniel Boone coonskin hat, and a Captain Midnight decoder ring. He was such a docile and meek nonthreat that the principal let him register for classes.

My father fondly recalled the laughs and cold celebratory summer vacation Dixie beers he shared with the good ol' boy senior class after their macabre reenactment of the Schwerner, Goodman, and Chaney murders. Rölf played Chaney, two Down syndrome kids from the special-ed class reprised the roles of the hapless miscreant Jews, and three carloads of football players acted as the vigilante sheriffs. My father and the two "Jewish" boys drove down Route 17 toward Meridian with the ersatz peace officers right behind them. After a few miles of horn-blaring, bumper-to-bumper tailgating and beer cans sounding off the windows like tin hailstones, Yeehaw's phony finest grew bored and forced my father's car to a stop. My father smiled weakly as the starting quarterback, Plessy "Go Deep" Ferguson, purposefully approached the driver's side. The strong-armed wishbone navigator par excellence opened the door with his scholarship hands and asked my father, "What are you SNCCering about? Get it, fellas? SNCC — snickering?" The rest of the team burst out in laughter and proceeded to pull the scared "student activists" out of the car, taking turns cuffing my dad and the retarded kids about the face, swinging them by the ankles into the muddy bog that ran alongside the highway. Later that night all the players in the living theater met in the glade behind the courthouse for a few wrap-party beers. A campfire's glowing flames lit up a keg placed next to a thick-trunked Southern pine known as a swing-low tree. Shadows of the strong-limbed branches flickered across soused contemplative faces. My father drank so much he passed out. He came to naked, his entire body spray-painted white, his face drool-glued against the trunk of the swing-low tree. He ran home under the sinking Mississippi moon, his white skin tingling with assimilation.

Three hours after graduating from high school in 1968, Dad joined the army. He served two tours in Vietnam. His commanding officer, elated with my father's patriotism, placed him in charge of a crazy Black Is Beautiful platoon of citified troublemakers. He led them on search-and-destroy missions through the sharpened thickets, eyes out for snipers, listening to his men gripe about the precipitation, the white man this and the white man that. After he joined the Los Angeles Police Department, he'd complain that he'd left the Indonesian jungle for the Iznocohesion jungle — "gone from fighting Viet Cong to King Kong." I remember one day he came home drunk from the LAPD's unofficial legal defense fundraiser for officers accused of brutality. (Dad later told me they showed *Birth of a Nation* followed by two straight hours of Watts riot highlights.) He sat me on his lap and slurred war stories. How his all-black platoon used to ditch him in the middle of patrols, leaving him alone in some rice paddy having to face the entire Communist threat by his lonesome. Once he stumbled on his men behind the DMZ, cooling with the enemy. The sight of the slant-eyed niggers and nigger niggers sharing K-rations and rice, enjoying a crackling fire and the quiet Southeast Asian night, flipped Pops the fuck out. He berated his rebellious troops, shouting, "Ain't

Paul Beatty

this a bitch, the gorillas snacking with the guerrillas. Hello! Don't you fucking baboons know that this is the goddamn enemy? The fucking yellow peril and you fucking Benedict Leroy Robinson Jefferson Arnolds are traitors to the democracy that weaned you apes from primitivism. You know, you're probably eating dog." The VC saw the disconcerted looks on the faces of the black American men, and a good colored boy from Detroit raised his rifle and put an M-16 slug inches from my pop's crotch. My father's men just sat there waiting for him to bleed to death. The Vietnamese had to beg them to take my dad back to the base. My father ended this confessional with the non sequitur wisdom that ended all our conversations: "Son, don't ever mess with no white women."

To my knowledge no male Kaufman had ever slept with a white woman, not out of lack of jungle hunger or for preservation of racial purity but out of fear. I'd watch my dad talk to white women, drowning them with "Yes, ma'ams," his darting eyes looking just past their ears. If the First Lady were to walk past my father naked with the original Constitution taped to her back like a "Kick Me" sign, my dad wouldn't even crane his neck. The last thing he'd want to see was some flabby butt and a hooded mob chasing him back to Niggertown.

On our custody outings to the drag races in Pomona, my father would tell me how he came back from the war and met my mother at a stock car race. They fell immediately in love — the only two black folks in the world who knew the past five winners of the Daytona 500 and would recognize Big Daddy Don Garlits in the street. Then he'd put his arm around me and say, "Don't you think black women are exotic?"

Kaufman lore plays out like an autogamous self-pollinating men's club. There are no comely Kaufman superwomen. No poetic heroines caped in Kinte cloth stretching welfare checks from here to the moon. No nubile black women who could set a wayward Negro straight with a snap of the head and a stinging "Nigger, puh-leeze." The women who allied themselves to the Kaufman legacy are invisible. Their existence and contributions cut off like the Sphinx's broad nose, subsumed by the mystic of an astronomical impotency. Every once in a while a woman's name tangentially floated from my mother's lips as a footnote to some fool's parable, only to dissipate with the vegetable steam. Aunt Joni's mean banana daiquiri. Meredith's game-winning touchdown run vs. Madame C. J. Walker High. Giuseppe's second wife Amy's Perry Como record collection. Cousin Madge, who was the complexion of pound cake dipped in milk. These historical cameos were always followed by my mother's teeth-sucking disclaimers, "But that's not important" or "Let's not go there." I wondered, where did my male predecessors find black women with names like Joni, Meredith, and Amy? Who were these women? Were they weaker than their men, or were they proverbial black family linchpins? I spent hours thumbing through photo albums, fearful that I was destined to marry a black Mormon Brigham Young University graduate named Mary Jo and become the spokesperson for the Coors Brewing Company. They say the fruit never falls far from the tree, but I've tried to roll down the hill at least a little bit.

Paul Beatty

two

My earliest memories bodysurf the warm comforting timelessness of the Santa Ana winds, whipping me in and around the palm-tree–lined streets of Santa Monica. Me and white boys Steven Pierce, Ryan Foggerty, and David Schoenfeld sharing secrets and bubble gum. Our friendship was a buoyant one based on proximity, easy-to-remember phone numbers, and the fact that Ryan always had enough money for everybody. We were friends, but didn't see ourselves as a unit. We had no enemies, no longstanding rivalries with the feared Hermosa Beach Sandcastle Hellions or the Exclusive Brentwood Spoiled Brat Millionaire Tycoon Killers. Our conflicts limited themselves to fighting with our sisters and running from the Santa Monica Shore Patrol. My co-conspirators in beach terrorism and I suffered through countless admonishments from overzealous officers lucky enough to grab one of us in some act of mischief that was always a precursor to a lifetime of incarceration bunking with society's undesirables. "Young man, try to imagine a future behind bars."

"What you in for, young buck?"

"I garnished the potato salad of this obese family of Orange County sea cows with sand crabs."

"Premeditated?"

"Hell, yeah! The entire clan beached themselves fully clothed twenty feet from the water. Tourists. Fucked up the local vibe."

"Hey, that's worth a couple of years, easy. Chow's at six o'clock."

After I was escorted home by the police "one too many times," my mother made me join Cub Scout Pack #251, starting me on the socialization treadmill toward group initiation and ceremonial induction. I was kicked out after three meetings for failing to learn the pledge, but the experience stayed with me. It was as if somebody assigned a den mother to point out the significance of campy blue uniforms with buttons in every imaginable place, flags, and oaths. My salt-air world began to subdivide into a series of increasingly complicated dichotomous relationships. Thankfully, I still remember when my worldview wasn't "us against them" or "me vs. the world" but "me and the world."

I was an ashy-legged black beach bum sporting a lopsided trapezoidal natural and living in a hilltop two-story townhouse on Sixth and Bay. After an exhausting morning of bodyboarding and watching seagulls hovering over the ocean expertly catching french fries, I would spend the afternoon lounging on the rosewood balcony. Sitting in a lawn chair, my spindly legs crossed at the ankles, I'd leaf through the newest Time-Life mail-order installments of the family's coffee-table reference library. *Predators of the Insect World, Air War Over Europe, Gunfighters of the Old West;* I loved reading about red ant–black ant wars, dogfights at fifteen thousand feet, and any cowboy "who was so mean he once shot a man for snoring." The baseball game would crackle and spit from the cheap white transistor radio my father gave me for my seventh birthday. The tiny tweeter damp with drool from Dodger play-by-play man Chip Parker salivating over Rusty Lanahan's agility around the bag and how despite allegations of spousal abuse the first baseman with the All-American *punim* remained a shining role model for the city's youth. If I still swore on my mother, I'd swear that between pitches I could hear the fizzing of the sun setting behind me, cooling down with a well-earned bedtime dip in the Pacific. I liked to twist the glossy Time-Life photos in the fading yellow light. When the praying mantis's chalky lime green changed to ghostly white and a B-26 Marauder bomber's drab army olive melted away into a muddy dark brown, it was time for dinner. The call of the irate mother could be heard over the roar of the airplanes flying off the page.

"Gunnar, set the fucking table."

"'kay, Ma."

Before making my way to the silverware drawer, I'd lean over the balcony, squinting into the dusk, and look out toward the nearly empty waterfront six blocks away. The elongated shadows of beachcombers and their metal detectors skimmed across the dimpled and paper-cup–laden sand in hopes of finding lost sandwich baggies full of quarters stolen long ago from the bottom of parents' dresser drawers. Lifeguard Station 26 is boarded up and shut down for the evening. The sandy-colored hairy-legged lifeguard walks quickly toward his classic convertible VW Beetle, his cherry-red vinyl shorts and windbreaker barking, "Caution! Dangerous riptide!" and fluttering in the strong sea breeze. Two shimmering wetsuit-clad surfers straddle fiberglass Day-Glo boards bobbing offshore, waiting for the last good wave of the day to take them home. The sandpipers play tag with the receding tide, scampering just outside the stretching reach of the waves dying at their knobby feet. Every once in a while the birds call time out to take water breaks, sticking their thin beaks into the moist sand. The sun stops fizzing, though Chip Parker remains excited, haranguing the listening audience about leftfielder Nathaniel Galloway's powerful Negroid hindquarters and seguing smoothly into the ad copy for Farmer John's ham, "hickory smoked just the way you like it."

The lights at Dodger Stadium and the streetlamps flicker on, and throughout Santa Monica the obedient kids wave goodnight to their delinquent friends as the community goes into the seventh-inning stretch. "Jesse Stewart retires the side in order, one, two, three. And after six it's the Dodgers three, the Mets one." Life was full of Cracker Jacks, root-root-rooting for the home team, and fucking with my mother.

"Gunnar! Set the table!"

"Ma? You know what?"

"What?"

"That's what."

"Very funny. Set the table or I'll wash your sharp-tongued mouth out with the whetstone."

I was very funny, in a sophomoric autodidactic knock-knock-who's-there sort of way. I learned timing, Zen and the art of self-deprecation from the glut of Jewish standup comics on cable TV, who served as living Chinese acupuncture charts of comedic pressure points: dating-yin, parents-yin, daily absurdities-yang. The ancient texts of Bennett Cerf and the humorous anecdotes from Grandma's waterlogged *Reader's Digests* were, if not the I Ching, at least Confucian hymnals.

I was the funny, cool black guy. In Santa Monica, like most predominantly white sanctuaries from urban blight, "cool black guy" is a versatile identifier used to distinguish the harmless black male from the Caucasian juvenile while maintaining politically correct semi-type-otics. If someone was planning a birthday party, the potential invitees

always asked, "Who's going to be there?" The conversation would go:
"Shaun, Lance, Gunnar . . ."
"Gunnar? Who's that?"
"You know, the funny, cool black guy."

Some kids had reps for shredding on skateboards or eating ear wax. My forte was the ability to hold a straight face and pull off the nervy prank. I learned early that white kids will believe anything anybody a shade darker than chocolate milk says. So I'd tell the gullible Paddys that I was part Gypsy and had the innate ability to tell fortunes. Waving my left index finger like a pendulum over their sticky palms, I'd forecast long lifetimes of health and prosperity. "You'll have a big house in the hills. Over here on the love line is your tennis court. Right here by the life line is your heliport. Now where do you want your pool?" The unsuspecting dupe would point to a spot usually midway between the mystic cross and the creative line, and I'd spit a wad of saliva somewhere near the designated area. "There's your pool."

I was the only cool black guy at Mestizo Mulatto Mongrel Elementary, Santa Monica's all-white multicultural school. My early education consisted of two types of multiculturalism: classroom multiculturalism, which reduced race, sexual orientation, and gender to inconsequence, and schoolyard multiculturalism, where the kids who knew the most Polack, queer, and farmer's daughter jokes ruled. The classroom cross-cultural teachings couldn't compete with the playground blacktop lessons, which were cruel but at least humorous. Like most aspects of regimented pop-quiz pedagogy, the classroom multiculturalism was contradictory, though its intentions were good.

My third-grade teacher, Ms. Cegeny, liked to wear a shirt that read:

Whenever she wore it she seemed to pay special attention to me, Salvador Aguacaliente (the silent Latin kid who got to go home early on Cinco de Mayo), and Sheila Watanabe (the loudest Pledge of

Allegiance sayer in the history of American education), taking care to point out the multiculturalist propaganda posted above the blackboard next to the printed and cursive letters of the alphabet: "Eracism — The sun doesn't care what color you are."

On hot stage-three smog-alert California days Ms. Cegeny would announce, "Okay, class, put away your pencils and take out your science books. Turn to page eighty-eight. Melissa, please read starting from 'Fun with Sunshine and Thermodynamics.'" Melissa Schoop-mann would begin in her deliberate relentless monotone. "This may sound funny . . . to the novice . . . third-grade scientist, . . . but sunshine is cool. . . . Without it . . . the earth . . . would be . . . as lifeless as a . . . Catholic funeral on a . . . rainy, dreary day." I'd try to fall asleep, but it was too hot even to daydream. My sweat-soaked Suicidal Tendencies *You Can't Bring Me Down* tour shirt clung to the inversion layer of grit on my skin. Melissa droned on. "Dark colors . . . such as . . . black absorb sunlight . . . and light colors . . . such as . . . white reflect sunlight." I looked up and down my skinny dark brown arms and turned to my lab partner, Cecilia Peetemeyer, the palest kid in school. Cecilia's skin was so transparent that one week during health Ms. Cegeny used Cecilia's see-through skim-milk-white limbs to show the difference between arteries, capillaries, and veins.

"Cecilia, are you hot?" I asked.

"No."

"Shit."

"Gunnar, what was the last thing Melissa read?"

"Uh, she said um. She said dark colors soak up the sun's rays through processes called conduction and convection and the lighter colors of the spectrum tend to alter the path of the radiation through reflection and refraction."

"Good, I thought you weren't paying attention. Melissa, please continue."

Everything was multicultural, but nothing was multicultural. The class studied Asian styles of calculation by learning to add and subtract on an abacus and we then applied the same mathematical principles on Seiko calculators. Prompting my hand to go up and me to ask naively, "Isn't the Seiko XL-126 from the same culture as the abacus?" Ms. Cegeny's response was "No, we *gave* this technology to the Japanese after World War II. Modern technology is a Western construct." Oh. To put me in my place further, Sheila Watanabe hummed "My country 'tis of thee, sweet land of liberty" loud enough for the whole class to hear.

One year during Wellness Week a MASH unit of city health workers set up camp in the gymnasium to ensure that America would have an able-bodied supply of future midlevel managers ready to lead the reinforcement brigades of minimum-wage foot soldiers to their capitalistic battle stations. A free-enterprise penologist was a physically fit one. We answered the patriotic call one girl and boy at a time. Allison Abramowitz and Aaron Aaronson were the first to go. Brave warriors, they left with no send-off party save the frightened faces of their classmates. Ten minutes later Allison returned unharmed. She skipped over to her desk, sat down, and covered a sly I-know-something-you-don't smile with her hand. Kent Munson quickly asked for permission to sharpen his pencil. He dropped the pencil next to Allison and asked her what happened. She hissed, "None of your beeswax," sending Kent slinking back to his seat defeated. When copycat and cootie-infested Katie Swickler tried the same technique, Allison greeted her with a message whispered in her ear. Then girls throughout the classroom giggled and smiled at Katie, thanking her for the reassurance. It was as if they were communicating through gender-specific telepathy, leaving us guys looking more confused than usual.

Then Aaron Aaronson walked in, his face drained of color, his arms stuck tightly to his sides, and a newly acquired tic violently tossing his head back at a sickeningly acute angle every two seconds. Zombiefied, he walked a few steps into the classroom, stopped, and shouted, "Oh shit, you guys. They touched my balls and made me cough."

Ms. Cegeny ignored Aaron's pederastic pronouncements, called two more names, and continued her lecture on the importance of living in a colorblind society. "Does anyone have an example of colorblind processes in American society?"

Ed Wismer raised his hand and said, "Justice."

"Good. Anything else?"

Millicent Offerman, who as teacher's pet spoke without raising her hand, shouted out, "The president sure seems to like people of color."

"Anyone else think of anything that's colorblind? Gunnar?"

"Dogs."

Paul Beatty

"I believe that dogs are truly colorblind, but they're born that way. Class, it's important that we judge people for what?"

"Their minds!"

"And not their what?"

"Color!"

The response to Ms. Cegeny's call was mostly soprano. I know none of the boy altos were into it — too busy cursing ourselves for wearing the same drawers two days in a row. Colorblind? I hoped the doctor would be totally blind, or he might pull down my underwear, see the brown skid marks on my white Montgomery Ward cotton briefs, and recommend me for placement in special education.

Eventually Ms. Cegeny called my name and I left to be examined by a quiet nurse and a doctor so old he may have cowritten the Hippocratic oath. I was weighed and measured. The doctor banged on my knees with a rubber tomahawk, then asked me to pull down my drawers. Ignoring my stains, he wrapped his trembling and wrinkled hand around my equally wrinkled scrotum. I didn't flinch. Which surprised him.

"Anyone ever do this to you before, son?"

"No."

"Do you know what I am doing, son?"

"Touching my balls."

"Do you know why? Cough."

"Ah-hem. To practice your juggling?"

"Oh, you're one of those funny cool black guys, aren't you. No, I'm testing you for a hernia. Cough."

"Ah-hem! How do you test the girls?"

"I pinch their nipples and ask them to whistle. Pull up your pants and we'll test your sight."

I sat on a stool and read the eye chart with no problems. The nurse placed an open book on my lap and asked if I saw any numbers in the pattern of colored dots. I pointed out the yellow-orange eight-six in the sea of gray dots and asked the nurse what I was being tested for. The doctor stopped shaking long enough to interrupt the nurse and answer, "Colorblindness."

"Our teacher says we're supposed to be colorblind. That's hard to do if you can see color, isn't it?"

"Yeah, I'd say so, but I think your teacher means don't make any assumptions based on color."

"Cross on the green and not in between."

"They're talking about human color."

"So?"

"So just pretend that you don't see color. Don't say things like 'Black people are lecherous, violent, natural-born criminals.'"

"But I'm black."

"Oh, I hadn't noticed."

I went back to class and told the still-nervous boys in the back rows whose last names began with the letters L through Z that the physical wasn't too bad other than when the doctor measures your dick with a ruler and calls out to the nurse, "Penis size normal," or "teeny-weeny," or "fucking humungous." Ann Kurowski, who was twice as blind as Helen Keller but determined to go through life without wearing glasses, asked me if I remembered the letters on the bottom of the eye chart. I told her "F-E-C-E-S" and opened my primer to the story about a war between a herd of black elephants and a herd of white elephants.

I don't remember what the elephants were fighting about — something about hating each other for the colors of their sponge-rubbery skins. It wasn't as if the black elephants had to use the mosquito-infested watering hole and rely on white elephant welfare for their quinine. After heavy casualties on both sides, a cease-tusking was called. The elephants, as wounded and bedraggled as elephants could possibly be, headed off into the hills, only to return to the plains years later as a harmonious and homogeneous herd of gray elephants.

I never could figure out why that story was so disquieting. Maybe it was the unsettling way Eileen Litmus would loudly slam shut her reader and stare at me from across the room as we completed the assignment at the end of the story.

1. *Why did the elephants not get along?* A folded note would soon find my hand under the desk.

2. *How come the elephants came back gray?* I'd open the note, trying my best not to rustle the paper. The scrawl read:

> Fuck the stupid elephants. I like the tortoise and the hare
> story much more better. I challenge you to a race. Meet me

Paul Beatty

after school for a race from the baseball diamond to the handball courts and back. Do you accept the challenge or are you a pigeon-toed wuss? P.S. You have big ears so you must be an African elephant.

3. *Can we apply this story to real life?* I'd look up and see Eileen's hand raised high in the air, her eyes' radar locked on mine. "Ms. Cegeny! Ms. Cegeny! Gunnar's passing notes!" Ms. Cegeny would squeak her pudgy sandal-shod feet over to my desk and read the entire note to the shrieking delight of the class. As punishment for my misdemeanor, I'd have to stand up and read aloud my answer to the last question regarding the elephant story.

4. *What do you think will happen to the elephants in the future?* "Just like some human babies are born with tails or scales, some unfortunate baby elephants are going to be genetic flashbacks and come out albino white and summer's nap black. Then the whole monochrome utopia is going to be all messed up."

✿

My first crush was on Stan "the Man" Musial, an old first baseman with a corkscrew batting stance who played for the St. Louis Cardinals in the 1940s and 1950s. Eileen Litmus was my second love. She had a vindictive sense of humor, power to left-center, and was faster than winter vacation, three qualities I admired in a third grader. Despite our age, Eileen and I were easily the fastest kids in the school. Kids would bet movie money on who would win our Friday marathons around the schoolyard backstops. The "Ready, get set, go!" often caught me flatfooted, staring at her lean figure, my arms frozen in prerace Tiberian Olympic-statue readiness. The sudden *whoosh* of Eileen's departure would roust me from my trance, her thick dirty-blond hair streaming behind her like jet vapor, denim hip-huggers blurring past the tetherball courts. Pumping my arms and puffing my cheeks like I'd seen the track stars do on TV, I'd try to make up ground just so I could catch a glimpse of her round tan tomboyish face. If the grass near the hopscotch boxes was soggy and she wore the heavier Nike Cortezes, not the lighter Adidas running shoes, I stood a chance of catching her near the handball court, the inner thighs of my corduroys rubbing and buzzing down the stretch. Usually Eileen crossed the finish line first, wading into a welcoming committee of high fives and hugs from the girls. The boys wreathed me with humiliation. "Dude, why did you let her win? I lost four grape Pixie Stix. What the fuck is wrong with you, man? You're supposed to be fast. When's the last time a white sprinter won a race? Would you bowl with a white bowling ball? No, you wouldn't."

After a long schoolday of moralistic bombardment with the aphorisms of Martin Luther King, John F. Kennedy, Cesar Chavez, Pocahontas, and a herd of pacifist pachyderms, my friends and I were ready to think about color on our own terms. We'd make plans to spend the weekend at the beach, sunning in the shoreline's warm chromatics and filling in childhood's abstract impressionism coloring books with our own definitions of color, trying our hardest not to stay inside the lines.

Blue

Those without bikes rode on the handlebars. We pedaled side by side in wobbly tandems, yelling our blue profanities, sharing our blue fantasies. We bombarded the windows on the Big Blue municipal bus with wet baby-blue toilet-paper grenades. We splashed in the postcard blue of the ocean and stuck out our Slurpee blue tongues at the girls two towels over. Eileen's light-saber blue eyes cut through me like lighthouse beacons lancing the midnight.

Psychedelic

When you're young, psychedelic is a primary color and a most mesmerizing high. Santa Monica was full of free multihued trips. The color-burst free-love murals on Main Street seemed to come to vibrant cartoon life when I passed them. The whales and dolphins frolicked in the clouds and the sea lions and merry-go-round horsies turned cartwheels in the street. The spray-any-color-paint-on-the-spin-art creations at the pier were fifty-cent Jackson Pollock rainbow heroin hits that made your skin tingle and the grains of sand swell up and rise to the sky like helium balloons. Looking into the kaleidoscopic eyes of a scruffy Bukowski barfly sitting in the lotus position along the bike trails fractured your soul into hundreds of disconnected psychedelic shards. Each sharp piece of your mind begging for sobriety.

White

Santa Monica whiteness was Tennessee Williams's Delta summer seersucker-suit blinding. The patchy clouds, the salty foams of the cresting waves, my friends, my style — all zinc oxide nose-cream white. My language was three-foot swells that broke left to right. "No waaaay, duuuude. Tuuubular biiitchin' to the max. Tooootalllyyy fucking raaad." White Gunnar ran teasingly tight circles around the recovering hollowed-out Narc Anon addicts till they spun like dreidels and dropped dizzily to the ground. White Gunnar was a broken-stringed kite leaning into the sea breeze, expertly maneuvering in the gusty gales. White Gunnar stabbed beached jellyfish with driftwood spears and let sand crabs send him into a disco frenzy by doing the hustle on his forehead. White was walking to school in the fog. White was ignoring the crossing guards and trying to outrun the morning moon. White was exhaling crystallized plumes of carbon dioxide and knowing it was the frozen exhaust of our excited minds. White wasn't the textbook "mixture of radiations from the visible spectrum"; it was the opposite. White was the expulsion of colors encumbered by self-awareness and pigment.

Black

Black was an unwanted dog abandoned in the forest who finds its way home by fording flooded rivers and hitchhiking in the beds of pickup trucks and arrives at its destination only to be taken for a car ride to the desert. Black was hating fried chicken even before I knew I was supposed to like it. Black was being a nigger who didn't know any other niggers. The only black folks whose names I knew were musicians and athletes: Jimi Hendrix, Slash from Guns n' Roses, Jackie Joyner-Kersee, the Beastie Boys, and Melody the drummer from Josie and the Pussycats.

Black was trying to figure out "how black" Tony Grimes, the local skate pro, was. Tony, a freestyle hero with a signature model Dogtown board, was a hellacious skater and somehow disembodied from blackness, even though he was darker than a lunar eclipse in the Congo. The interviews in *Shredder, Rollerbladers Suck,* and *Stoked* magazines never mentioned his color.

Stoked: So, dude?

Tony: Yeah.

Stoked: Gnarly frontside ollie 180 fakie at the Laguna Pro-Am.

Tony: Nailed it, bro, want another hit?

Now and then we'd see Tony Grimes, our deracinated hero, in Coping 'n' Doping Skateshop on Ocean Street next to the Tommy Burger. "What's up, Tony?" we'd all ask coolly, yet with genuine concern in our voices. We'd receive an over-the-shoulder "What's shakin', dude?" and fight over who he'd acknowledged. "He called me dude. Not you, you nimrod."

Tony Grimes strolled around the shop, a baseball cap magnetically attached at some crazy angle to his unkempt thick clumpy Afro. His lean muscular legs loped from clothes rack to clothes rack as he eyed the free shit he would take home after he got through rapping to the manager's girlfriend.

Black was a suffocating bully that tied my mind behind my back and shoved me into a walk-in closet. Black was my father on a weekend custody drunken binge, pushing me around as if I were a twelve-year-old, seventy-five-pound bell clapper clanging hard against the door, the wall, the shoe tree. Black is a repressed memory of a sandpapery hand rubbing abrasive circles into the small of my back, my face rising and falling in time with a hairy heaving chest. Black is the sound of metal hangers sliding away in fear, my shirt halfway off, hula-hooping around my neck.

✿

That summer of my molestation, my sister Christina returned from a YMCA day camp field trip in tears. My mother asked what was wrong, and between breathless wails Christina replied that on the way home from the Museum of Natural History the campers had cheered, "Yeah, white camp! Yeah, white camp!" and she had felt left out. I tried to console her by explaining the cheer was, "Yeah, Y camp! Yeah, Y camp!" and no one was trying to leave her out of anything. Expressing unusual concern in our affairs, Mom asked if we would feel better about going to an all-black camp. We gave an insistent "Noooooo." She asked why and we answered in three-part sibling harmony, "Because they're different from us." The way Mom arched her left eyebrow at us, we knew immediately we were in for a change. Sunday I was hitching a U-Haul trailer to the back of the Volvo, and under cover of darkness we left halcyon Santa Monica for parts unknown. Ma driving, singing a medley of Temptations hits, my sisters passed out in the back seat, twitching in exhaustion from moving and packing.

Ma's voice dropped a couple of octaves as she segued from "My Girl" into "Papa Was a Rolling Stone." I rolled down the window, trying to capture the last vestiges of the nighttime salt air, and began writing mental letters to friends I knew I'd never see again.

❋

Dear Ryan Foggerty,

Later, man. Thanks for the ticket to the Henry Rollins/Anthrax show at the Civic Auditorium and for lending me your Slidemaster trucks and the Profane Insane Urethane wheels, I'll send 'em back to you. Rock and roll will never die.

> Be cool,
> Gunnar

❋

Dear Steven Pierce,

I'll miss the weekend speedboat outings with your red-haired ex–Playboy Bunny mom and her loaded boyfriend who always wore the stupid Skipper from *Gilligan's Island* hats. I remember how you hated the way he winked at you, one hand on the steering wheel, the other stroking your mother's behind. We did the right thing by pissing in the gas tank, so what if his engine stalled and he nearly died of exposure off the coast of Mexico. I'm sorry, but Larry, not Shemp or Curly or Moe, was the funniest Stooge. "Susquehanna Hat Company"?

> Slowly I turn,
> step by step,
> Gunnar

❋

Dear Eileen,
    I never told anyone. I know you didn't.

XXOXOXX,

Gunnar

❊

Of all my laidback Santa Monican friends, I miss David Joshua Schoenfeld the most. He was off-white and closest to me in hue and temperament. Strangers would come up to him and ask if he was Mediterranean. David would shake his head, his dollar-bill-green eyes trying to convey that he was a tanned Jewish kid originally from Phoenix and perpetually late for the Hebrew school bus. Every Tuesday and Thursday after bar mitzvah classes we'd meet at the public library and pore through the WWII picture books, doing our best to fight the bewitching allure of Fascist cool. Our obsession wasn't a clear-cut Simon Wiesenthal Dudley Do-Right always-get-your-war-criminal fixation. We concerned ourselves with whether it would be more fun to fantasize about world domination attired in crushed Gestapo black velvet with red trim or in crumpled green Third Army gum-chewing schleppiness.

> Himmler is wearing the Aryan autocrat's summer ensemble, designed for maximum military foreboding with a hint of patrician civility. Ideal for a morning jaunt through the death camps or planning an autumn assault on the Russian front.

By sixth grade we'd read the junior warmongers' canon: *Mein Kampf, Boys from Brazil, Thirty Seconds over Tokyo,* and Anne Frank, and our allegiances were muddled. On the way to Laker games we'd talk about the atrocities at Buchenwald and Auschwitz. David's father, looking for a parking space, would ask us whether he should feel guilty about playing the serial numbers branded onto his father's forearm in the state lottery. During time-outs we'd test each other on the design specifications and flight capabilities of the Luftwaffe arsenal.

"The blitzkrieg clarion the Polish heard whistling out of the clouds in 1939?"

"Please, the Stuka dive-bombers."

"Top speed for the Messerschmitt 109 K-model."

Paul Beatty

"Easy, 452 miles per hour, climb rate 4,880 feet per minute."

"Someone's been studying."

"Knock this out. Give me the wingspan and ceiling for the Focke-Wulf 190 D-series."

"You know that's my favorite plane of all time. Wingspan 33 feet and 5 inches, ceiling 32,800 feet. Don't Focke with me, man. Chu wanna go to war? Okay, we go to war."

Later that night, with permission to sleep over at David's house, we went to war. On our last reconnaissance sortie before bedtime we found a trail of ants on a Bataan death march to underground bunkers beneath his front porch. After five passes with the aerosol deodorant, we applied the matches and watched the soldier ants burn, shouting, "Dresden! Dunkirk! Banzai!" and strafing their shriveling exoskeletons with plastic scale-model airplanes. Then it was inside to watch our favorite video, *Tora, Tora, Tora*, stuffing handfuls of Jiffy Pop popcorn in our mouths and cheering for the Japanese.

When David's parents were asleep we played Hiroshima-Nagasaki in the bedroom. In our astronaut pj's with the crinkly plastic soles we moved the armoire into the hall and cleared enough space for Little Boy and Fat Man to land. Fake radio transmissions from the backs of our throats: "Come in, Los Alamos kkksssk. Come in, this is the *Enola Gay*, do you read? Kkksssk."

"Loud and clear, this is Oppenheimer, copy."

"Oppy baby, is this thing goin' to work?"

"Oh yeah, equivalent to twenty thousand tons of TNT. Do you copy?"

"Roger, ten-four, over and out."

We'd simulate the atomic flash by switching the bedroom light on and off as fast as we could, catching strobe glimpses of ourselves as nuclear shadows. Frozen in our positions, we mimicked death, writing letters home, pruning bonsai trees, playing with Hot Wheels, bent over mid butt-wipe.

Before going to bed, we brushed our teeth in the cramped bathroom. I noticed that David put the toothpaste on his brush before passing it under the cold water. I, like most folks, wet my brush, then put on the toothpaste, but I copied him because he was white and I figured maybe I was doing it wrong.

The only time race entered our war was when we sat over a basket of french fries drinking root beer and debating who Hitler would kill first, David the diabolical Jew or me the subhuman Negroid. It was on our excursions to the library that I stumbled across my first black heroes: the Tuskegee airmen, the Redball Express, some WAC nurses from Chicago, Brigadier General Benjamin O. Davis, Sr., Jesse Owens, and the mess cook who shot down a couple of Japanese Zeros from the sinking deck of the *Arizona*. I kept these discoveries to myself. I didn't think David would find it as juicy as when I told him that Hitler had only half a package.

✿

Dear David Schoenfeld,

I'm still high from the model airplane glue-sniffing session in the alleyway behind Pic 'n' Save. Remember the waterfalls of vomit rushing down our chins and our contest to see who could find the largest chunks of undigested potato chips in their pool of throw-up? Fuckin' cool. David, somehow through being with you I learned I was black and that being black meant something, though I've never learned exactly what. *Barukh atah Adonai.*

Shalom, motherfucker,
Gunnar

✿

I don't remember helping my mother unload the trailer, but the next morning I awoke on the floor of a strange house amid boxes and piles of heavy-duty garbage bags jammed with clothes. The venetian blinds were drawn, and although the sunlight peeked between the slats, the house was dark. My mother let out a yell in that distinct-from-some-where-in-the-kitchen timbre: "Gunnar, go into my purse and buy some breakfast for everybody." I acknowledged my orders and got dressed. Rummaging through my personal garbage bag, I found my blue Quicksilver shorts, a pair of worn-out dark gray Vans sneakers, a long-sleeved clay-colored old school Santa Cruz shirt, and just in case the morning chill was still happening, I wrapped a thick plaid flannel shirt around my skinny waist. I found the front door, and like some lost intergalactic B-movie spaceman who has crash-landed on a mys-

Paul Beatty

terious planet and is unsure about the atmospheric content, I opened it slowly, contemplating the possibility of encountering intelligent life.

I stepped into a world that was a bustling Italian intersection without Italians. Instead of little sheet-metal sedans racing around the fontana di Trevi, little kids on beat-up Big Wheels and bigger kids on creaky ten-speeds weaved in and out of the water spray from a sprinkler set in the middle of the street. It seemed there must have been a fire drill at the hair salon, because males and females in curlers and shower caps crammed the sidewalks.

I ventured forth into my new environs and approached a boy about my age who wore an immaculately pressed sparkling white T-shirt and khakis and was slowly placing one slue-footed black croker-sack shoe in front of the other. I stopped him and asked for directions to the nearest store. He squinted his eyes and leaned back and stifled a laugh. "What the fuck did you say?" I repeated my request, and the laugh he suppressed came out gently. "Damn, cuz. You talk proper like a motherfucker." Cuz? Proper like a motherfucker? It wasn't as if I had said, "Pardon me, old bean, could you perchance direct a new indigene to the nearest corner emporium." My guide's bafflement turned to judgmental indignation at my appearance. "Damn, fool, what's up with your loud-ass gear? Nigger got on so many colors, look like a walking paint sampler. Did you find the pot of gold at the end of that rainbow? You not even close to matching. Take your jambalaya wardrobe down to Cadillac Street, make a right, and the store is at the light."

I walked to the store, not believing that some guy who ironed the sleeves on his T-shirt and belted his pants somewhere near his testicles had the nerve to insult me over how I dressed. I returned to the house, dropped the bag of groceries on the table, and shouted, "Ma, you done fucked up and moved to the 'hood!"

"young, dumb, and full of cum"

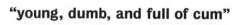

three

My MAGICAL mystery tour ground to a halt in a West Los Angeles neighborhood the locals call Hillside. Shaped like a giant cul-de-sac, Hillside is less a community than a quarry of stucco homes built directly into the foothills of the San Borrachos Mountains. Unlike most California communities that border mountain ranges, Hillside has no gentle slopes upon which children climb trees and overly friendly park rangers lead weekend flora-and-fauna tours.

In the late 1960s, after the bloody but little known I'm-Tired-of-the-White-Man-Fuckin'-with-Us-and-Whatnot riots, the city decided to pave over the neighboring mountainside, surrounding the community with a great concrete wall that spans its entire curved perimeter save for an arched gateway at the southwest entrance. At the summit of this cement precipice wealthy families live in an upper-middle-class hamlet known as Cheviot Heights. At the bottom of this great wall live hordes of impoverished American Mongols. Hardrock niggers, Latinos, and Asians, who because of the wall's immenseness get only fifteen minutes of precious sunshine in summer and a burst of solstice sunlight in the winter. If it weren't always so hot it would be like living in a refrigerator.

We lived in a pueblo-style home with a cracked and fissuring plaster exterior my mother said provided an Old Mexico flavor. Even she had to laugh when I walked up to a peeling section of the house, broke off a yellow paint chip, popped it into my mouth, rubbed my tummy, and said, "Mmmmmm, nacho cheese." Our back yard nestled right up against the infamous wall. I often marveled at the unique photosynthesis that allowed the fig, peach, and lemon trees to thrive in a dim climate where it often rained dead cats and dogs, rotted fish, and droplets of piss. Apparently rich folks have an acerbic sense of humor.

After a week in our new home, a black-and-white Welcome Wagon pulled up in front of the house to help the newcomers settle into the neighborhood. Two mustachioed officers got out of the patrol car and knocked on our front door with well-practiced leather-gloved authority. Tossing courtesy smiles at my mother, the cops shouldered their way past the threshold and presented her with a pamphlet entitled "How to Report Crime and Suspicious Activity Whether the Suspects Are Related to You or Not." It wasn't the day-old macaroni casserole she'd been expecting. My sisters and I sat in the living room, half listening to the news on the radio, half listening to the cops asking Mama questions to which they already knew the answers.

"Kids, Ms. Kaufman?"

"Yes, three."

"Two girls, ten and eleven, and a boy, thirteen, all of them left-handed, right?"

"That's correct."

"Ma'am, may we speak to the boy, Gunnar?"

My mother turned around and waved me over with the hated come-hither crooked index finger. I lifted my sheepish carcass off the couch and shuffled like a reluctant butler toward the interrogation. The cop with gold stripes on his sleeves cut Mama a look and said, "Alone, Ms. Kaufman," and she deserted me with a satisfied smirk, happy that I was finally getting a bitter taste of her vaunted "traditional black experience."

I stood there, perched directly under the doorjamb, as I'd learned to do when your earth quaked. My slumping shoulders trembled. My kneecaps shook. These weren't some Santa Monica cops sporting Conflict Resolution ribbons, riding powder-blue bicycles, this was the LAPD, dressed to oppress, their hands calmly poised over open holsters like seasoned gunfighters'. I tried to distance myself from the rumbling in my ears, clamoring for one of those out-of-body experiences only white folks in midlife crises seem to have. I felt the gases rising from my queasy stomach to inflate my body. My arms and legs began to swell, and slowly I began to float away. I was just getting off the ground when I let out a long silent fart. Apparently, my escape fantasy had a slow leak.

"Son, you smell something?"

"Nope."

Paul Beatty

"Well, something reeks."

"Oh, that's the chitlins."

My would-be out-of-body experience hovered there, wafting in the flatulent fumes. I wasn't going anywhere; I felt like a Macy's Thanksgiving Day Parade balloon — tethered, and grounded to reality by fishing lines looped through my nose and eyeballs. I was a helium distraction until the arrival of Santa Claus. "Look, Daddy, Snoopy with an Afro."

The squat grayish-blond officer removed his cap and introduced himself and his partner as officers Frank Russo and Neal Salty.

"Gunnar, we know you had some problems with the Santa Monica police department. Son, here in" — the officer took a deep breath — "Nuestra Señora la Reina de Los Angeles de Porciuncula, we practice what we like to call 'preventative police enforcement.' Whereby, we prefer to deter habitual criminals before they cause irreparable damage to the citizenry and/or its property."

"You mean you put people who haven't done anything in the back seat of your squad car and beat the shit out of 'em so you don't have to do any paperwork. Thereby preventing any probable felonious assaults on the citizenry."

"And/or its property."

"And/or it is. You know, my father is a sketch artist down at Wilshire Division. Does that carry any weight?"

"Yeah, he gets to visit your ass in jail without being strip-searched."

Taking out a small notebook from his supercop utility belt, he continued the inquest. "What's your gang affiliation?"

"Gang affiliation?"

"Who do you run with? Who are your crimeys, your homies, your posse? You know, yo' niggers."

"Oh, I see. Well, on weekends I'm down with the Gang of Four."

"Who?" To his partner, "Geez, these fucking turds are incredible, there's a new gang every frigging week." Then he turned back to me. "So, Gunnar, who you banging with in this Gang of Four?"

"You know, it's me, my homegirl Jiang Qing, Wang Hongwen, Zhang Chuqiao, and my nigger even if he don't get no bigger Yao Wenyuan. Sheeeeit, we runnin' thangs from Shanghai to Compton."

Although I had only lived in Hillside for a few days, it was impossible not to pick up a few local catchphrases while running errands for Mother. Language was everywhere. Smoldering embers of charcoal etymology so permeated the air that whenever someone opened his mouth it smelled like smoke. Double-check the mailbox to see if your letters had fallen through and the lid shrieked, "Dumb-ass motherfucker, have you ever looked and letters were still there? No! Shut the goddamn lid." Press the crossing button at the intersection and the signal blinked a furious "Hurry the fuck up!" Call information and the operator answered the phone with a throaty "Who dis?" Nothing infuriated my mother more than me lounging on one elbow at the dinner table slinging my introductory slang with a mouth full of mashed potatoes: "Sheeeeit, Ma, I'm running thangs, fuck the dumb."

"Seriously, son, judging by your previous nefarious history, we feel that you have a proclivity for gang activity. Do us all a favor and come clean."

"Okay, fuck the dumb. On Mondays, Wednesdays, and odd-numbered Fridays when my mother lets me stay out late, I be down with the Our Gang He-man Woman Haters Club. Matter of fact, we have a rumble with the Bowery Boys next week. If you see that schmuck Muggs, tell da bum I'm gonna kick his ass."

"Okay, we're going to put you down as unaffiliated. For now keep your big black nose clean."

Gang affiliation? I didn't even have any friends yet. My sisters and I had no idea how to navigate our way around this hardscrabble dystopia. Each of us had already been beaten up at least once just for trying to make friends. Deciding there was safety in numbers, we took to traveling in a pack. Nervously, traipsing through the minefield, we tiptoed past the suspected ruffians and kept on the lookout for snipers. Shots would ring out from nowhere, forcing us into sacrificial heroics, diving onto verbal grenades to save the others.

"Say, bitch-ass, com'ere!"

"Who, me?"

"Must be you, you looked."

"You guys, go on without me. Get away while there's still time. Tell Mama I love her. I regret that I have only one life to give for my family."

By day six of the ghetto hostage crisis my sibling captives and I were avoiding the dangers of the unexplored territory along the banks of the Harbor Freeway by sitting in the den playing Minutiae Pursuance, substituting our own questions for the inane ones on the cards. "Sports and Leisure, for the pie."

"Oh, this one's a toughie. How many dimples on a golf ball?"

"Four hundred sixty-three. Give me my piece."

Mom was not the kind of matriarch to let her brood hide up under her skirt, clutching her knees, sheltered from the mean old Negroes outside. Under the guise that she was worried about our deteriorating social skills, she suggested we go to Reynier Park and play with the other kids in the neighborhood. She might as well have told us to play in the prison yard at Attica. Reynier Park was an overgrown inner-city rain forest that some Brazilian lumber company needed to uproot. You needed a machete to clear a path to the playground. The sandbox was an uninhabitable breeding ground for tetanus and typhus. Shards of broken glass and spent bullet shells outnumbered grains of sand by a ratio of four to one. Hypodermic needles nosed through this shimmering sinkhole like rusted punji sticks.

Despite our pleas for a pardon, Mom invoked the death penalty and sentenced us to an afternoon at the park. For the record, the condemned ate last meals of liverwurst and mustard on white bread and drank grape Kool-Aid (extra scoop of sugar) before departing. We were somberly alternating turns on the only working swing when two girls about ten years old, smoking cigarettes and sharing sips from a canned piña colada, approached us. The taller of the two was wearing denim overalls and had so many pink and blue barrettes clipped to the thinning patches of braided hair on her head it looked as though she was under attack by a swarm of plastic moths. The other girl had on orange polyester hot pants and a matching polka dot halter top that was so small it barely succeeded in halting her two BB-sized nipples. Her hair was heavily greased into a rigid elliptical disk that sat precariously on the crown of her head. Every few seconds she'd stoop down to pick up a discarded needle and deposit it in her little red Naugahyde purse. She resembled a Vietnamese woman wearing a straw hat and toiling in a paddy. I listened for bleating water buffalo but heard only the bigger one's mouth.

"Get out of our swing now!" she shouted at Nicole. Nicole wanted to get off the swing, but she was catatonic with fear. It didn't help that out of sheer nervousness Christina and I kept pushing, propelling her stiff frame higher and faster.

Kicking off their dime store flip-flops, the two badly coiffed bullies marched through the sandbox without a flinch or grimace. A little diaper-clad boy waddled up, blew a kazoo tribunal, and heralded the dyspeptic duo: "That my sister Fas' Betty and her bestest friend Vamp a Nigger on the Regular Veronica. They fixin' to kick y'all's ass." Betty and Veronica went into a loud hands-on-hips, call-and-response, head-bobbing tirade on how they owned the entire park from the calcified jungle gym to the busted teeter-totter. Betty's braids stood on end as she demanded that Nicole get off the swing before she heated up every piece of broken glass in the sandbox, affixed them to the end of one of those pointy 7-Eleven Slurpee straws, and blew glass bubbles in her tight black bourgeoise booty.

The thought of this snake-haired demon shoving molten glass in her rectum gorgonized Nicole even further. Her sphincter tightened and her rock-hard butt sat heavy in the swing. Betty picked up a piece of broken glass, lit a Bic lighter, and teasingly passed the piece of glass through the flame, her fireproof fingers impervious to the heat. Nicole's hands fastened themselves to the chains; her legs spread out in front of her and locked at the knees. Mistaking our silent petrification for hincty insolence, Betty and Veronica tried to rush us. The alcohol must have affected their bullying judgments, because they charged into Nicole chin first just as her legs were in the high kicking up-stroke of a swing filled with panic-stricken kinetics. Fas' Betty caught a sneaker in the trachea and Veronica Vamp a Nigger something-or-the-other got kicked in the solar plexus.

Wiggling in spasmodic waves like dying fish on the filthy playground, the girls somehow managed to find enough air to moan raspy Miles Davis "motherfuckers" and threats that every ex-con cousin, pyromaniac auntie, serial killer uncle, and pit bull in the neighborhood would soon be coming to "put that head out" and "peel our caps." Within moments, as if some silent gangster medical alert alarm had gone off, a small army of nepotistic enforcers magically appeared at the entrance near the basketball courts, parting the underbrush and yelling, "Y'all fucking with my cousins?" The three of us instantaneously burst into a waterfall of tears. Begging for a sympathetic détente, Christina and I mindlessly continued to push Nicole's swing. Her whooshing arc through the air, accompanied by the rusty swing set's rhythmic creak, became a foreboding, metronomic pendulum counting down our deaths. "We didn't know! We didn't know! Please leave us alone." A screaming vortex of punches and kicks answered our pleas with a firm *ignorantia juris neminem excusat.*

The ghetto intelligentsia had kindly provided the young Kaufmans with our first lesson in street smartology: never, ever cry in public — it only makes it worse. If we hadn't bawled we might have been let off with a polite cursory thrashing, just to maintain protective appearances. Since we sobbed like wailing refugee babies, we received a full-scale beatdown designed to toughen us up for the inevitable cataclysmic Italian opera ending of black tragedy. Usually when the fat lady sings in a black community, it's at a funeral. I've seen kids get hit by cars, ice cream trucks, bullets, billyclubs, and not even whimper. The only time it's permissible to cry is when you miss the lottery by one number or someone close to you passes away. Then you can cry once, but only once. There is no brooding; niggers got to get up and go to work tomorrow.

My sisters and I walked home routed, picking bits of gravel out of one another's tattered Afros and holding our heads back to stanch our nosebleeds. I thought about Betty's flecked bouffant, Veronica's flying-saucer-like do, and the oily Jheri curls, rock-hard pomade cold waves, and horsehair weaves of our attackers, and I realized that every day for the black American is a bad hair day.

"We haven't seen Daddy since we moved."

"Mommy told me he knows where we live, but he won't come by."

"Fuck that nigger."

"Listen to you. So, tough guy, I think Betty and Veronica kind of like you. Did you notice the tender look in their eyes when they stomped on your head? Which one you gonna choose, Archiekins?"

"Oh, be quiet. I could swear that little baby knee-dropped me in the balls."

The night of the Reynier Park beating I slept with a cold pack on the left side of my face and dreamed I lived in a museum diorama with the Hottentot Venus and Ishi, Last of the Yahi. Surrounded by stuffed mastodons and saber-toothed tigers, we played dominoes on a small round table in front of a hastily oil-painted backdrop of the Hollywood Hills. All the dominoes were blank, and inexplicably I spent long periods of time considering my next play. Ish and Hottie would scream at me in Z-talk to hurry up. "Plizzay dizza fizzucking dizzzominoes!" As I pulled dominos from the pile, I tried to explain that it wasn't a matter of playing a blank domino, it was a matter of playing the right blank domino. "Dizzumb bizzastard." At feeding time the caretaker would give me a pack of Oreos and the visitors would yell "Cannibal" and throw their yellow metal visitor buttons at me. The buttons turned to snow as they passed through the glass partition.

I woke up comfortable in the knowledge that I was a freak. If I had walked the streets with a carnival barker to promote my one-boy sideshow, I could have made some money. "Hurry! Hurry! Step right up! All the way from the drifting sands of whitest Santa Monica, the whitest Negro in captivity, Gunnar the Persnickety Zulu. He says 'whom,' plays Parcheesi, and folks, you won't believe it, but he has absolutely no ass what-so-ever."

My inability to walk the walk or talk the talk led to a series of almost daily drubbings. In a world where body and spoken language were currency, I was broke as hell. Corporeally mute, I couldn't saunter or bojangle my limbs with rubbery nonchalance. I stiffly parade-marched around town with an embalmed soul, a rheumatic heart, and Frankenstein's autonomic nervous system. Puberty wasn't supposed to be like this. The textbooks said something about a little acne, some chest hair, and that I could use this special time in life to grow closer to my parents by discussing my nocturnal emissions with them. "Mom! Dad! Six cc's of jizz last night. Am I a man or what?" Instead, my adolescence was like going to clown college. I found myself clumsily walking on a set of size thirteen feet, bumbling through the streets of Hillside and ricocheting off inanimate objects and into the pathways of hypertensive and equally embattled pedestrians. I constantly found myself cowering under raised umbrellas and fists, hurriedly apologizing and kowtowing for forgiveness for stepping on someone's heel.

I learned the hard way that social norms in Santa Monica were unforgivable breaches of proper Hillside etiquette. I'd been taught to look someone in the eye when speaking to them. On the streets of Hillside, even the briefest eye contact wasn't a simple faux pas but an interpersonal trespass that merited retaliation. Spotting a potential comrade, I'd catch his eye with a raised eyebrow that said, "Hey, guy, what's up?" — a glance I hoped would open the lines of communication. These silent greetings were often returned in spades, accompanied by the angry rejoinder "Nigger, what the fuck you looking at?" and a pimp slap that echoed in my ears for a week. I'd rub my stinging cheek, dumbfounded, and find myself staring into a pair of dark sullen eyes that read, "Verboten! Stressed-out ghetto child at work. Keep out."

The people of Hillside treat society the way society treats them. Strangers and friends are suspect and guilty until proven innocent. Instant camaraderie beyond familial ties doesn't exist. It takes more than wearing the same uniform to be accepted among one's ghetto peers. The German spies in those late-night World War II movies who tried to infiltrate U.S. Army units by memorizing baseball trivia and learning to chew gum with a certain snappy American flair had it easier than I did. I couldn't just roll up on some folks and say, "I know the Black National Anthem, a killer sweet-potato pie recipe, and how to double-dutch blindfolded. Will you be my nigger?" Dues had to be paid, or you wasn't joining the union.

I had my overbite corrected and an impacted molar removed when I approached a crew of kids sitting on the fender of a metallic gold 1976 Monte Carlo with white interior. The boys were playing the dozens, snapping on each other's mothers; I walked directly up to the fattest kid, playfully punched him in his doughy shoulder, and said, "Hey, I don't even know your name, but your mother soooooo black she sneezes chimney soot and pisses Yoo-Hoo." The family dentist said she couldn't have done a better job herself.

The Hillside tribe wasn't going for no ghetto fakery. If I wanted to come correct, I'd have to complete some unspecified warrior vision quest. The gods of blackness would let me know when I was black enough to be trusted. I walked the dark streets of Hillside with my head down, looking for loose change and signs that would place me on the path to right-on soul brother righteousness.

In early September, bruised and toothless, I realized that my search for companionship was becoming too painful. Trying to foist myself on these people wasn't going to work; I needed a more transcendental approach to locating my soul. To achieve this soulful enlightenment, I started playing Thoreau in the Montgomery Ward department store over in the La Cienega Mall, turning its desolate sporting goods department into a makeshift Walden. I moved the pond, a flimsy dark blue plastic wading pool decaled with big-eyed, absurdly happy black and yellow ducks, next to the eight-man tent tucked away in the wilds of the camping section. The tent was pitched in a four-tree forest of plastic redwoods and dead nylon leaves in various states of factory decomposition. A phalanx of cuddly foam forest creatures, née archery targets, roamed the grounds: a whitetail deer with its nose in a Kodiak bear's ass, and a wild turkey propped against a Ping-Pong paddle so it wouldn't fall over on its side. A few passes of aerosol mosquito repellent and I had all the scents and sounds of the wild. "Ms. Palazzo, you're wanted in shipping."

Fun Facts for Department Store Campers
Did you know that you can tell the temperature by counting the number of high-pitched department store dings in a
minute, then dividing that number by five?

I spent entire days in the tent, snuggled up in a down sleeping bag reading Kant, Hegel, and the Greek tragedies by flashlight. Whenever I felt the need to stretch my legs, I'd break out my Cub Scout compass and go orienteering around the store. Grabbing a fishing pole, I'd blaze trails from the glacier-white kitchen appliances up the steep back stairwells and traverse the lawn furniture outback until I reached the bluffs of television sets that overlooked the pet store. From the balcony I'd cast my line into the aquariums below, sip a cream soda, and commune with nature, waiting patiently for a bite. The end of a good day's fishing would yield a cooler filled with angelfish, oscars, and tiger barbs, but since I wasn't much of an angler, it was usually guppies, guppies, and more guppies.

The day after Labor Day I was sitting in the tent reading Homer when I overheard some voices outside excitedly commenting on the nearby display of hunting rifles and bows and arrows. Ahh, intrepid explorers! Cautiously, I peeked my nappy head out from between the tent flaps and saw a group of black and Mexican boys a little older than I assembled in Household Weaponry. The glass case was broken and most of the guys were peering down the barrels of shotguns. One was passing a sharp Bowie knife under the nose of the terrified salesperson and asking if he could slash some prices. If I planned to trade pelts for foodstuffs and form a working relationship with this barbarous bunch, I'd have to try the avuncular approach.

I placed both hands in my pockets and sauntered over to the group in as nonthreatening a manner as possible. Each kid was dressed from head to toe in various shades of blue. Baby blue baseball caps, navy blue scarfs, and from the back pockets of those loose-fitting midnight blue chinos, Dodger blue handkerchiefs bloomed like cottony autumn delphiniums. What did the Venice Beach queers say about dark blue hankies in the right rear pocket — was it dominant or submissive?

While I tried to remember, a dwarf-sized freckle-faced big-headed redbone kid the others called Pumpkin nocked an arrow into a powerful compound bow. He took aim at a smug-looking mannequin who was standing up in an aluminum dingy, holding a rod and reel and modeling a black-and-red checkerboard lumberjack jacket with a matching hat, the kind with wool earflaps. One of Pumpkin's cronies gently placed an apple on the dummy's head and stepped back. Pumpkin lifted the bow, pulled back on the string till his hand touched his ear, shot an arrow that pierced the mannequin's forehead and exited through the back of his plaster skull, landing somewhere in the young miss section.

"I shot an arrow into the air, it fell to the earth I know not where," I said by way of introducing myself. The pint-sized William Tell looked in my direction and twisted his hands in some arthritic gesticulation. I interpreted his double-jointed gesture as a sign of welcome and replied in kind with the only high sign I knew. I raised the back of my left hand to my chin and wiggled my fingers, giving him the high sign popularized by Stymie and Alfalfa in the Our Gang comedies. I felt I was speaking a sort of gangland Esperanto, but Pumpkin stiffened, pursed his lips, and scrunched his face in displeasure. To dampen his anger, I commented on the expensive sheepskin quiver strapped across his chest.

"Nice quiver."

"Quiver? You saying I'm scared of your ass?"

"No, I'm talking about the holder for arrow shafts."

"You saying you Shaft? Oh, you that cat, that baaaad mother . . . shutyourmouth, but I'm talkin' about Shaft. Oh, I can dig it, motherfucker."

knowing what to say next in a game of who's on first that was
ng increasingly hostile, I said nothing and looked longingly
the tent, but his stare hadn't yet given me permission to go
anywhere. Pumpkin and each of his merry men in turn threw up the
hand signal again, waiting for me to acknowledge it. I knew better
than to give the Little Rascal high sign again, so I stalled.

"That thing you do with your hands is awfully cryptic."

"Damn straight, nigger, because I'm a goddamn Crip. Where from,
punk? Represent, fool, fo' me and my potnahs break you off something
proper-like."

I felt someone place that apple that had once been on top of the
mannequin's head on my head. Pumpkin furrowed his brow, nocked
a shiny brass-tipped arrow in his bow, and said, "Wuddup, fool? You
Cuz or Blood?"

My shiftless free will leaned lazily against my brain stem and
flipped a coin onto its clammy palm, whistling a chorus of "eeny,
meany, miney, moe, catch a nigger by the toe." From somewhere
inside my head a game show host with a majestic voice welcomed me
to Final Jeopardy. "What is Blood?" I answered.

The Little Lord Fauntleroys stopped shuffling in place, clenched
their teeth, and stood up straight. Their fists knuckled into iron black
ballpeens.

"Ennnhhh," a tall, crazy-looking Mexican boy in the rear said.

"Wink, tell the boy what he's won as a consolation prize."

The circle of boys tightened.

"Okay, Bob. Our contestant has won a matching set of contusions
and bruises with possibly some lacerations of his internal organs
courtesy of that infamous gang, the" — my eyes closed and someone
rolled his tongue in a mock drumroll — "Gun Totin' Hooligans."

The quills of an arrow brushed past my ear and I turned just fast
enough to see it plow into the foam head of the deer with its nose
nuzzled in the bear's ass. The deer wobbled, then fell on its side, dead.
The bear looked relieved and the blows crackled and crunched on my
head, rearranging my already lumpy phrenological topography. Steel-
toed boots explored the depths of my rib cage and waves of pain
rapelled up and down my spine. Periodically, my persecutors would
rest and step back from my bloodied carcass, share bites of the apple,
and admire their handiwork. "Yo, Joe, how do you get both eyes to

Paul Beatty

swell with such symmetry and purple robustness?" Then they'd swallow, spit the seeds in my general direction, and resume whipping my ass. Between thumpings I remained optimistic, hopeful that this would be the beatdown that certified my worthiness, stamped me with the ghetto seal of approval.

Maybe this was one of those jumping-in rituals I'd seen on the PBS documentaries titled *Our Youth at Risk* or something equally forlorn. My mother would watch these melodramatic shows, angrily addressing the screen. "What they talking about, 'our youth'? Those aren't my kids, and if they were, they'd damn sure be at risk. At risk of me putting some euthanasia shotgun pellets in their bellies." I'd never thought that one day I would be in the center of a maelstrom of "our youth," pacifying myself with thoughts of possible acceptance into their world. Maybe the Gun Totin' Hooligans would beat me senseless, then revive me with dousing buckets of water, welcoming me into the fold with snappy French Foreign Legion kisses on both cheeks and Leo Buscaglia gangster bear hugs. "My nigger. What it be like, black? Gimme some love, dawg." The secret password would be whispered in my ear, and the sacred soul shake taught. I'd raise off the linoleum floor with swollen lips and a gang affiliation, pumping my fist in the air, screaming to the gods, "That's right, motherfuckers, you don't know who you fucking with, I'm down with the Gun Totin' Hooligans. Get back, Jack. Up your milk money before I regulate you and all your punk-ass disciples."

I was squirming on the ground, contorted into a bloody fetal mess, too sore even to groan when they rifled my pockets. Finding nothing but the book I had been reading, one of the fistic coterie bemusedly read the title. "*The Odyssey?* Ain't that some club over on Slauson and Normandie?" He carelessly flung it back at me, and the book fluttered through the air like a teal-colored paperback butterfly and landed lightly on my chest, face down and open somewhere in the middle. I picked it up, looked at the triumphant, swaggering backs of my conquerors, and read aloud:

> Athena, gray-eyed goddess, then replied:
> Take heart: you need not fear such things.
> But now, in the recess of that beguiling cave,
> let's set your treasures, there they will be safe.

Not the ironic profundity I hoped for, but it portended better times. Junior high started in a week; I couldn't wait. I wondered what the nurse's name would be and if she disinfected cuts and slashes with Mercurochrome or the wimpy ouchless spray. I'd have to remember to ask my mother to call the office to ensure they knew how to make butterfly bandages out of those "flesh"-colored Band-Aids.

four

I ARRIVED forty-five minutes early for my first day of school at Manischewitz Junior High. A tattered and faded U.S. flag snapped solidly in the wind, full of bluster despite bearing only half its original fifty stars. The stars that remained hung on to the blue field by only one or two points. The putrid pink, dirty gray, and filthy baby blue of Old Glory had seen better days.

I opened the steel front door and stepped into the deserted vestibule, looking for some middle school guidance. There was none to be found. No smiling faces welcomed me to the smelting factory of young widgethood. No signs directed me toward fall registration. I walked through the metal detector and went looking for the dean's office to pick up my schedule. Walking through the halls, I couldn't keep my eyes off the glossy panorama photographs of Manischewitz graduating classes past that adorned the walls.

CLASS OF '23: Scads of white students and teachers dressed in pleated flannel skirts and pants. A young colored custodian with a mop in his hand stands next to a metal bucket. The name tag on his overalls reads "Melvin Samuels." A close examination of the principal reveals the outline of a flask in the breast pocket of his suit jacket.

CLASS OF '41: Other than the smattering of Asian faces lousing up the Anglo homogeneity, very similar to the previous photograph. A student in the front row holds a sign that reads, "Get out of jail soon, Melvin. The wastebaskets miss you."

CLASS OF '42: There are only two male teachers, one of whom has his arms wrapped around the waists of two female teachers. The other stands in the middle of the nursing staff, holding a stethoscope and smiling from ear to ear. There are no Asian students.

In the years following 1944 the staff gets fatter and there are always three or four black and Chicano faces dotting the photos like grease smudges. Each year's colored faces bear a striking resemblance to those from the previous year. Unless there is a change in sex, it's hard to tell if the minority kids are the progeny of single families passing through the school system or the same kids repeating ninth grade year after year.

CLASS OF '67: The first class photo in color. The student population is still overwhelmingly white, but they no longer wear staid plain white shirts and blouses to school. Instead they sport groovy colorful tartans, stripes, and paisleys. One teacher in the front row is wearing an African dashiki and giving the peace sign. Standing in the back next to a metal bucket and holding a mop is a graying janitor outfitted in a blue jumpsuit. His name tag reads "Melvin Samuels."

CLASS OF '68: If it weren't for the same crew-cut gym teacher and bifocaled principal standing like bookends in both photographs, this picture could be a negative of the Class of '67's portrait. The faces of these graduating ninth-graders are dark and overwhelmingly Latino and black. Mr. Samuels is standing in the back, dressed in a bright orange leisure suit and smoking a cigarette, with a mop slung over his shoulder like a rifle. The teacher with the dashiki has a black eye and his arm in a sling.

CLASS OF '86: The last photograph in the series. The number of students in the picture is smaller than ever before. The faces, including those of most of the staff, are Latino and black, with a sprinkling of Asians. A man in gray overalls whose name tag reads "Mr. Samuels, Jr." is standing in the back, mopless and sharing a joint with a couple of kids. Every boy in the front row has his penis sticking out of his button-fly jeans. Close inspection reveals the outline of a flask in the breast pocket of the principal's suit.

✿

The dean's office was just around the corner. The receptionist awoke when he heard the heavy wooden door slam shut. Wiping the sleep from his eyes, he looked up at the clock.

"Damn, you early." He asked my name and retrieved my schedule from a thick leather binder with "Gunnar Kaufman — Records" embossed on it in shiny gold flake. I'd never seen my records. Supposedly filled with my black marks, accolades, test scores, and aptitude results, this fabled folder was preordained to follow me throughout my entire life, passing from school to university to employer to jailer and finally ending in the hands of Saint Peter or the Devil.

"You're the first one here. The principal hasn't even arrived yet. Is there some trouble at home?"

"No."

The receptionist skimmed my file, using his tie as a reading ruler. He glanced up at me, shook his head, returned his gaze to the file, and spoke.

"You're not from around here, are you?"

"Nope."

Handing me my schedule, he grabbed my wrist and, in the sympathetic voice adults use to raise money for handicapped and troubled kids on late-night television, said, "Boy, you know if you find yourself having trouble getting to and from class, the school provides an escort service and you can be placed in protective custody."

"No thanks," I said. I couldn't stop smiling at the irony. The police thought I was a potential criminal mastermind and the school district thought I was an easy target for junior high hit men in training. Seeing that I'd touched a protective nerve, I pointed toward my records and asked the receptionist, in the helpless voice teens use to ask adults for a favor, "What's the aptitude part say?"

"I'm not allowed to reveal that without state and parental consent."

"Come on, man. Be cool. I won't tell. You can trust me. Look, I'm the first kid in school on the first day of school — is there anything less intimidating than that?"

He opened the eternal dossier, placed his glittery synthetic tie on the page, and started reading. "Okay, it says, 'Despite his race, subject possesses remarkable intelligence and excellent reasoning and analytical skills. His superb yet raw athletic ability exceeds even the heightened expectations normally accorded those of his ethnicity. Family background is exemplary, and with the proper patriotic encouragement Gunnar Kaufman will make an excellent undercover CIA agent. At a young age he already shows a proclivity for making friends with domestic subversives and betraying them at the drop of a hat.' Satisfied, Double-O Seven? Your homeroom is on the first floor of the Science Building, next to the vineyard. You'll see a sign saying *Vitis vinifera* on your left."

Amazed at what the government can glean from a few timed tests and laps around the track, I slunk to homeroom imagining I was wearing dark glasses and a trench coat. The halls began to fill with Manischewitz Junior High's administrative and security personnel, and my best espionage moves served me well. Pressing my back against the walls and peeking coolly around corners, I managed to avoid detection and made it to homeroom twenty minutes early. I opened the door slowly, index fingers loaded and ready to blast holes into any purveyors of injustice not taken in by my stealth. To my disappointment, there were no enemy agents wearing headsets and minding computer consoles.

Homeroom was an antiseptic classroom buzzing not with hostile anti-imperialist activity but with humming overhead fluorescent lights. A pair of dingy felt banners hung at both ends of the room. The purple-on-gold one at the back of the room read, "Karibuni! Bienvenidos! Welcome!" Its obverse gold-on-purple cousin at the front read, "Conceive It! Believe It! Achieve It! Imagina! Cree! Realiza!" I took the middle seat in the middle row. The desk looked like a modern Rosetta stone, etched with penknifed legacies that begged to be deciphered.

Kathleen y Flaco para siempre con alma
Pythagoras the Congruent Truant —
$A^2+B^2=C$ square punk busters get killed

Eventually the hallways stopped echoing with the footsteps of the Oxford wingtipped and high-heeled administration. In their place was the sound of brand-new sneakers squeaking on the waxed floors and the heavy clomp of unlaced hiking boots. The walkie-talkie communiqués were soon drowned out by the FM stereo meta-bass of the Barrio Brothers' morning show on KTTS. Steadily, the students entered the classroom and slid into the empty seats around me. First to arrive were the marsupial mama's boys and girls. These sheltered kids had spent the entire summer sequestered indoors by overprotective parents. They entered the classroom with pale complexions and squinting like possums to adjust their eyes to the light.

The reformed and borderline students followed. They crept into class, carefully trying to avoid last year's repercussive behaviors, and sat upright at their desks, face front and hands folded, mumbling their September resolutions to themselves. "This year will be different. I

Paul Beatty

will do my homework. I will not slap Mr. Ellsworth when he calls me a loser. I will only bring *my* gun to school." I admired the determination they showed in ignoring their corruptive friends, standing in the doorway and egging them on to join the excursion to McDonald's for breakfast McMuffins, orange juice, and a joint.

Two minutes before nine o'clock signaled the grand entrance of the fly guys and starlets. Dressed in designer silk suits and dresses, accessorized in ascots, feather boas, and gold, the aloof adolescent pimps and dispassionate divas strolled into homeroom smoking Tiparillos and with a retinue of admirers who carried their books and pulled chairs from desks with maitre d' suaveness.

I'd never been in a room full of black people unrelated to me before, and as the classroom filled, the growing din was unlike anything I'd ever heard. I sat like a tiny bubble in a boiling cauldron of teenage blackness, wondering where all the heat came from. Kids popped up out of their chairs to shout, whispered, tugged at each other. Homeroom was a raucous orchestral concerto conducted by some unseen maestro. In the middle of this unadulterated realness I realized I was a cultural alloy, tin-hearted whiteness wrapped in blackened copper plating. As my classmates yelled out their schedules and passed contraband across the room, I couldn't classify anyone by dress or behavior. The boisterous were just as likely to be in the academically enriched classes as the silent. The clotheshorses stood as much chance of being on a remedial track as the bummy kids with brown bag lunches. Many kids, no matter how well dressed, didn't have notebooks.

At exactly nine o'clock the bell rang and Ms. Schaefer stormed into the room. Disheveled and visibly nervous, she never bothered to introduce herself or say good morning. She wrote her name on the board in shaky, wavering strokes and took attendance. The class instantly interpreted her behavior as a display of lack of trust and concern. That day I learned my second ghetto lesson: never let on that you don't trust someone. Even if that person has bad intentions toward you, he will take offense at your lack of trust.

Ms. Schaefer spat off the names like salted peanut shells.

"Wardell Adams?"

"Here."

"Varnell Alvarez."

"Aquí."

"Pellmell Atkinson?"

"Presentemente."

"Praise-the-Lord Benson?"

"Yupper."

"Lakeesha Caldwell?"

"What?"

"Ayesha Dunwiddy?"

"Who wants to know?"

"Chocolate Fondue Edgerton."

"That's my name, ask me again and you'll be walking with a cane."

"I don't know how to pronounce the next one."

"You pronounce it like it sounds, bitch. Maritza Shakaleema Esperanza the goddess Tlazotéotl Eladio."

"So you're here."

"Do crack pipes get hot?"

Then the gangsters trickled in, ten minutes late, tattooed and feisty. "Say man, woman, teacher, whatever you call yourself. You had better mark Hope-to-Die Ranford a.k.a. Pythagoras here and in the house. Nobody better be sitting at my desk. I had the shit last year and I want it back for good luck."

"Mr. Pythagoras, take any available seat for now, okay? Who's that with you?"

"Why you ask him I can speak for my damn self? This is Velma the Ludicrous Mistress Triple Bitch of Mischief Vinson."

Ms. Schaefer's unfazed approach to maintaining classroom comportment didn't last long. By the end of the year we called her Ms. Sally Ride, because she was always blowing up at us.

After growing accustomed to police officers pulling students out of class for impromptu interrogations, bomb scares, and locker searches, I started to make friends, mostly with the nerdier students. We'd meet after school at the designated neighborhood safe houses on the ghetto geeks' underground railroad: the library, the fire station's milk-and-cookie open houses. The safest place was the basement of the Canaan Church of Christ Almighty God Our Savior You Betcha Inc. Pretending to be engrossed in Bible study, we traded shareware porn samplers downloaded onto our home computers. The computer was the only place where we had true freedom of assembly. Electronic mail allowed

Paul Beatty

us shut-in sissies to talk our dorkian language uncensored by bullies who shoved paper towels soaked in urine down our throats and teachers who awoke from their catnaps only long enough to tell us to shut up. I tried to appreciate Spock's draconian logic, Asimov's automaton utopias, and the metaphysical excitement of fighting undead ghouls and hobgoblins in Dungeons and Dragons, but to me *Star Trek* was little more than the *Federalist Papers* with warp drives and phasers. "Set Democracy on stun. One alien, one vote." I was cooler than this, I had to be — I just didn't know how to show my latent hipness to the world.

The change in semesters brought new electives and a chance to make new friends. All the exciting choices, like Print and Electric and Wine-making Shop, were gang member bastions and closed to insouciant seventh-graders such as myself. During spring registration I stood in line behind sloe-eyed bangers and listened to kind liberal guidance counselors derail their dreams. "Buster, I know you want to take Graphic Design, but I'm placing you in Metal Shop. Mr. Buck Smith will know how to handle you, and it'll be a good prerequisite for license plate pressing. You've got to plan for the future, Buster, ol' boy. Can't be too shortsighted, Mr. Brown. Remember, the longest jail sentence starts with one day."

I was left with a pitiable choice between sycophant havens: Home Economics II and Drama. A memory of last semester's beginning home ec, where Lizard Higgins's contorted, charred, and smoldering body was lifted into the ambulance and then sped toward the burn unit, was fresh in my mind. Drunk from sneaking sips of cooking sherry behind Ms. Giggscombe's back, Lizard spilled some libations on his clothes and absently leaned too close to his peach flambé assignment. Using his alcohol-soaked Washington Redskins football jersey as kindling, the fire crept up Lizard's torso and enveloped him in an eerie blue flame. (Ms. Kramer, the science teacher, said it was the kirsch and slivovitz distillates that accounted for the blue flame.) In a panic, Lizard ran, somersaulted, and cartwheeled down the hall, desperately trying to extinguish his blazing body by trying to drop, roll, and cover all at the same time. Ms. Giggscombe extinguished him with a flying body tackle and an old army blanket.

I showed up for Drama with a blithesome smile on my face and greeted my computer geek friends with cheery hellos and Shakespearean "How now, nuncles." The citywide Shakespearean Soliloquy Championship was in two weeks. Our teacher, Ms. Cantrell, determined to show that her impoverished Negro thespians could compete with kids at the well-funded oceanfront and Valley schools, entered us and notified the media that her domesticated niggers would soon be on parade. In a predictable attempt to inject some cultural relevance, she decided to do *Othello* and assigned parts by having the class draw roles from a hat. There weren't enough characters to go around, so each monologue would be learned by two students. The girls drew from a church bonnet and the boys from a bowler. Gretchen and Ursula, the bespectacled stone foxes of dweebdom, each drew Desdemona and pleaded with Ms. Cantrell to cast me in the lead role as the noble but paranoid blackamoor. Thankfully, Osiris, god of shy little black boys, fated me to play Iago, the scheming Venetian puppeteer, sparing me from having to place any necromantic kisses on Gretchen's or Ursula's cheek.

My dramatic confrere was Nicholas Scoby, a thuggish boy who sat in the back of the class, ears sealed in a pair of top-of-the-line Sennheiser stereo headphones and each of his twiggish limbs parked in a chair of its own. Rocking back and forth in his seat and seemingly oblivious to Ms. Cantrell and life's lesson plan, Nicholas Scoby seemed like an autistic hoodlum. His pea head lolled precariously on his wiry neck like a gyroscope; he snapped his fingers in some haphazard pattern and muttered to himself in a beatnik word-salad jibberish. "Dig it. This nigger's tonality is wow. Like hep. Like hepnotic. It's contrapuntal glissando phraseology to bopnetic postmodernism. Blow, man, blow. Crazy." Much to the dismay of those who paid attention to the burned-out teachers, Scoby was a straight-A student.

Ms. Cantrell divided the class into study groups. I reluctantly approached my partner, his eyes closed, a stream of guttural pablum escaping from his mouth accompanied by a barrage of spittle: "Bleeeet eet eeeet raaaaant dit dit dent ting ting. Send me, Jackson, send me. Oop-pop-a-da." Tapping Nicholas on the shoulder, I interrupted. "Hey man, what you listening to?"

Apparently able to read lips, he arched his eyebrows to the highest regions of his forehead and answered, "Cannonball Adderley."

"Who?"

"Jazz, daddio, jazz." Then carefully removing his headphones, he

Paul Beatty

continued, his pallid ears clashing with his brown-veneer skin. "You don't listen to jazz? The only truly American art form other than the sit-com."

"I listen to jazz. David Sanborn, Al Di Meola, and Spyro Gyra. Jeff Lorber is funky."

"Funky? Fool, that ain't jazz any more than Al Jolson and Pat Boone is soul. That shit is fusion. A superficial fusion at that. A little black style with weepy bland white sedative sensibilities. White boys with the blues tinged with some Caribbean high-end percussiveness."

"So what should I listen to?"

"Do like me, start at the beginning."

"With what, the New Orleans Rhythm Jazz Kings?"

"No fool, with *a*. My plan is to listen to everything recorded before 1975 in alphabetical order. No white band leaders, sidemen cool. No faux African back-to-the-bush bullshit recorded post-1965. Though I'm going to have to make an exception for Anita O'Day, she could pipe. What's your name, cuz?"

"Gunnar. Gunnar Kaufman."

"You dark as fuck for someone with Teutonic blood."

"Naw, strictly Negro hemoglobins."

Nicholas introduced himself with a grin. "Nicholas Scoby."

"I know."

"Do I have a cool-ass name or what? Sounds like I'm on some old secret agent cloak 'n' dagger type shit. I should get a card to hand out to motherfuckers, 'Nick Scoby — Espionage.'"

"You wanna learn the monologue together?"

"Wouldn't it be cool to be the most famous spy in the world? Makes no practical sense, everybody'd know I'm spying on them, but I'd be appealing to the inflated superego of the evildoer. Be a bad motherfucker, CIA needs to get with me. Yeah, nigger, let's get together later this week. Cool? Later."

He called me "nigger." My euphoria was as palpable as the loud clap of our hands colliding in my first soul shake. My transitional slide into step two was a little stiff, but I made up for it with a loud finger snap as our hands parted. Scoby gently placed his headphones over his ears and I skated away cool, dipped my right shoulder toward the ground, and with some dapper spinal curvature pimp-daddied back to my seat. I picked up the mimeographed Shakespearean sonnets Ms.

Cantrell had handed out at the start of class, pressed my nose against the damp page, and inhaled the delirium of blue-inked love poems and newfound friendship. I'd have to remember to ask Nicholas Scoby about the blues. I stood up to read.

> That thou art blamed shall not be thy defect,
> For slander's mark was ever yet the fair;
> The ornament of beauty is suspect,
> A crow that flies in heaven's sweetest air.

"More erudition," Ms. Cantrell said, "more erudition."

Scoby and I rehearsed in his bedroom while his mom sat in the basement den watching old tapes of her roller derby days at the Shrine Auditorium. The Scobys relocated from Chicago's West Side when the Windy City Tornados traded their star jammer, Beleeta "Queen Nairobi" Scoby, to the Los Angeles Thunderbirds for Skeets McNeely, Fat Jasper Perkins, and fifty sets of brake pads. During study breaks we'd join her on the couch, munching cheese puffs and directing muffled cheers at the television set.

I never understood the game, but invariably with time running out and the Thunderbirds down by five points, a plump man in a garish burgundy three-piece suit waved Ms. Scoby off the bench. Queen Nairobi skated around the ring in long slow strides to the roar of the small but rambunctious crowd of drunks, kids in tattered T-shirts, and wheelchair-bound senior citizens. Measuring her opposition and plotting her offensive strategy, she'd fasten the chin strap to a shiny yellow helmet that sat on her beachball-sized Afro like a plastic yarmulke. Picking up speed in the banked turn, Scoby's mom would extend a skinny arm to Big Dan Party Hardy, who'd whip her into a gauntlet of obese bearded and big-tittied enemy buffalos on wheels. Arms cocked at the elbows for combat, she wriggled and scratched her way to hero worship, scoring points by ducking under the legs of the St. Louis Gateways, dodging the sucker punches of the Pennsylvania Black Lung Sputums, and sailing over the body blocks of the Bay Area Seismics. Skating on one leg, arms flailing like windmills, Ms. Scoby was so athletic that she sent the opposition hurtling over the rails and into the ringside seats, where crazed fans pelted them with fistfuls of stale popcorn, cups of flat beer, and metal folding chairs. As Nicholas's mother rolled off the track, bent at hips and unsmiling, the PA announcer would yell, "Six big T-bird points!" and the big man in the burgundy suit would greet the winded Queen Nairobi with a kiss. They were oblivious to the flying aluminum walkers and whisky bottles that zipped past their intertwined bodies, and flashes of sweet pink tongue victory darted from their lips.

Nicholas and I returned to our studies.

"Yo, is that mauve-suited kumquat your father?"

"I think so. Mama won't say. They call him Gene 'the Dream' Beasley."

"You got any dreams, yo?"

"Yeah, I have a dream. Dream and a half, really. You ever hear of a Brocken specter?"

"Who?"

Nicholas put down his monologue. "A Brocken specter. If you stand on real high ground, say Mount Everest, with your back to the sun and look down, you'll see your shadow on top of a fogbank or a cloud. That shadow is a Brocken specter."

"Oh snap, your shadow on a cloud? That's cool as hell."

"But wait, there's more. As an added bonus for those who act early, you get your very own glory."

"Your own what?"

"Your own *glory*. As you look down at your shadow, there's a corona around your head. Even if you're standing next to a gang a niggers looking at they own Brocken specters, you can only see the glory around the shadow of your head."

"That's deep."

"Gunnar, do you have any dreams?"

"Nope, but listening to you carry on, I'm working on one now. I once heard about some shit called a Flächenblitz."

"Yeah?"

"It's lightning in reverse. A Flächenblitz strikes *up* from the top of a cumulonimbus cloud and ends in clear air."

"You're a fucking reincarnated Prussian Hun Bohemian. No doubt in my mind, homeboy."

❖

The city Shakespearean soliloquy finals were held at Anita Bryant Junior High in the Valley. First to arrive, Ms. Cantrell's third-period drama class entered the plush auditorium and sat in the back, testing the incredible acoustics with ghetto whoops and urban yodels. "Hey yo! Awwwight! Manischewitz Drama Club in the house, y'all! Yo mama-mama-ma-ma-aaa!" We were prepared to do well; we had all memorized our monologues, and our Old English diction was popping with sexual innuendo and abba rhyme schemes. What we weren't prepared for was the lily-white cocksureness of the students from the Valley and the ritzy L.A. County woods: Brentwood, Westwood, and Woodland Hills. The auditorium filled with suburbanites costumed in Renaissance finery. The white kids had metamorphosed from surfers, stoners, and student council members into medieval gold-digging courtesans and horny lords. We picked the wrong day to wear our "Don't ask me 4 shit" shirts. The white girls glided onto the stage in towering hairstyles and billowy velvet gowns, and the white boys wore ruffled silk shirts, skintight pants, peacock-feathered hats, and pointy suede Robin Hood shoes. It didn't seem to matter much when they flubbed their lines; their parents and housekeepers stood and applauded, and the judges murmured among themselves in low voices and nodded approvingly.

Whenever Manischewitz Junior High trundled onstage, our hiking boots clomped between deliveries and our baggy jeans hindered our emotive histrionics. When we stumbled over a line of Shakespearean blather, the judges looked down at their score sheets with self-satisfied smirks, tapped their pencils, and stared at us with bored expressions masquerading as smug impartiality. Paul Robeson was turning over in his grave.

By the time Scoby's turn to recite came, we had managed to cultivate an atmosphere of good-natured white liberal pity among the audience. Scoby shakily introduced his monologue; "*Othello*, act one, scene three. After plotting with Cassio to kill Othello, Iago . . ." Then Nicholas, choking on the patronizing sympathy, began. "Thus do I ever make my fool my purse . . . ummm . . ." He froze. Gathering his wits, he waved his arm majestically across his chest. "Thus do I ever make my fool my purse . . . fuck."

The crowd started cheering him on as if he were one of those kids stricken with cystic fibrosis taking his first baby steps on a telethon at two o'clock in the morning: "Come on, guy, you can do it." Two white girls, one of whom had just nailed Desdemona minutes earlier, boldly strode onstage and massaged Scoby's rock-hard hypertensive shoulders and whispered honey-voiced encouragement in his ear: "You can do it, big boy." Nicholas blurted out a spiritless "Thus do I ever make my fool my purse . . ." that died as soon as it left his lips. He slunk off the stage, his face hidden in his hands, his ears ringing with a deafening applause for failing. The defeated Manischewitz Drama Club sank in our seats and drowned under a tidal wave of shame.

A booming announcement from the emcee jolted the crowd from its collective condescension. "Next up, Manischewitz's Gunnar Kaufman as Iago, *Othello*, act two, scene one." I sauntered onto the stage and squinted into the spotlight, never feeling more misplaced, more burdenish, mo' niggerish. I found it difficult to breathe. I was growing allergic to the powdery mask of Elizabethan whiteface. I could hear Scoby whimpering in the back as I cleared my throat.

"I'm junking Iago's envy-laden 'What a stupid moor-ronic nigger this Othello is' speech for a less traditional bit from *King Lear*, act two, scene two. Note how the fusion of Goneril's vile lackey Oswald and the loyal Kent's lines give the monologue a self-hating and introspective spin." Gazing directly at the judges, I grabbed my dick and ripped into my makeshift monologue. "What dost thou know me for? A knave, a rascal, an eater of broken meats; a base, proud, shallow, three-suited, hundred-pound, filthy, worsted-stocking whoreson . . . one-trunk-inheriting slave . . . beggar, Nigger . . . I will beat you into clamorous whining if thou deny'st the least syllable of thy addition." I walked off the stage into a stunned auditorium of dazed crash dummies adrift in post-car-accident silence. At the top of my voice I yelled, "Is everyone all right? Anyone hurt?"

On the ride home Scoby saved me a seat in the back of the bus. I sat next to him, and like two shock absorbers we bounced up and down in the initial stages of lifelong friendship.

"Gunnar, you a crazy nigger."

"Yeah, I guess so. Nick, where you be at lunchtime? I be looking for your ass, but I can never find you."

"Monday meet me at the wine vats near the back gate."

When Monday's lunch bell rang I tore out of class and ran to the back gate to meet Scoby. He was already there with nine boys and one girl silently huddled about a tape deck. Those who weren't lacing their sneakers and adjusting sweatbands were whipping a basketball around with a sharp crispness that seemed to singe the hands of whoever was on the receiving end. One boy was pulling on tube sock after tube sock until his feet looked as if they were encased in plaster casts. He winced as he placed his padded feet in a pair of hightop sneakers. I turned to the kid and said, "How many pairs of socks do you have on?"

"Seven."

"Why?"

"For good luck, stupid."

"Oh, yeah, right. Sure. My bad, I should've known."

Nicholas Scoby peeked around the corner of the wine vats and said, "Okay, Mr. Uyeshima isn't looking, let's go." The chainlink fence groaned and sagged under the weight of ten kids scaling it like boot camp Marines. From the other side Scoby looked back at me with a pained expression. "Yo, cuz, the radio." I tossed the radio over and began climbing, catching my pants leg in the barbs at the top of the fence. None of the kids had bothered to wait for me; they were running down Airdrome Avenue, heading for the park.

"Kaufman!" It was Mr. Uyeshima, the dean of boys, yelling and blowing his whistle. He marched toward me, swinging his paddle. I flung myself onto the sidewalk, ripping my pants in the process, and ran after the rest of the gang.

I caught up with them at the park. There wasn't much time and they were in a hurry to get started, kissing their talismans and pleading with Nicholas, "Scoby, fuck that nigger, let's play."

"Chill." Nick Scoby turned toward me, whisking the ball behind his back and through his legs and looking me in the eye. "C'mon, Gunnar. It's us five. Me, you" — he quickly pointed out three other boys — "Dontévius, Snooky, and Spoon."

The kid who had painstakingly put on all those socks whined, "What about me? That's fucked up. That skinny mark motherfucker can't even play no ball."

"Look, Patrick, sub for Spoon every six baskets."

Patrick was right, of course. I'd never played a game of basketball in my life and told Nick so.

"Nick, I ain't no ballplayer."

Paul Beatty

"I know you ain't. I seen you looking at those sonnets, drool dripping out your mouth. You either a poet or a homosexual."

"Oh shit, that's fucked up. Why can't I be both?"

"True. Well, you can be a ballplayer too. If you want to hang with me, you're gonna have to play ball. Awwright? Press the play button."

I pressed the tape deck's play button and a deep bass line rumbled over the blacktop. The music set the tempo and provided the ballplayers with a grooveline around which to improvise. They spun, twisted, lunged, and chased each other from pole to pole as I ran in circles, determined to stay as far away from the ball as possible and still look busy.

The Santa Monica school district didn't have a physical education curriculum. Participation in organized sports was looked down on as the taboo dominion of society's underprivileged. During Proletarian Pastimes Week, instead of playing sports we learned the rules. Ms. Cegeny had a nephew who was the UCLA basketball team's manager. After he explained to us the intricacies of handing out towels to sweaty giants and the importance of liquid electrolyte replacement, he taught us the game, using two wastepaper baskets and a globe.

I jogged near the sidelines, trying to recall the nephew's lessons. The other kids ran purposefully up and down the court. Adrianna Carros put Scoby on her hip, pump faked, spun left, and smartly banked the ball in the basket.

1. *Double Dribble* — No dribbling with two hands.

2. *Foul* — Touching an opposing player with ball results in a defensive foul.

3. *Traveling* —?

I remembered the UCLA team manager had had trouble explaining traveling, saying it was a vague rule that was often dependent on the referee's interpretation. Deciding that visual demonstration would best explain the ambiguous violation, Ms. Cegeny's nephew grabbed the globe firmly between two hands and ran about the room feigning a dribbling motion. Suddenly he stopped and jumped high in the air without shooting the metallic earth into the trash basket. When he landed he said, "If you do that, you've traveled."

Perplexed, I asked him, "Traveled where?"

The college boy got indignant and tried to bluff his rulebook mastery across. "If a player in possession of the ball leaves the playing surface with the ball and lands at a location other than the original takeoff still in possession of the ball and without having dribbled the ball, said player has created an unfair advantage and 'traveled'."

"What if you come down in the exact same spot? Then you haven't gained an advantage, you're right back where you started."

"Impossible."

The student manager must have been a physics major, because he jumped up and down a few more times to prove that landing in the same spot was an impossibility.

"But, what if?"

"Traveling, you little fuck."

As the game wore on, I began to notice that whenever anybody on my team rebounded a missed shot, everyone ran at top speed toward our basket. I got cocky and decided to take an active role in the game. I began by playing defense. It looked easy enough; you just stood in front of whoever had the ball and wiggled your body until you exasperated your opponent to the point of distraction. A boy named Weasel Torres dribbled toward me and I leapt out in front of him, placing my lanky frame between him and the basket. Weasel's feints and pivots couldn't shake my unorthodox jumping-jack defense, and for good measure I burped in his face, causing Weasel to shoot a wild shot that clanged off the rim like a cannonball.

Scoby rebounded and I took off down the court, my speed boosting me ahead of the pack. With a devilish look in his eyes, Scoby fired a bullet pass that hit me right in the hands about fifteen feet from our team's basket. I caught the ball, took the one dribble my coordination allowed, then jumped as hard as I could, my eyes closed tight. I could hear Ms. Cegeny's testy nephew: "You land with the ball, traveling!" I must have stopped breathing, because I could feel my legs kicking in midair as if I were suspended from an invisible noose. What the fuck was I doing with a basketball in my hands? I opened my eyes and saw that my momentum was hurtling my fragile body toward the basket and the steel rim was closing in on the bridge of my nose. I raised my arms in self-defense and crashed into the basket, the ball slamming through the hoop with an authoritative boom. Instinctively, I grabbed onto the rim to stop myself from flying into the pole. When I slowed to a gentle sway, I let go and dropped to the ground with a soft thud, just as the bell ending the lunch period sounded in the distance.

Paul Beatty

The game stopped. The other players looked at each other, per-plexed, for a brief second and then burst out in a frenzy of high-pitched whooping, high fives, and high-stepping jigs.

"Oh *shit*."

"Yo, that nigger had legs akimbo."

"Oh *shit*."

"Scoby, your boy's got like crazy hops."

"Ain't no seventh-grade ballers in the city dunking."

"This nigger has high-flying kung fu triple-feature you-killed-my-teacher-you-dirty-bastard rise."

"Oh *shit*."

On the walk back to school, Scoby looked at me as if he knew something I didn't. Mr. Uyeshima met us at the gate. He sent the rest of the boys and the lone girl to class. I had a swat coming to me because I had ignored a direct order. As Mr. Uyeshima marched me over to the wine vats for corporal enlightenment, Patrick turned around, cupped his hands to his mouth, and shouted, "Uyeshima, don't hit Gunnar too hard, he dunking with two hands nasty-like pow."

Bent over in the musty shed catching heat with my pants puddled in a denim heap about my ankles and my elbows dug into my knees, I'd received three of the prescribed five swats when Mr. Uyeshima asked me did I really dunk. I said yes and he sent me back to class with a stinging pat on my tender behind.

"Way to go," he said.

"Way to go where?" I snapped back.

I sat in Spanish class, my warm ass simmering in the seat of my pants, trying to concentrate on the infinite conjugations of the verb "escribir" scribbled on the board. I thought of Swen Kaufman taking lashes for his farcical dreams of being a dancer and realized I had taken my swats for the sake of friendship. Not for some orchestrated *semper fi* cultish fraternal bonding or a Huck Finn Nigger Jim "love the one you're with" friendship, but because I'd met a special mother-fucker whose companionship was easily worth a middle-school beating.

"Gunnar, haz una oración utilizando la palabra 'escribir,' por favor."

"Yo voy a *escribir* poemas como Octavio Paz y Kid Frost."

"Quienes?"

"Octavio Paz era un poeta gordiflón y activista de Mexico."

"Y Kid Frost?"

"El es un poetastro hip-hop de la vieja guardia, de la vieja escuela quien vivo en Pomona o en la este."

"Vieja escuela?"

"Si, de la *old school.*"

"Bueno."

"Mata a los pinché gringos. No hablo este lingo y yo quiero jugar bingo. Ya estuvo, time to show and prove-oh."

"Bastante, Gunnar."

I spent the next Saturday perched on the front steps, lazily watering the lawn, waiting for a poem to descend from the midday Los Angeles haze. Paying special attention to the dry patches, I slowly turned the front yard into a grassy swamp, forcing the ants and beetles to scramble over one another as they sought higher ground on the aluminum Montgomery Ward fence that surrounded the yard.

There was a different vibrancy to 24th Street that day. The decibel level was the same, but a grating Hollywood hullabaloo replaced the normal Hillside barking dog and nigger cacophony. The newest rap phenoms, the Stoic Undertakers, were filming a video for their latest album, *Closed Casket Eulogies in F Major.* Earlier in the day I had wandered into the production tent to audition for a part as an extra. The casting director blew one expanding smoke ring in my direction and dismissed me with a curt "Too studious. Next! I told you I want menacing or despondent and you send me these bookworm junior high larvae."

Moribund Videoworks was on safari through the L.A. jungle. A caravan of film trucks and RVs lurched through the streets like sheet-metal elephants swaggering through the ghetto Serengeti. Local strong-armed youth bore the director over the crowds in a canopied sedan chair, his seconds shouting out commands through a bullhorn. "Bwana wants to shoot this scene through an orange filter to make it seem like the sun's been stabbed and the heavens are bleeding onto the streets." "Special effects, can you make the flames shoot farther out from the barrel of the Uzi? Mr. Edgar Barley Burrows wants the guns to spit death. More blood! You call this carnage! More blood." My street was a soundstage and its machinations of poverty and neglect were Congo cinema verité. "Quiet on the set. Camera. Roll sound. Speed. Action!"

Carloads of sybaritic rappers and hired concubines cruised down the street in ghetto palanquins, mint condition 1964 Impala lowriders, reciting their lyrics and leaning into the camera with gnarled intimidating scowls.

"Cut!"

The curled lips snapped back into watermelon grins like fleshy rubber bands. "How was that, massa? Menacing enough fo' ya?"

"You got 'em pissing their pants in Peoria. Now one more take, and this time make sure they defecate their dungarees in Dubuque."

Our local councilman, Pete "Hush Money" Brocklington, walked past my house wringing his hands and bragging to the passersby about the loads of money pouring into the neighborhood coffers. I only saw the bulge in his pocket. When the civic carpetbagger ventured into firing range, I pressed my thumb into the nozzle and sprayed him with a water jet from my Montgomery Ward Birmingham Special garden hose. He was about to chastise me when my mother, obviously of voting age, opened the screen door. "Gunnar, stop playing with the hose!" Councilman Brocklington waved to her. My mother ignored him and sloshed across the lawn to inspect my job, then joined me on the steps. I looked down at her sopping wet feet; as she wiggled her toes, tiny bubbles squeezed through her canvas sneakers.

"Mom, I need some new tennis shoes."

"What's wrong with the ones you have on now? They're damn near new."

"These are skateboard sneakers. I can't play basketball in these."

"What, you stopped skateboarding?"

"I played basketball for the first time the other day, and I think I'm gonna be pretty good. Besides, the streets out here are all fucked up — cracks, potholes, broken glass. You can't skate on that. Every time I fall, I get cut to ribbons and my wheels get all thrashed."

"Well, what kind of shoes do you need?"

"I don't know, something like the ones they advertise on television, I guess. Something expensive, I suppose."

"Don't people get shot for wearing those shoes?"

"Ma, it's not the shoes, people get shot because someone decides to shoot 'em. Anyway, I'll get Nick to go with me to the store."

"Okay, I'll give you the money tomorrow."

A member of the film crew yelled "Sound!" and the beats to the Stoic Undertakers' latest single, "Exhume the Dearly Departed and

Take Their Watches," kicked in. Reflexively, my eyes closed halfway, my shoulders hunched toward the ground, my right foot tapped softly on the stair, and my head began a faintly perceptible bob.

"Your taste in music sure has changed."

"How can you tell? I thought you were tone-deaf."

"When you used to listen to that rock 'n' roll, your head used to bang so hard I thought it was going to snap off and roll into the street. Now you look like you're strung out on heroin. Your body just teeters from side to side like you have an inner ear infection — reminds me of Gene Kelly in those sailor movies. Gunnar, why don't you buy some tap-dancing shoes instead? It'll be safer — no one would shoot you for your tap-dancing shoes."

"Gene Kelly, Ma? Tap dance? Vaudeville is dead. You want me to change my name to Bubbles and start singing them 'Call me Shine' songs? No one would have to shoot me, I'd die of shame."

"Geez, you're sensitive. What topics of importance are these hoodlums singing about, anyway?"

"The spoils of war, I guess."

My mother and I stopped to watch lead rapper MC Smarty-Pants wave his flamethrower over his head and recite his frenzied verse.

> Aaaahhh yeah, I'm the ghetto fascist,
> inner-city black Mussolini.
> The cruel druid dousing your dick in lighter fluid
> then eating it up like roast wienie.
> Oh what the fuck, ketchup, mustard, relish;
> I bar-b-cue niggers so why embellish the hellish
> Full of hate, casting my fate with Satan I'm the
> devil's prime mate . . .

"What's with all the homoeroticism? People talk about the white man's penis envy. The white man ain't got nothing on these genital-obsessed hip-hoppers."

"I know, Ma. You should hear the guys at school. 'Suck my dick, slob on the knob, lick my stick,' non-fucking-stop. There's this one boy whose nickname is Big Dick Black, and if someone asks him, 'How big is it?' he yells back, 'Three fists and tip!'"

"I don't get it."

"Never mind." I paused. "Mama?"

Paul Beatty

"Hmmm."

"Where do poems come from?"

"Why? You a poet too?"

"Soon as I write a poem I will be."

"It's corny, but I think poems are echos of the voices in your head and from your past. Your sisters, your father, your ancestors talking to you and through you. Some of it is primal, some of it is hallucinatory bullshit. That madness those boys rapping ain't nothing but urban folklore. They retelling stories passed down from chicken coop to apartment stoop to Ford coupe. Hear that rhyme, boy. Shit, I could get down and rap if I had to. MC Big Mama Osteoporosis in the house."

"That reminds me, I did the family tree in Ms. Murphy's class last week and everyone believed me. I couldn't believe it."

"Gunnar, what kind of poet do you plan to be?"

"I don't know, the cool tantric type. Shaolin monk style. Lao Tsu, but with rhythm."

"You'll do the Kaufman legacy proud, I'm sure."

The bullhorn crackled — "Okay, that's a wrap" — and the video shoot was over. Hillside's indigenous population stopped clamoring for attention. The Hollywood ethnographers were no longer examining the traditional native dances, and the dancers' hands slowly dropped down to their sides, their rumps stopped shaking. Like photogenic Riefenstahl Nubians watching the white god's helicopter pull away, the Hillside denizens watched the film crew coil the cables, load the trucks, and hustle off, leaving us to fight over the blessed remnants of Western civilization they left behind. My tribe wrestled for the rights to broken doughnuts and oily ham 'n' cheese croissants, then scattered back to our hovels, triumphant from a good day's hunt. Plastic cups clattered in the gutter; paper napkins and signed release forms fluttered about the village like lost leaves.

It occurred to me that maybe poems are like colds. Maybe I would feel a poem coming on. My chest would grow heavier, my eyes watery; my body temperature would fluctuate, and a ringing in my ears would herald the coming of a timeless verse.

Betty and Veronica sashayed up to my front gate, their faces powdered white with doughnut dust. This time Betty's hair was in two ponytails that stood straight up and then branched off at right angles like antelope antlers. Veronica's flapper-style pageboy was dyed silver and sprinkled with blue flakes. Betty slipped a pair of brass knuckles onto her right hand, tossed lightning-fast jabs at the fence post, and started cooing, "So Gunnar, I know you want to play hide-and-go-get-it with us." *Ping.* The clang of Betty's fist slamming against the fence sounded like a navy radar honing in on an enemy submarine. *Ping. Ping.*

"No."

Ding. Ping. Ping. Pang. A hook and two jabs followed by a stiff right uppercut put a small dent in the post, and sparks flew off the aluminum. I could smell the tangy scent of charred metal.

"But I'm the only boy. That's not fair, two against one."

Ping. Ping. Bing. Veronica removed a lead blackjack from her back pocket. "Look, motherfucker, either you play or I gives you some bruise tattoos." She whipped the satchel at the gate and it gonged against the Montgomery Ward "quality" insignia, sending the fence's lattice into rattling waves. When the aluminum convulsions died down, Betty and Veronica about-faced with military abruptness and loudly began to count backward from one hundred. I clicked my heels and gave the girls one of those casual halfhearted Sieg Heil salutes and hurdled over the fence. I sped down the street like an escaped convict, trying not to panic and running through the list of hackneyed movie tricks for outwitting the search party.

Ninety-six, ninety-five, ninety-four

Rule Number One — Change your appearance.

I zipped through the Willoughbys' back yard and ripped a burgundy-and-gold USC sweatshirt from the clothesline. Their bull mastiff, Thor, began to bark, but I pacified him with a scratch between the ears and a stomach rub. Then it was over the back fence, through the alley, and past the Thrifttown liquor store.

Seventy-three, seventy-two, seventy-one

Rule Number Two — Make an effort to disguise your scent.

Despite California's water conservation laws and a completely inorganic front yard consisting of a small patch of Astroturf, a porcelain turtle, and a plastic pink flamingo, weird Mr. Quigley's sprinklers were on full blast twenty-four hours a day. I ran under the makeshift waterfall and, soaking wet, made my way around the corner and into the courtyard of the Piccadilly Arms apartments.

Forty-nine, forty-eight

Rule Number Three — Convince a member of the local populace that you are worthy of his or her assistance by recounting your tale of false imprisonment and the brutality you've suffered at the hands of the guards.

Dexter Sandiford was playing jacks in front of the laundry room, wearing only a pair of loose-fitting white polyester Montgomery Ward briefs. Sitting on his rump, tossing a bright orange ball in the air, and sweeping the jacks into the palm of his chubby little hand, he looked like Cupid. I talked fast.

"Hey Dex, you waiting for your clothes to dry?"

"Uh-huh."

"What you on?"

"Sixies."

"Oh, sixies is tough. Your hands big enough to pick up six jacks scattered from here to Koreatown?"

"Uh-huh."

"You know Betty and Veronica, them two wild banshees who live on Corning Street in the yellow apartments?"

"Uh-huh."

"They chasing me. They're going to kill me. Here's two dollars. I'm going to hide in the laundry room. If they come by, don't tell 'em where I'm at. Okay? Say you seen me run through here headed for Al's Sandwich Shop. My life is in your chubby hands, don't drop it."

"Uh-huh."

Ready or not, here we come!

I slipped into the cramped laundry room. Dexter's clothes were spinning in the dryer. The sound of his size five P.F. Flyers caroming around the steel drum drowned out my heavy breathing. Confident that Betty and Veronica would never find me, I stripped down to my soggy size 26 white polyester briefs and tossed my wet clothes in the dryer. Dexter sat outside the door playing jacks and I sat on top of the washing machine playing with my dick.

"Dexter, you seen Gunnar?"

Damn.

"Uh-huh."

"Where is he?"

"He gave me two wet dollar bills and said to tell you he was running over there near Al's Sandwich Shop."

"Dexter, tell you what I'm not gonna do. I'm not gonna take your two dollars out your hand. I'm not gonna tear them dirty drawers off your little pitch-black behind, shove the stupid two dollars in the crack of your ass, insert one of them jacks in your wee-wee pee hole, and toss you butt-naked into the fucking street if you tell me where Gunnar is."

The silence told me that Dexter was breaching our contract with a cherubic pout and a point of his finger toward the laundry-room door.

Seeing my scrawny near-nakedness, Betty and Veronica licked their lips and shut the door behind them. "Mmmmmm, tap-tap on the fine nigger sittin' on top of the washing machine."

Veronica cradled my limp body in her arms and placed me gently on the floor. The dryer gave off a strange half-buzzing, half-ringing sound and continued to rumble. Betty's teeth clamped down on my nipples and sucked the chill from the damp concrete out of my body. Warm rivulets of her spit meandered past my abdominal muscles and pooled in my bellybutton. Veronica crept around my body, teasingly snapping the elastic band on my underwear and grinding her crotch on my thigh, my shin, and begging to tickle her love button with my big toe. At some point during the torturous fury of this menage à trois noir, my undies slid down to my ankles and shackled me into complete submission. The horny furies took tag-team turns squeezing my genitals. Betty's cold hands ran against the grain of my prickly pubic hair, then cupped and kneaded my balls into a shriveled sack of testosterone mush. Veronica stretched my limp dick with one hand, plucked it like a bass string, and the girls broke into a dueling chorus of gospel double-entendre. Veronica opened with "Go down, Moses, waaaay down to Egypt's land," forcing my face between her legs. Betty side-stepped and countered in an Easter Sunday vibrato of "Touch me, Lord Jesus, mmmmmmmm, with thy hand of mercy," ramming my hand into her crotch. Veronica, reeling from Betty's blows, pointed at my flaccid member and slid into a storefront Pentecostal soprano: "Fix it,

Paul Beatty

Lord Jesus, you fixed it for my mother, now fix it for me." Betty reached into my mouth, grabbed my tongue and placed its pointy tip on her knee, and started singing Mahalia Jackson's subliminal hit, "Move On Up a Little Higher." Feeling left out, Veronica snatched me by the Afro, smothered my lips with kisses, and forced her long tongue down my throat until it tickled my larynx. Betty extracted her spongy plumber's helper from my ear and whispered, "Why don't you sing, Gunnar? Give your frigid spirit wings and just imagine if niggers could fly."

There was a knock on the laundry-room door. It was little Dexter's mother come to collect her clothes and wanting to know what all the moaning was about.

"If y'all in there fucking, you better save some for me. I'll give a motherfucker a shot of life."

"Just a minute, Ms. Sandiford."

Rescued at last. As I removed my clothes from the dryer, Betty and Veronica took one last hunk of buttcheek and then started arguing on the appropriate term for a boy's losing his virginity.

"Deboned."

"Spit-shined."

"Bitch-dipped."

I walked home basking in the warmth of newly tumble-dried clothes, singing "Oh Happy Day" at the top of my lungs. I was still singing when I got home.

A musclebound shirtless boy of about sixteen covered in soapsuds was in Ms. Sanchez's driveway, washing the hell out of her Buick LeSabre. He heard me singing and stopped rubbing the caked-on bird shit long enough to greet me.

"What's up, little man?"

"Cooling."

The wind blew a cloudbank of suds across his chest, revealing a shiny gold crucifix that seemed imbedded in his massive brown torso. It was Ms. Sanchez's son, Juan Julio, known around the neighborhood as Psycho Loco. I'd never seen him before, but knew all about him. His mother used to tell me how Juan Julio's voice was the best missionary religion ever had. On Sundays he'd sing with the choir and his baritone would make the babies stop crying and the deacons start. Ms. Sanchez would hold a crucifix exactly like his up to the sky and swear that drunks, bums, prostitutes, hoodlums, even police officers, people who'd never been in church a day in their lives, would walk into the original First Ethiop Azatlán Catholic-Baptist Church and Casa de Sanctified Holy Rolling Ecumenical Sanctification, kneel at Juan Julio's feet to plead forgiveness, renounce sin, accept the Lord Jesus Christ as their savior, and put all the money they had in the collection plate. When the service ended, the collection plate would be filled with car keys, crack vials, and stolen credit cards.

The neighborhood kids told me the story of Juan Julio's life outside the House of God. On the street the angelic Juan Julio was Psycho Loco, leader of the local gang the Gun Totin' Hooligans. I'd heard how as a strong-arm man-child for a loan shark, when he tired of a debtor's sob story on why that week's payments were late, he'd heat his crucifix with a nickel-plated lighter and press the makeshift branding iron into the victim's cheek and scream, "Now you really have a cross to bear, motherfucker!"

One day I asked Snooky how come his Uncle Kahlil always wore earmuffs, even in the summer. He told me that his uncle and Psycho Loco got into a tussle over who was going to get to smash the jewelry cases at Declerk's Discount Diamonds during a robbery they were planning. Juan Julio grabbed Uncle Kahlil by the ears and pulled like he was opening a bag of potato chips. The pop of his ears being snatched off the sides of his head was the last thing Uncle Kahlil ever heard. Out of pity, Juan Julio let him break the glass during the robbery, but Snooky's uncle got caught, because he couldn't hear Juan Julio telling him the cops were coming.

Here was Psycho Loco, home on parole for killing a paramedic who refused to give his piranha Esta Lleno mouth-to-mouth resuscitation after the fish choked on a family of sea monkeys.

"What you singing, cuz?"

"Some song."

"That's more than some song. That song got me through four years in the Oliver Twist Institute for Little Wanderers and Wayward Minority Males. I sang that shit from lights on to lights out. Oh happy day, oh happy day, when Jesus washed, when Jesus washed, he washed my sins away."

Paul Beatty

Psycho Loco was still singing and putting a shine on the LeSabre's chrome bumpers when I went inside. It took me eight hours and two boxes of frosted flakes to write my first poem. It was a fitting end to a long day.

Negro Misappropriation of Greek Mythology
or, I know Niggers That'll Kick Hercules's Ass

i lift the smoggy Los Angeles
death shroud
searching for ghetto muses

anyone seen Calliope?
heard she emigrated to the San Fernando Valley
fulfills her ranch-styled dreams
with epic afternoon soap operas
and bong water bubble baths

outside, listening for voices,
i hear nothing
the leaves are silent
and the chichi birds look at me
like i'm crazy

you tell that dime-dropper Clio
she better not
leave her witness protection program
i seen some stone killers passing her picture
down by the 7–Eleven

on the sloped banks of the L.A. River
i sit cross-legged
classical guru pose;
my 50-cent Bic pen taut with possibilities

Thalia's bloated body
floats by, zigzaggin' between Firestone radials
finally catching itself on the rusted barbs
of a shopping cart
seriously lost at sea

Euterpe is at the talent show
begging entrance into the church basement
permission to sing her Patti Labelle covers
promising a big record label she won't
smoke up the production money like last time

on my knees
I place my ear to the concrete
I hear nothing
no thundering cavalry hooves
    kicking up dust
no war whoops
not even the ghost-town winds of massacre

    i have a notion
    that if i could translate
    the slobbering bellows of Ray-Ray
    the ubiquitous retarded boy's
    swollen-tongued incantations
    i'd find Melpomene reciting the day's obituaries
    anyone here speak Down syndrome or crack baby?

running my hands over tree-bark Braille,
swashbuckling with palm tree leaves
nothing, paper cuts
en garde, motherfucker

    ham radio signals
    s.o.s. a.p.b. 911 electronic prayers
    to the goddess Urania's voicemail
    go unanswered

    late last night my man picked up a jailhouse phone
    "Yo, nigger, you got to come down and get me out."
    and i was inspired

✿

The next morning I rummaged through the attic and found a can of
black spray paint and the stencils my great-great-uncle Wolfgang used
to do his Jim Crow handiwork. I painted the poem on the wall that

Paul Beatty

surrounds Hillside. Surprisingly, my still-wet verse didn't look out of place between the specious rest-in-peace calligraphic elegies and the fading *Übermensch* graffiti already splashed on the wall.

I was eating cereal and watching the Sunday morning TV journalists discussing the prospect of substantive black rule in South Africa when Nick Scoby knocked on the door. He had his headphones on and his arms were filled with a Montgomery Ward trimline steam iron that dripped water, an ironing board, a can of starch, and a pile of brand-new white T-shirts. He walked in, propped up the board with a loud squeak, and plugged the iron into a nearby socket.

"What you listening to?"

"Toshiko Akiyoshi."

"Who?"

"A piano player. You met Psycho Loco last night, I heard."

"Yeah, so?"

"Listen to you — 'Yeah, so?' Can you imagine the Indians meeting Christopher Columbus and saying, 'Big deal, some midget with syphilis and a bad cold, so fucking what? Pass the buffalo meat'? You're Psycho Loco's next-door neighbor and he likes you."

"Likes me how?"

"He likes you. Ever had a murderer like you before? Psycho Loco is going to come over to your house and ask you for favors. Borrow a cup of sugar, hold on to his gun, put your sister in a headlock and ask you to kindly tell the police he spent the night at your house playing Scrabble, shit like that. You're involved, homes. You're gonna have to respect something more than yourself. You know that saying, 'Fate chooses our relatives, we choose our friends'?"

"*Malheur et Pitié*, canto one, 1803."

"Well, here in the street, that shit works in reverse. Fate picks your friends, and you choose your family. Everybody starts out an orphan in this hole. Gunnar, you gonna have to respect Psycho Loco, the neighborhood, and the way things get done here. Psycho Loco and the Gun Totin' Hooligans try to kill people. People their perception of fate has slated as the enemy. This ain't Hatfields and McCoys, nobody's birth certificate says Joe Crip, Sam Piru, and I definitely don't know no niggers surnamed Hooligan — some Irish homies, maybe. If Psycho Loco says you're his friend, there ain't nothing you can do about it. You're friends 'cause he says so. Now there might be some fool who lives on the other side of town who thinks you're his arch-enemy simply because Psycho Loco likes you. That is fate, black. Maybe people with money can skew fate in their favor, but that ain't us. I seen that poem you wrote on the way over here. There was a gang of motherfuckers reading it like a wanted poster. Oh yeah, nigger, thirteen years old and you involved now."

Scoby ripped open a plastic bag, pulled out a T-shirt, and stretched it over the pointy end of the ironing board. He sprayed the starch over the shirt, licked his finger, pressed it to the bottom of the iron, and listened to the sizzle. "Watch," he said. The iron cackled and spit as it glided over the shirt. When Scoby got to one of the factory wrinkles, he pressed the steam button and the iron exhaled plumes of vapor and the wrinkles vanished. After ironing the front and back of the shirt, he snatched it off the end and laid the sleeves on the board. Carefully aligning the hems, he dug the iron into the material, putting a stiletto-sharp crease in each sleeve. "Don't put no creases anywhere else. No crease down the back, that's the east side. No military double creases down the front from the collar to the end of the sleeve like them buster-ass niggers from XXY Chromosome Recidivists. Now go get a pair of pants."

"I don't care what happens, I will never put a fucking crease in my Levi's. No fucking way, man. I will never be that involved."

Scoby laughed and asked if my mother had given me enough money for basketball shoes. I pulled two hundred dollars from an envelope marked "Basketball Paraphernalia" and fanned the crisp twenty-dollar bills, wondering if it was enough to change my fate.

The Shoes

Buying basketball shoes was much harder than I thought. Unlike the skate shop, where there are only three different brands and maybe ten styles to choose from, Tennies from Heaven was the footwear equivalent of an automobile showroom. A sneaker emporium where the walls were lined with hundreds of shoes and salesmen dressed in silk sweatsuits patrolled the floor, handing out brochures, shaking hands, and checking credit ratings.

The basketball section took up the entire third floor. An eighty-dollar sneaker caught my eye and I hefted it in my hand as if its weight might tell something about its quality. I was about to call for a salesperson when I heard Scoby snickering behind my back and singing, "Buddies, they cost a dollar ninety-nine. Buddies, they make your feet feel fine." I put the shoe down and Nicholas pushed me through a sliding glass door into an area of the store called the Proving Grounds. A section of the store where the state-of-the art, more expensive models were on display. Before the staff allowed me to try on any shoes, I had to sign a release stating that if my new sneakers were forcibly removed from my feet and the crime received any media attention, I would blame the theft on the current administration and not on niche marketing.

Even with all the paperwork I could only try on one shoe at a time, since I wasn't accompanied by a bonded legal guardian or a basketball coach. Whenever I slipped my foot into a new shoe I'd hobble over to the mirror like Tiny Tim Cratchit and blink really fast, trying to create an optical illusion so I could imagine what wearing both sneakers at the same time would look like. After some eyestrain I managed to convince the guy to let me try a different shoe on each foot and teetered over to Nicholas to ask his opinions. He vetoed the sporty Barbarian on my left foot because they were sewn by eight-year-old Sri Lankans who worked in open-air factories, received no lunch breaks, and were paid in candy bars. The Air Idi Amin Fire Walker on my right foot, a colorful suede high-top designed to look like a traditional African mask, was nixed because although the shoes performed well on asphalt, they tended to slip on gym floors, and besides, the kids chanted "Coup d'état, coup d'état!" at anyone who wore them. Nick suggested the high-tech Adidas Forum II's, an outrageously expensive pair of plain white basketball shoes, computer-designed for maximum support, something called "wearability," and exactly like the pair he was wearing.

The salesperson, smelling commission, closed the deal with a spiel about French cowhide hand-sewn with French thread by French seamsters who were paid by French entrepreneurs who donated a percentage of every shoe sold to help build basketball courts in ghettos throughout the world. I wanted to comment on how building more basketball courts just created a demand for more sneakers, but instead gimped around the store, hopped up and down on one foot, and put one hundred and seventy-five dollars on the counter. The salesman smiled and handed me the other shoe and the carbon copy of my release form.

The Haircut

I had twenty-five dollars left and felt that my next purchase should be a basketball, but Nicholas insisted that having the proper haircut was more important than having a basketball. He recommended Manny's Barbershop and Chiropractic Offices on the corner of 24th Street and Robertson Boulevard. Manny Montoya was a tall curly-haired Chicano whose mission in life was to improve the posture of every hunchbacked ex–farm laborer, swaybacked prostitute, and stoop-shouldered hoodlum in the neighborhood. Manny only offered one haircut, the "Sunkist Special," which was a concentration-camp baldy with a hint of stubble. Ballplayers and bangers lined up for haircuts, sharing copies of *Jet*, *Pocho*, and *Guns & Ammo* till a barber called their names.

"Hey bro', peep this *firmé cuete*. Air-cooled, magnesium-plated, single-action Gepetto Pinnochio long-nosed .22 caliber."

"Naw, cuz, you want one of these fingerprint-resistant Buger GAT polymer ten-millimeters with the emerald handle."

"Well, I think we can both agree that this centerfold *jaina del mes* is fine."

"What's her hobbies?"

"The usual — scuba diving, horseback riding, and skiing."

"Where in fuck does *Jet* magazine find all these colored cowgirls who ski?"

On the other side of the room, near the plastic skeleton, lowriders who'd gotten whiplash from taking corners on two wheels and thrown their backs out because they'd spent last night bunny-hopping their Oldsmobile Cutlasses down Crenshaw Boulevard waited patiently for adjustments, pretending the cricks in their necks didn't hurt. Manny excitedly pointed out the window and exclaimed, "Hey look, there's Gilbert Suavecito's cherry '45 DeSoto convertible and Iris Chacon riding on the hood in a bikini." The hot-rodders' heads spun around for a look at Gilbert's champion lowrider and the Mesopotamian-buttocked televison star Ms. Chacon. A chorus of agony rang throughout the shop as the men rewrenched their necks for nothing more than a glimpse of Rafael Muñoz giving a ride to Gina "Scullybones" Sanders on the handlebars of his custom Schwinn Stingray five-speed.

Manny laughed and dug his thumb into the nape of my neck. The pain forced my head down and he sheared long furrows down the middle of my scalp.

In the far corner of the shop, a circle of old men, Indios and Africans, played electronic poker games and swapped migration stories. I sat in the barber chair concentrating on keeping my head still and straining to hear the stories of how their families ended up in Los Angeles, far from their ramshackle southwestern and southern roots.

One man, Mr. Tillis Everett, the attendant at Zoom Zoom Gas, chewed on beef jerky and talked about how one day in Biloxi his father came home with blood on his shirtsleeve. "It was a Tuesday, and Daddy walked in the door, kissed Grandma on the cheek, and said, 'Momma, I have to go.' Grandma said, 'I'll have your stuff ready in five minutes.'" The mechanic spit out a wad of unchewable gristle, picked his teeth with a thumbnail, and continued. "Things was understood down south. If you made a decision to hit a white man, you made the choice to kill him and relocate. Wasn't no left, right, left, 'Don't fuck with me no more,' shake hands and let's be friends. They used to say, 'Hope the man with the rope ain't got no telescope.' It wasn't no running in the water to throw the dogs off your scent. They bring the hounds round to the other side and pick you up soon enough. You had to get to a chicken coop and rub handfuls of chicken shit on your shoes real thick-like. Dogs would get tired of smellin' that shit and they'd refuse to follow the scent. My daddy arrived in Los Angeles smelling like a henhouse toilet. Niggers out here is out of luck. Ain't no chicken shit in Los Angeles. Lots o' chickenshit niggers, no real chicken shit. Couldn't run away from Los Angeles if you wanted to."

I couldn't keep my hand off my newly shorn skull. It sprinkled on the way home and the droplets of rain soothed my tender scalp. When I got home my mom pressed my noggin into her breasts and sobbed that I looked as if I were on a hunger strike. My sisters were taking turns doing bongo solos on my head when the phone rang. It was my father.

The Ball

"Boy, you see my portrait of the Northbrook Necrophiliac in yester-day's paper?"

"Yup. Looks a little bit like Dwight Eisenhower. Is it true this guy goes round fucking skeletons and shit?"

"Yeah, some janitor at the medical school caught him sticking his dick in an eyesocket."

"What a numskull."

"Very funny. Your mother tells me you've started playing bas-ketball."

"Yeah, me and some of the fellas . . ."

"Just don't get one of those Jack-Johnson-black-buck-hey-look-at-me-I'm-an-athlete baldheads, you hear me."

"Dad, I need a basketball."

"Only scrubs *buy* basketballs."

"Dad!"

"I'll see what I can do. Put your mama on the phone."

About two hours later a police cruiser drove by the front of the house and chirped the siren. I looked out the window and saw a hairy white arm fling a brand-new basketball into the front yard. As I ran out to retrieve the ball, a book landed at my feet. The book was a thin paperback entitled *Heaven Is a Playground*. From what I could glean from the back cover, it was a sports journalist's treatise on a pack of inner-city Brooklynites who spent the better part of their days scam-pering around a basketball court known as the Hole. Inside my father had scribbled a note: "Read this and remember you're a Kaufman, and not one of the black misfits sociologically detailed herein."

❖

Soon it was time to try out my new sneakers, new basketball, and new haircut. Scoby and I sauntered into the park and he pointed out some of the aging local legends seated under the trees, sipping from crinkled brown bags. Ben "Yoda" Morales reputedly was so quick that when he changed directions, the sneaker-to-concrete friction caused his shoes to spontaneously combust. Over the years he'd lost a step and all anyone ever saw was puffs of smoke wafting from his soles as he slithered to the basket. In his prime, Nathan "Sadhu" Ng could go up for a rebound and leave a dirty footprint on the backboard. Now he was a shoeless stumblebum begging dimes from the younger kids. Scoby too had a rep. Blind Melissa "Sonar" Kilmartin, who could do anything on the court but chase the ball when it went out of bounds, turned in our direction and raised her beer to him. "What's up, Scoby, you gonna serve niggers today like I used to, baby? Who that with you?"

That first day Nick and I went to the park, about fifty players were standing in the hot sun, waiting their turn to play. When the game in progress ended, Scoby walked onto the court, touched his toes, alternately lifted his feet by the insteps until his heels touched his butt, and waited for whoever had winners to tell him who else was on his team. There was some unspoken protocol at work, and Nicholas apparently had diplomatic status. Soon a huge crowd gathered around the sidelines. Right from the start there was an intensity on the court that hadn't been present in the previous game. Players who usually spent most of their precious court time arguing and disputing every call were silent and stealing glances at Scoby whenever they made a shot or did something particularly impressive. Scoby's pregame announcement — "Niggers who come here for the attention best to leave now" — seemed to have had some effect.

I watched Nicholas play a few games and tried to figure what the big deal was. His team always won, but it wasn't like he was out there performing superhuman feats. He didn't sprout wings and fly, he didn't seem to have eyes in the back of his head. There was always someone who jumped higher than he could, handled the ball better. Nick would make five or six baskets and that was it.

After winning his fourth straight game, he told me to walk over to the basket and dunk the ball.

"Huh?"

"Do what you did at school the other day."

I walked under the basket with my brand-new ball cradled under my arm and flushed the electric orange orb through the hoop with two hands. A tall boy wearing a dark gray T-shirt that read "Wheatley High Varsity Basketball" in faded green letters sauntered over to me and started to small-talk.

"You know Scoby?"

"We go to Manischewitz together."

"Your name Gunnar Kaufman?"

"Uh-huh."

"You wrote that poem?"

"Mmmm-hmmm."

"You wanna run?"

In as low a voice as I could muster, I said, "Yeah." I had a rep before I ever played a game at the park, although I wasn't sure exactly what for.

We played until nightfall. During what was shaping up to be the last game of the evening, it became impossible to see the basket farthest away from the streetlight. It was as if we were playing at the lunar surface during the half-moon. One side of the court was in complete darkness and the other fairly well lit. The score was tied at ten-ten and someone suggested we call the game a draw on account of darkness before someone got hurt. Scoby said, "Next basket wins." My team had the ball and we were shooting at the visible basket. The high schooler in the gray shirt took a short shot that circled around the rim and fell out, right into Nick's hands. Scoby took two speed dribbles, losing the man who was guarding him, and headed upcourt. When he crossed half-court he disappeared into the darkness, then quickly reappeared in the light without the ball. A second later you heard the crashing of the chain net as the ball arced through it.

"Game."

Skipping the ball through my legs, imitating the moves I'd seen during the course of the day, I rounded the corner onto Sherbourne Drive and realized what Scoby's rep was for: he never missed. I mean never.

five

SUMMER BEFORE my first year of high school was the summer niggers stopped sitting next to each other in the movies. We jaywalked, spit on the sidewalk, broke curfew, but strictly abided by the unwritten law prohibiting black boys over fifteen from sitting next to each other in the dark. One yawning unoccupied chair always belied our closeness, separating us like a velvet moat filled with homophobic alligators and popcorn as we solved cinematic mysteries with deductive streetsmart reasoning.

"The pockmarked motherfucker from the country club gots to be the killer."

"Nigger-ro, is you crazy? It's the lefthanded honey with the juicy Maybelline lips and the fucked-up German accent. It's always the foreigner. Kill again, you sexy thing, you."

"Both you Sherlock Holmes cokeheads are wrong, it's the Doberman pinscher. The mutt is hypnotized by the psychologist to kill on his say-so. Didn't you see the bloody paw prints?"

In the past three years me, Nicholas, and Psycho Loco had become a heroic trio of sorts. We were the Three Musketeers, all for one and one for all, sipping watery lemon-lime soda from the same straw, galavanting in the streets, sounding off like wind chimes in the city breeze. By high school I was no longer the seaside bumpkin, clueless to the Byzantine ways of the inner city. But I hadn't completely assimilated into Hillside's culture. I still said "ant" instead of "awwwnt" and "you guys" rather than "y'all," and wore my pants a bit too tight, but these shortcomings were forgiven because I had managed to attain a look. My sinewy physique drew scads of attention. I'd be on the bus or standing in line at the store and strangers would come up to me and knowingly nod their heads as if we shared some secret. The more straightforward ones would speak up and interpret my dreams for me.

"You play ball? Don't say no, you got that look. I can tell by your calves. Skinny, powerful legs and the way you walk. Pigeon-toed, small ass 'n' all. You ain't nothing but a ballplayer."

Despite the pigeonholing, it was fun to answer the inquiries and watch the populace swoon.

"How tall are you?"

"Six-five, baby, six-five." I'd exaggerate by an inch and a half.

Not everyone was enamored of my height and athletic ability. There were those who didn't care that I'd spent hours in the city's gyms and parks perfecting my game. Not that I had ever asked anyone to care, but to some ghetto subcultures I was nothing more than a tall wise-ass punk who deserved a serious comeuppance.

Whenever I stopped to listen to the street-corner sermons of the all-albino brothers and sisters of NAPPY (New African Politicized Pedantic Yahoos), the speakers always singled me out as a traitor to my race, the dreaded heretic of the nation of sun people. After prophesying the founding of New Africa, a glorious day when the United States government would turn over five southern states to legions of turbaned pink-eyed heliocentrists, their leader, Tasha Rhodesia, would defiantly ask, "Any questions from the unbelievers?"

I'd raise my hand with a puzzled look on my face. A look that differed from my basketball mien, a look that said, "Maybe if I heard the right syllogism I'd make a worthy convert?"

Tasha Rhodesia would wave a light-skinned arm lined with copper bracelets cast from precious African metals ceremoniously over the crowd. "You, the proud young warrior, obviously of Watusi stock — what white propaganda infests your fertile African mind?"

"How can a bunch of people such as yourselves, who give themselves names like Wise Intelligent, P-Knowledge, and Erudite Judicious, be so fucking stupid?"

In Afrocentric slapstick, an offended neophyte would smush a bean pie in my face and banish me from the promised land.

Then there were the bands of bored Bedouins who roamed Hillside, silently testing my resolve by lifting their T-shirts, revealing a bellybutton and a handgun tucked in their waistband. "S'up, nigger?"

In response I'd lift my T-shirt and flash my weapons: a paperback copy of Audre Lorde or Sterling Brown and a checkerboard set of abdominal muscles. "You niggers ain't hard — calculus is hard."

Paul Beatty

"All right, Gunnar, you keep talking smack. Psycho Loco ain't going to be around forever."

My friendship with Psycho Loco did have its perks, but Scoby was right, Psycho Loco asked for a lot of favors. My back yard became a burial ground for missing evidence; warm guns and blood-rusted knives rested in unmarked graves under little mounds of dirt. I had nightmares about the ghosts of convenience-store clerks and ice-cream-truck drivers floating among the fruit trees, stuffing their puncture wounds with rotted fruit poultices.

One Halloween night Psycho Loco rang the doorbell in a black knit whodunnit mask and with a nickel-plated nine-millimeter in his hand. I opened the door with a mocking "Trick or treat?" and put a candy bar in his flannel shirt pocket. "Look at you, nineteen years old out here knocking on doors begging candy. Why you ain't bag snatchin', homie?"

Psycho Loco walked past me, snatched off his mask, and asked in a shaky voice if he could take a shower.

"Ma, can Juan Julio take a shower?"

"Yes, long as he cleans the tub afterward."

After a few minutes I noticed clouds of steam drifting down the hallway and into the living room. *He must've forgotten to close the door,* I thought, and walked to the bathroom. Psyco Loco was standing naked, looking at himself in the mirror. Eye to eye with his demons and crying so hard he had tears on his knees. I pulled back the shower curtain and handed him a bar of soap. He stepped into the mist and slipped a hand into my mom's loofah mitt and said, "Don't go nowhere, okay?"

"Yeah, yeah," I said, trying not to embarrass either of us by acknowledging Psycho Loco's pain. "Just don't use my mom's Australian chamomile shampoo. Use the red jojoba extract."

I sat on the toilet and turned on the radio so I wouldn't have to listen to Psycho Loco's cathartic wailing while he scoured his skin raw through two weather reports and three traffic updates. When he finally got out of the shower, he told me to get dressed and meet him at the wall in ten minutes. I rinsed the tub clean of slivers of skin and curlicue body hairs swimming in rivulets of his blood like microscopic bacteria.

When I arrived at the wall, the Gun Totin' Hooligans were waiting for me, their raffish frames casting impatient shadows in the moonlight. Smoking generic cigarettes, cradling unopened quart-size bottles of Carta Blanca like brown glass-skinned babies, they raised their eyebrows to say hello and cavalierly tossed up gang signs. Those who weren't propped up against the wall in gangster leans squatted on the ground, flat-footed, perfectly balanced in the refugee tuck. The squat was a difficult position that most yoga teachers have problems assuming, but the disenfranchised in all societies do it with ease. I knew better than to assume the poor indigene pose. I always ended up on my tippy-toes, my wobbly equilibrium betraying my privileged upbringing.

Joe Shenanigans waved me over and I braced myself against the wall next to him. I folded my arms and wondered why Psycho Loco had invited me to the party. Joe offered me a sip of pink swill from a pint of Mad Dog 20/20, which I declined. It was tempting, but I heard that after drinking that shit you glowed the next morning.

"Thought you stopped drinking, Joe?"

"Only on special occasions."

"Like what, sundown?"

"Watch your back, the paint is wet."

I looked over my shoulder and saw a dripping scrawl that read,

> Pumpkin raising hell in hell
> October 31   R.I.P.
> Happy Halloween

Pumpkin was dead. I tried to conjure up some grief, but it was hard to feel any sympathy for the pudgy redbone devil who had almost pierced my ear with an arrow in the Montgomery Ward sporting goods department.

"Who killed him?"

"Not for nuthin', but him and Psycho Loco was trying to fuckin' rob the fuckin' Koreans."

Joe Shenanigans was a skinny boy, black as a penny loafer, who claimed he was a Sicilian from a long line of mafiosi. He had a cheesy wisp of a mustache, and his skin sagged at the joints because his diet consisted entirely of frozen Italian foods like turkey tetrazzini, fettuccini alfredo, and chicken parmigiana with linguini. Holding a conversation with Joe was like talking to someone who was simultaneously channeling Martin Scorsese, Al Pacino, and Mama Celeste.

Paul Beatty

"Badda bing, badda bam, badda boom, Psycho Loco and Pumpkin, the gun to Ms. Kim's chin, 'Open the register.' But Mama mia, Ms. Kim ain't listenin'."

Ms. Kim was the half-black, half-Korean owner of the corner store. Fathered by a black GI, she was born in Korea and at age seventeen was adopted by a black family and raised in Fresno. To us, when she was behind the counter in her store, Ms. Kim was Korean. When she was out on the streets walking her dogs, she was black. Ms. Kim and I used to kid each other as to who had the flattest rear end.

"Ms. Kim busy cussin' Psycho Loco out. You know how she be talking Korean and black broken English at the same time. 'First you steal my eggs and now you're gonna steal money? Naw, motherfucker. How you be so cold-blood? I feed you kim-chee when you baby. Break north befo' I call mother.' So Psycho Loco fires a warning shot to get her attention, and he hits one o' dem huge inflatable Maelstrom 500 malt liquor bottles. The fucking ting falls on Pumpkin's ass and suffocates him. Fugettabodit. Fucking jay."

"You mean A."

"Yeah, fucking A. Hey, where your boy Nick Scoby?"

"He's listening to Miles Davis and refuses to come outside. Maybe tomorrow, he says."

Psycho Loco situated himself in the epicenter of the gathering, looked over his incompetent troops, and spoke in a soft voice.

"Do we have a quorum?" he asked.

"Hell naw!" the boys responded.

With that Psycho Loco theatrically twisted the cap off his beer bottle. Most groups of boys pay homage to a slew of dead homies by saying, "This is for the brothers who ain't here," spilling a swallow of drink onto the sidewalk. Not the delinquents from the Gun Totin' Hooligans. Though less elaborate than a Japanese tea ceremony, the GTH drinking ritual was equally reverent and definitely longer.

The Gun Totin' Hooligans started out as a local dance troupe called the Body Eccentric. When Los Angeles's funk music scene was in its heyday, kids from different neighborhoods met at the nightclubs and outdoor jams to dance against one another in "breakin'" or "poppin'" contests. After losing battles to companies known as the Flex-o-twists and the Invertebrates, the kids from Hillside often limped home with sprained ankles and broken bones from botching a complicated move.

The citywide ridicule became unbearable when, after a humiliating defeat by the Lindy Poppers, a one-legged Hillside boy named Peg-Leg Greg beat a contestant to death with his artificial limb. To ensure the survival of the species, the dance troupes evolved into gangs and the war was on. Countless drive-bys and handkerchief purchases later, the Gun Totin' Hooligans were the bravest but most inept gang in Los Angeles. Suffering more casualties than the rest of the city's gangs combined, the Hooligans had developed a tradition that required that the thirsts of every parched and perished comrade be quenched. Thus the endless beer ceremony.

"Riff-raff, rest in peace." Pour.

"Tank-tank, sweet dreams." Dribble.

"Weebles, six feet under." Splash.

"L'il Weebles, smoking weed with the angels." Spatter.

"Baby Weebles, dozin' and decomposin'." Bloop. Bloop.

When GTH finally finished honoring their dead, they'd gone through six containers of beer and Psycho Loco was standing ankle-deep in a pool of beer foam.

The main reason for GTH's high death rate was that initially the gang didn't tote guns. They fought their enemies with antiquated weaponry such as blow darts, tomahawks, and spears. The founding members thought the moniker would be a good subterfuge. Who'd suspect a gang called Gun Totin' Hooligans in a vicious gangland lassoing?

The gang owed its formidable notoriety to Psycho Loco's ruthlessness. Tattooed with naked women and adorned with a chain of paper doll figurines, Psycho Loco's arms resembled the kill tally on the cowling of a World War II airplane. The red Swiss cross on his right forearm represented the paramedic whose death had resulted in the bid upstate.

The mourning party for Pumpkin heated up into a war dance; the boys got antsy and began sloshing beer on one another and hollering hoodlum apothegms. "What we gonna do when a GTH Crip takes the final dip? Take a set trip, load the clip, cruise the strip, give a punk-ass buster a hellified fat lip. Nothing is even steven till everybody's bleedin'. Pumpkin, we love you! We'll make 'em pay!"

Psycho Loco yelled for everyone to shut up and grabbed a boy named Butane by his eyelids. Everyone flinched in vicarious pain and uttered a barely audible but collective "Ow." Psycho Loco went into his proud drunken warrior tirade. "What do you mean, we? Every time one of us gets capped, who does the revenge killing? My ass. When I first moved here, you motherfuckers was scared of every vato on the block, especially Raymond Keniston. 'Juan Julio, Juan Julio, Raymond took my money. Raymond threw my bike off the roof. Raymond threw my father into the garbage truck.' Punk-ass yellow rat bastards. Joe Shenanigans, when Raymond stepped on your pet frog Kermie on purpose, didn't I make him eat it and every fly that landed on your screen door for two weeks?"

"That's 'cause you my gumba. My main molan-yan from the old country."

"Fuck it, I'm tired of doing y'all's dirty work. After the payback for Pumpkin, that's it, I quit bangin'."

Every gangster in GTH dropped to his knees and started kowtowing. "You can't quit, Psycho Loco. We need you." They knew if Psycho Loco quit, there would be a mini-pogrom on GTH members.

Psycho Loco laughed, released Butane's eyelids, and plopped down next to me. We drank some beers, and eventually a few of us made a foray through Cheviot Heights in Psycho Loco's van. We celebrated Halloween and tried to forget about Pumpkin by taking turns smashing car windows with a crowbar. The BMWs and Mercedes Benzes were all small fish when we saw our Moby Dick, a thirty-five-foot motor home parked in front of a huge three-story house complete with marble portico and a set of tall wooden doors. While Captain Ahab and the rest of the crew harpooned and skinned the mobile home, this sailor, drunk with jealousy and resentment, crept across the lawn and uprooted a small metal sign that read THIS PROPERTY GUARDED BY CHEV-TEC SECURITY.

After an hour of crippling cars, we weaved down Nalgas Drive back home. Psycho Loco made a left onto Wiltern Boulevard, reached under his seat, and pulled out his nine-millimeter. The boys passed the gun around, commented on its weight, barrel length, muzzle velocity, then stuck their arms out the window and into the humid air. With a pop the streetlights flashed, then burst into incandescent amber mini-novas, the plate-glass windows collapsing like families.

"Shoot this shit, Kaufman."

I didn't hesitate. Grabbing the gun in two hands, I squeezed off a three-shot sound poem that slapped a complacent hot southern California night to attention.

"Aim, nigger."

"I am."

"What you shooting at?"

"God, motherfucker."

Nothing goes faster than fifteen bullets. In need of another fix, we stopped by Lettie's, Psycho Loco's girlfriend, for more ammunition. Hopping back into the car with a sly look on his face, Psycho Loco showed us a handful of bullets and put the car in gear. As we sped away, he announced with a hint of contriteness in his voice, "You should have seen the look on the old girl's face. 'Where you going?' Like I know."

Riding in the back seat of the car, I felt as if I were circling the neighborhood on some R-rated carousel. Familiar landmarks blurred into the sunrise, the stupid merry-go-round music refusing to go away. When I arrived home, I planted the metal Chev-Tec flag in the crab grass, threw up on my mother's lone flowering rosebush, and tried to tear a set of unwanted chevrons from my memory.

"Gunnar, Pumpkin's funeral is at four-thirty tomorrow afternoon."

"I'll be there." I slammed the front door a little too loudly, distracting my mother from her morning eggs and crossword puzzle.

"Gunnar, where you been?"

"Shooting up the neighborhood. Ma, I'm becoming so black it's a shame." I wanted to explain to her that living out there was like being in a never-ending log-rolling contest. You never asked why the log was rolling or who was rolling the log. You just spread your arms and kept your feet moving, doing your best not to fall off. Spent all your time trying to anticipate how fast and in what direction the log would spin next. I wanted to take a seat next to my mother and use this lumberjack metaphor to express how tired I was. I wanted to chew my runny eggs and talk with my mouth full. Tell her how much I missed the calm equipoise of my old life but how I had grown accustomed to running in place, knowing nothing mattered as long as I kept moving. I wanted to say these things to her, but my breath smelled like wet dog shit with a hint of sulfur.

Paul Beatty

That morning I dreamed of chasing a brown-haired white boy down a flight of stairs and into the normally busy but now empty intersection. The boy and I used to be friends, but he had wronged me somehow, though I couldn't say exactly how, and he and I both knew that the transgression merited death. The streets looked as if they'd been evacuated because of a nuclear threat or a hurricane gathering momentum off the coast. I chased the boy past a row of abandoned cars and caught him in the middle of the street under a traffic light stanchion that was swaying wildly in the wind. I shot him twice in the chest and he fell in the crosswalk. When I inspected the body, there were no bullet wounds, no blood, just two frayed holes in his yellow oxford shirt. Bending down, gun in hand, I opened his closed eyes as the noise of sirens and bystanders filled the streets. Was I hero or criminal? Psycho Loco ran over and wrested the gun from my hands, saying that he'd take the fall so I could go to college. I awoke recalling that it hadn't been long ago when I was the only black person in my dreams; now I was shooting white kids in the street.

At church I slumped in a pew worn smooth by restless rear ends shifting from side to side trying to keep their owners awake through another young-black-man-done-gone sermon. Scoby, Psycho Loco, and the gang had heard this speech so often they called out the biblical passages before the reverend: Corinthians 7:13, Leviticus 2:10, Peter 4:25, Book of Job 1:17. The reverend gripped the sides of his podium and tried to outshout his hecklers and impress upon the rowdies how Orwell "Pumpkin" Ferguson had wasted his precious youth. "If the young man had only spent more of his time in church, he might have spent a little less time in that box." I picked up a Bible and attempted to follow along with the reverend's eschatological harangue, but I didn't know where the books of Corinthians, Peter, and Job were. Flipping back and forth between Old and New Testaments, I ripped the book's thin pages to shreds.

As the mourners prepared to file past the corpse, the minister asked the aged organist to play some sorrowful hymn the family had requested to accompany their son's soul to the hereafter. The organist's knobby fingers methodically pounded out a lifeless tune, halted every two bars by violent coughing attacks and sticky organ keys that re-quired a butter knife to pop them back up into position. Pumpkin's sendoff dirge was more like one long emphysemic wheeze. His parents started to cry, and I imagined Pumpkin sitting up in his coffin saying, "Get me to the fucking hearse, already" and disassociating himself from the fiasco.

Scoby removed a tape from his portable cassette player and popped it into the church's sound system. The mewling strains of Miles Davis echoed off the panelled walls. The grateful organ player stopped sweating and lit a cigarette. The Hooligans strolled past the open casket, tossing bullets, shotgun shells, joints, switchblades, and cans of beer into it. If Pumpkin found himself in need of money, he could open a general store in the afterlife.

When it was my turn to pay my respects, his diminutive Creole-colored parents shook my hand with tearful solemnity. "It's mighty nice of you to stop by. Our son used to tell us how he beat you to a pulp when you first moved into the neighborhood. Good luck with the basketball and the poetry." I looked into Pumpkin's brittle face and tried to hide my indifference. Propped on one knee, I placed my elbows on the edge of his box and started to utter a phony prayer. Then I noticed a black-light painting of a black Jesus bathed in purple light hanging over Pumpkin's body like a guardian angel, a lime-green crown of thorns imbedded in his fuzzy crushed-velvet Afro. Clearly Pumpkin was in reliable company. I asked Jesus if, after he'd taken care of Pumpkin's wounds, he could help him clear customs and grant him permission to enter the afterworld despite the armaments, marijuana, and alcoholic beverages laid across his chest. I ended my request with an earnest "Amen," loud enough for everyone to hear.

During the eulogy at Immaculate Lawns Cemetery, I was absent-mindedly shooting imaginary jump shots into the empty grave when Psycho Loco told the reverend to shut up and asked me to recite a poem before they laid Pumpkin in the ground. I composed the following poem.

Elegy for a Vicious Midget

Pumpkin, his homunculus casket
only big enough for four pallbearers,
is lowered into earth
next to his grandfather

Paul Beatty

a diminutive light-skinned black man
who passed for white Munchkin
in the Wizard of Oz
offered a lollipop to Dorothy
then drank himself to death
with pint-size blended whiskey residuals

a squat family cries
and shakes pudgy fingers
at the wicked witch
of the West Side

The reading signified my unofficial ascension to *poète maudit* for the Gun Totin' Hooligans and by extension the neighborhood. My duties were similar to those of a Li Po or Lu Chao-lin in the employ of a Tang dynasty warlord: immortalize the rulers and say enough scholarly bullshit to keep from getting my head chopped off. It wasn't all bad. As word spread of my lyrical prowess, I earned movie money as a human Hallmark card, reading sappy epithalamiums at weddings and dour elegies at funerals.

Once in a while a poet from another fiefdom seeking to challenge my reputation would swagger into the neighborhood demanding a poetic showdown. We'd duel in impromptu verse; tankas at seven paces or sestinas at noon, no use of the words "love," "heart," and "soul." I sent many bards home in shame. Their employers carried them out on stretchers as they frantically thumbed through their rhyming dictionaries wondering how they had fucked up a rondeau so badly. I heard that one quixotic laureate I defeated has taken an eternal vow of silence and crisscrosses the country playing the bongos at the graves of famous poets for food.

Home Grown

young G puts down his joint for a moment
and through red-slitted eyes
checks out his burned-out homies
sprawled all over mama's burgundy leatherette corner group
asleep under a blanket of smoke
tucked in by the slow jams on the radio

who are these men
he's grown up with
traded comic books with
been tested for VD with

what are they really like when none of the others are around

do they . . .
>take bubble baths?
>stop and stare at the setting sun?
>like to vacuum?
>watch the MacNeil/Lehrer hour on the sly?

the young G rousts his boys. "Hey!
All I know about you motherfuckers
is that y'all are niggers who care."

one of his boys lifts his groggy head and shouts back,
"And that's all you need to know."

❖

Two days after Pumpkin's funeral I was in Psycho Loco's living room
helping him choose an appropriate eye shadow to go with his molé
brown skin and the tight blue chiffon dress he was wearing. We'd
narrowed it down to the chartreuse cinnamon and the peccadillo plum.
Admiring his lusty visage in his compact, Psycho Loco flapped his false
eyelashes, blew himself a kiss, and went with the peccadillo.

Today was the day the Gun Totin' Hooligans would avenge Pumpkin's ignominious death. Most of the boys wanted to dismember Ms.
Kim, the owner of the corner store where Pumpkin died, but Psycho
Loco talked them out of it, astutely pointing out that the families
of every fool in the room would starve to death, because Ms. Kim
carried them on credit for two weeks out of the month. It wasn't very
hard to find a scapegoat. The obvious choice was the Ghost Town
Black Shadows from the Bilkenson Gardens Projects. The Shadows
had been GTH's arch-enemies for so long that gang members on both
sides termed the animosities "the Crusades," and here was the GTH
strike force, dressed in drag and primping in preparation to go "Ghost-
busting." All the homeboys were "Hooliganed down," flaunting their
colors like rhesus monkeys in heat showing off their blue asses. They

fought over who would have the largest breasts and who would wear the expensive Wanton perfume. They stuffed halter tops with blue toilet paper, daintily knotted blue scarves about their necks, smoothed pleated blue skirts, cringed as they slipped their blue-painted toenails into blue high heels and blue-steeled .25 pistols into blue leather handbags.

The idea was to roll into Ghost Town and take their hideouts by surprise. I wished the homies luck and was headed home when out of nowhere Psycho Loco grabbed me by my throat and planted a sticky kiss on my cheek.

"Where you going, Gunnar?"

"I'm going home."

"You not coming on our little sortie?"

"Hell naw, not unless you got a bulletproof brassiere in the closet."

"Look, just come. You play ball and write, this is what I do. I shoot motherfuckers. You know I'm going to be at every one of your games this year cheering your ass, so you come and cheer mine. You'll be our date."

I sat in the back seat of a convertible Volkswagen Rabbit, squeezed between Joe Shenanigans, who looked stunning in a Liz Claiborne pantsuit, and fat No M.O. Clark, who wore a Macy's pregnancy jumpsuit set off nicely with silver hoop earrings. Pookie Hamilton drove and Psycho Loco rode shotgun. We went into battle, a three-car armada of horsehair-wigged corsairs sailing over the open concrete, sipping rum and listening to Pookie Hamilton tell sailor stories.

Pookie was something of a neighborhood celebrity. He had an unwanted cameo in *Peace Officer*, a nationally syndicated live-action video docudrama. In Pookie's episode, a clean-cut white cop is driving down a dark street, quickly glancing from the road to the camera and explaining what it's like to patrol the streets of West Los Angeles. A drop-top Volkswagen exactly like the one we were riding in speeds past the officer's patrol car. The cop looks into the camera as if he's talking to his partner and says, "See that. That nig . . . uh, turd . . . uh, guy is probably intoxicated." The camera pans to the windshield; you see the Volkswagen swerving in and out of its lane. Every five seconds or so, a fountain of vomit spews out of the driver's window. The police car's red and white lights turn the freeway into a disco. The police officer requests to see Pookie's license and registration.

Pookie hands the officer his papers and accidentally drops a beer can onto the street. The officer asks Pookie to step out of his car and tells him that he is being stopped for suspicion of driving while intoxicated. Pookie willingly but unsteadily steps out of the car to take the sobriety test. The cop says, "Sir, will you please count backward from a hundred?" Smiling into the camera, Pookie agrees and says, "Drednuh eno, enin-ytenin, thgie-ytenin, neves-ytenin . . ." The next scene shows Pookie handcuffed in the back seat of a patrol car and on his way to waking up with a hangover in jail.

The whole ride over, I watched No M.O. Clark dig his fingernails into the palms of his thick hands, peel off layers of skin, roll them into tiny flesh balls, and pop them into his mouth. No M.O.'s goal in life was to be a criminal mastermind. He thought if he could remove his fingerprints, he'd be the bane of the FBI, a mystery thief slipping in and out of the Federal Reserve, leaving nothing behind but greasy smudges. The drawback to No M.O.'s plan was that all the sandpapering and scraping had turned his hands into a blistery mass of flesh so tender he got paper cuts from counting money. Unable to hold silverware, No M.O. ate nothing but marshmallows, cotton candy, and white bread. When feeling brave, he bought large bags of french fries and waited for the hot morsels to cool so he could eat them without scalding himself. A favorite GTH parlor trick was to get No M.O. so excited about his grandiose dreams he'd want to slap hands with someone in celebration of his genius. The sound of a No M.O. high five was a sickening splat not unlike the scrunch of a family of snails being stepped on. No M.O. came away from these handclasps alternately screaming in pain and blowing on his hand to take away the sting.

Cruising down Central Avenue in the old business district, we were plainly behind enemy lines. The rusty alarm boxes over the barred doors to the pawnshops and soul-food kitchens all read, "Sears, Roebuck and Co. Alarm System" in lightning-bolt quotation marks. Mountains of Sears all-weather radial tires snow-capped with white Sears Kenmore appliances in disrepair filled the vacant lots. Feeling a little homesick and hoping to motivate the troops, Psycho Loco stood up and yelled, "Sears sucks. Montgomery Ward's rules." Following his lead, shouts rang from every car in the convoy. "Ward's! Ward's!" The outburst triggered a small avalanche of Sears Diehard batteries, which rumbled down a vulcanized slope, crushing a toaster oven, to the joy of the transvestite soldiers.

After we had driven for about fifteen minutes, No M.O. slowly removed his hand from the seat, green ooze momentarily clinging to Pookie's vinyl upholstery, and pointed to a metal archway. "There go Bilkenson Gardens," he said. We drove up to the main entrance. Psycho Loco pursed his lips and winked at the security guard. The guard smiled, removed a rubber from his wallet, opened the wrought-iron electric gate, then turned his attention back to a small black-and-white Sears television.

Bilkenson Gardens was a slight misnomer. There were no bee-pollinated flowering fields or lush meadows populated by butterflies and snapdragons. Just stagnant and algae-laden ponds formed by the run-off of leaky fire hydrants and clogged sewers, serving as landing pads for mosquitoes and flies.

"Let's be on da lookout for dese friggin' calzones," warned Joe Shenanigans. "I don't know about youse guys, but I wanna whack dese fucking strombolis."

The caravan broke up into search-and-destroy teams. Our platoon drove west, easing past rows of rundown bungalows till we saw five guys dressed in white Lacoste shirts and white golf hats standing on the porch of a small brick cabana. They looked like golf pros sipping lemonade at the nineteenth hole, leisurely rehashing the last round of play. As we got closer, Psycho Loco straightened his tits and whispered their names — "Casper, L'il Spooky, C-Thru, Opaque Nate, and the Invisible Nigger," all of whom were staring lustily at the "females" in the car. With a flirtatious squint in his eyes, Joe Shenanigans lasciviously ran his tongue over his top lip, sending the Ghost Town gangsters into a frenzy. The courtship ritual began with the sugary sweet words of budding love.

"Set that shit out, baby!"

"Goddamn, girl, your breastesses is big. A sandwich is a sandwich, but your titties is a meal."

"Hey, ho, com'ere and let me put a little something on your chin."

Pookie played coy and piloted the car around the block, the hard-ons of every Ghostbuster following us like dowsing rods.

"Damn, Joe, if you was a girl you'd be a fucking slut. You was looking at them niggers like you wanted some dick bad."

"Aw, nigger, fuck you, I bet we pull that skirt off your ass, your panties be wet as a motherfucker, stank bitch."

Psycho Loco put a cassette into the deck, barraging Bilkenson Gardens with a screeching aria. Mood music, he called it. The boys quieted themselves and made ready. I expected guns, but Psycho Loco and Joe Shenanigans removed fancy crossbows and arrows from under the seat. No M.O. was filling balloons with liquid drain opener.

"What about the guns?" I pleaded. "You do know that the Second Amendment gives you the right to form a militia and bear arms? By the fear invested in me, I hereby proclaim the Gun Totin' Hooligans a militia. So bear some goddamn arms."

Psycho Loco turned around in his seat, shook his head disapprovingly in my direction, and told me that whenever the Gun Totin' Hooligans acted vengefully, they stuck to the old ways, and tradition meant no guns unless absolutely necessary. The car wheeled around the last corner and I cowered in my seat as No M.O. knotted the end of his last liquid drain opener balloon and Psycho Loco and Joe Shenanigans wet their arrowheads with aerosol deodorant.

A fool from Ghost Town called out from the street, struggling to be heard over the wailing French contralto, "I knew you fine bitches would be back. Why don't you all come inside, drink a little Riunite on ice, and get busy?" The car braked to a slow glide; Psycho Loco and Joe lit a lighter, and the tips of their arrows flamed like giant aluminum matches. The boy in the white hat cupped his hands to his mouth. "Hey what's up with that music?" With a war whoop, Psycho Loco, No M.O., and Joe stood up, and a salvo of flaming arrows and balloons zipped through the air. The stunned homeboys from Ghost Town dove for cover, their hats flying off their cornrowed heads and parachuting down to earth as the arrows bounced harmlessly off the brick bungalow onto the concrete, where the fires petered out like dud Fourth of July fireworks. One projectile found a home in the rear tire of a Buick Supersport, causing the car to howl and list to one side. They wouldn't be chasing us.

No M.O. had the best aim; one of his balloons exploded on one boy's chest. Succumbing to the fumes, the kid dropped to the sidewalk, gurgling and clawing at his burning eyes. A hyped-up No M.O. hopped out of the car and yelled in the wounded boy's face, "Induce vomiting, motherfucker," and hustled back to the car.

Paul Beatty

Eventually Ghost Town rallied and rushed the car as we pulled away. The fastest boy pulled a sawed-off shotgun out of nowhere like an outlaw magician, and a knot of buckshot danced on the car's rear end like water droplets on hot oil. The opera singer sang on, her voice blowing past my ears as Pookie sped out the main entrance and toward the freeway.

"Psycho Loco, what are we listening to?"

"Delibes' *Lakmé*. It's from act two — the lovers declare their undying devotion, then they die."

I noticed none of the boys bothered to remove their wigs or makeup. I placed one hand over my heart and raised the other high in the air and celebrated life by hitting the high notes with the rest of the fellows. Somehow I knew the words.

six

IT WAS MANDATORY for every male student at Phillis Wheatley High to attend the monthly "Young Black and Latino Men: Endangered Species" assembly. Principal Henrietta Newcombe opened the meetings by reminding us that despite the portrayal of inner-city youth in the media (she didn't mention the name of the assembly), we weren't animals. These hour-long deprogramming sessions were supposed to liberate us from a cult of self-destructiveness and brainwash us into joining the sect of benevolent middle-class American normalcy. Once, before we listened to the motivational speeches, Principal Newcombe conducted an extemporaneous Gallup poll in hopes of uniting us against something other than ourselves.

"Raise your hand if

. . . you are on welfare.

. . . you don't live with your parents.

. . . you're a father.

. . . you've ever been handcuffed."

I raised my hand, much to everyone's surprise, especially that of Ms. Newcombe, who invited me to tell my story. "You all see how any colored boy, no matter how academically and athletically gifted, is a target? What happened, child?"

I was reluctant to testify, so Principal Newcombe prompted me in her gentle manner. "How old were you when the white man shackled you like a captured African animal?"

"Eight."

"You got arrested at age eight?"

"Well, I wasn't exactly arrested. When I was in third grade, this cop visited our class to talk about his job and shit."

"Young man!"

"Sorry. Then he started explaining what each item on his belt was

Paul Beatty

for. When he gets to the handcuffs, he asks for a volunteer to help demonstrate how they work and chooses me, although I didn't have my hand raised. Anyway, the cop asks me to pretend I'm the bad guy and he handcuffs me, both hands. In the middle of reading me my rights, he asks me if I can get out of the handcuffs. I was so skinny I lowered my arms and the cuffs slid to the floor. The whole class is laughing. Then the cop says, 'Don't worry, in a few years they'll stay on.'"

Principal Newcombe nodded compassionately. "See how they do a young nigger? Now I'd like to introduce this month's distinguished speaker."

The monthly orator was usually a local businessman, community activist, obscure athlete, or ex-con. He'd bound up onstage with lots of nervous energy, wave, and say a hearty "Wassup, fellas?" to prove he was hip and could speak our language. Some speakers tried to rouse us with scare tactics. The ex-con showed off his scars and told butt-fucking stories. During the question-and-answer session the kids only wanted to know how many bodies did he have, did the tattoos hurt, and did he know so-and-so's brother. The mortician from Greystone Bros. spoke about how business was good and asked us if we could kill a few more niggers this week because his twins were starting college in the fall. Other community leaders tried to sway our self-destructive sensibilities with the flashy, superbad, black businessman-pimp approach to empowerment. Great Nate Shaw, who owned Great Nate's Veal 'n' French Toast over on Centinela, made a grand entrance in a purple stretch limousine. Dressed in a tuxedo, cape, and top hat, twirling a pearl-handled walking stick, Great Nate strode down the auditorium's center aisle looking like a lost member of the Darktown Follies just bursting to sing "That Ol' Black Magic." His chauffeur trailed obediently behind him, carrying the shoeshine box that had catapulted "the black Ronald McDonald" to tacky affluence. Two weeks later some boys from Wheatley High in cahoots with his chauffeur followed Great Nate home, robbed his house, and kidnapped his wife. I heard they got more money from the Hollywood wardrobe agency they sold his clothes to than from the ransom Nate paid for his wife. The ex–football player scored points by passing around pictures of himself arm in arm on Caribbean beaches with bikini-clad white women. After his presentation, hands shot up, and Principal

Newcombe looked so pleased, figuring she'd finally made a break-through. The first boy held up a Polaroid and asked the former jock, "Did you fuck this one?"

No matter who the delivery boy, the message was always the same. Stay in school. Don't do drugs. Treat our black queens with respect. I made decent money taking bets on whether the distinguished speaker-of-the-month would say, "Each one, teach one" first or "There's an old African saying, 'It takes an entire village to raise one child.'"

I suppose I could afford to be snide. I had a personal motivational speaker, Coach Motome Chijiiwa Shimimoto. The stereotype is that most successful black men raised by single mothers had a surrogate father figure who turned their lives around. A man who "saw their potential," looked after them, taught them the value of virtuous living, and sent them out on the path to glory with a resounding slap on the butt. Coach Shimimoto didn't do any of those things. He just paid attention to me. The only time he ever told me what to do with my life was during basketball practice. There he constantly pulled and pushed me around the court. I was a skinny six-foot-four-inch pawn in the chess game unfolding inside his head. "Kaufman, where are you supposed to be?" Looking into his small hamster-brown eyes, which through his thick Buddy Holly glasses looked absolutely minuscule, I'd say, "I don't know, Coach." Coach Shimimoto, his face covered in perspiration, would snatch the bottom of my shorts and drag me to wherever it was I was supposed to be, droplets of sweat dripping off his nose and trailing behind us. "You're here, Gunnar," raising his hands and demonstrating the proper technique for denying the bas-ketball. "If Roderick Overton gets the ball on the box, we lose, weak-side help. Comprende, stupido?" I can't say that I learned any valuable lessons from Coach Shimimoto. He never gave me any clichéed phrases to be repeated in times of need, never showed me pictures of crippled kids to remind me how lucky I was. The only thing I remember him teaching me was that as a left-hander I'd have to draw from right to left to keep my charcoals from streaking. Coach Shimimoto was also my art teacher, and even there he was always looking over my shoulder, beads of his sweat splattering my water-colors.

Other than Scoby, there was no one I talked to more than Coach. After practice he'd try to fatten me up on churritos and chimichangas, while he told stories of how the GIs had taught him to play ball in the internment camp during World War II. He was never very good, but he was a hustler. It was his pluckiness and a front line comprising the Asazawa triplets, Ruth, Ruby, and Roy, that enabled his team to win the Internment Youth Championships in 1945. The prize was the team's picture in the camp newspaper and a Caesar salad made with lettuce picked from his family's repossessed farm.

Coach Shimimoto loved the "purity" of athletics, but the provincial protocol made him uncomfortable. Being a coach was tantamount to being knighted or elected president; the appellation and its circumscriptions stuck with you for life. Even Shimimoto's wife called him Coach. Shimimoto often pleaded with me to call him something else. "Gunnar, we're friends. Come up with a clever nickname for me, like Chi-whiz or Moto-scooter."

"Coach, if you're going to be an authority figure, you've got to live with the dehumanizing consequences."

I often think the real reason Coach Shimimoto feted me was to get inside Nicholas's head through me. Nicholas was his prize student, his ticket to high school coaching fame. Shimimoto knew that in thirty years reporters would call him at home and ask what it was like to coach, if not the greatest, the most unique basketball player in the world. Coach had his answer all prepared; he would tell them, "Nicholas doesn't understand the game, but the game understands him."

Both Nicholas and I entered tenth grade with solid basketball reputations. Nick was the wizard and I the sorcerer's apprentice. My duties were to get Scoby the ball so he could score, play tough defense so the other team wouldn't score, and bow reverentially after each dazzling feat. The first game went as expected. We played our archrivals, the Aeronautic High Wind Shears, in our first home game of the season. Aeronautic ranked fifth in the city, but Scoby made seventeen straight baskets to lead the Phillis Wheatley Mythopoets to their first basketball victory in four years. He made shots from all over the floor. He kissed one thirty-five-foot bank shot off the glass so sweetly that the shot left lip prints on the backboard. After each successive basket, the legend of Nicholas Scoby documented itself shot by improbable shot; what was once urban lore was now irrefutable public knowledge.

At one point Scoby shot a jumper from deep in the corner over the outstretched arms of three Wind Shears. The ball splashed through the net and the opposing coach turned red, stomped his feet, and yelled at his players to stop Scoby at all costs. One of the coach's obedient henchmen planted an elbow in Scoby's temple, which sent him into the stands head first. As he staggered dazedly back to the bench, Psycho Loco walked onto the floor and paced back and forth in front of the Aeronautic High bench, repeatedly slapping his thigh and challenging the team. "You fools see this two-and-half-inch thick length of pipe from my crotch to my knee? That's not my dick, it's a Remington twelve-gauge sawed-off. The next motherfucker to touch Scoby is going to be performing shotgun fellatio and become a victim of some seriously unsafe sex."

Unlike at the playground, here a collective self-esteem was at stake. People who didn't give a fuck about anything other than keeping their new shoes unscuffed all of a sudden had meaning to their lives. They yelled at the referees, sang fight songs, razzed the efforts of the other team. With the outcome of the game still in doubt, I was at the free-throw line going through my routine. Three dribbles, eye the front of the rim, deep breath. A voice barrel-rolled out of the stands, demanding attention. "Come on, Gunnar, we need these." We? I didn't even need these free throws. I missed the first one on purpose. The crowd moaned and spit, instantly stricken with psychosomatic bellyaches. "Please, make this next one, please, goddammit." They were hypnotized and didn't even know it, and I was the hypnotist. I had the power to make them cry or send them home happy, clucking like chickens. I sank the next one and fans stormed the court, and before I could look up at the scoreboard I was buried under a pile of exulting bodies. "We won! We won!" When I was finally exhumed by Coach Shimimoto, he asked me how did I feel, and I shrugged my shoulders with indifference. "What a competitor. What self-control. That hold on your emotions will take you far, wait and see, Gunnar." When he freed me from a playful headlock, I wanted to shout, "But Coach, I really don't give a fuck." But why spoil his joy?

It was Nicholas's and my first organized game, and afterward over the phone we joked about how we didn't know to wear jockstraps instead of underwear, when the referee needed to touch the ball, what to say when the team huddled around Coach Shimimoto and clasped hands.

"What did you say?"

Paul Beatty

"I said, 'One-two-three, eat me.'"

"You're supposed to say, 'One-two-three, Wheatley.'"

The next morning at school everyone was still in a trancelike state. Principal Newcombe, the district supervisor, and a photographer from the daily paper met us at the front entrance. We gathered around Phillis Wheatley's gigantic cast-iron bust and posed stiffly for the photographer. The district supervisor tried to shake Scoby's hand, but Nicholas yanked it away at the last second. He had more trouble wriggling free of Principal Newcombe's cheek-to-cheek embrace. I stood off to the side, propped up by an elbow, leaning on the crown of Phillis Wheatley's brass cranium. The caption in the next day's paper read, "Wheatley's Nicholas Scoby and Gunnar Kaufman, ace students, ace athletes, and ace boon coons."

Everywhere we went we were Wheatley High's main attraction. Teachers and students treated us with unwanted reverence. The murmur of everyone clamoring for our attention rang in my ears like a worshipful tinnitus. Girls slipped phone numbers into my pockets and rubbed the tips of their angora nipples on my shoulders. Boys bearhugged us and enthusiastically replayed the entire game for our benefit. "You niggers is bad. Money, when it was four minutes left in the half and you went baseline with that crossover and boofed, boom!, on that gorilla Aero High nigger, I swear my dick got hard." Mr. Dillard, the math analysis teacher, lectured on parabolas and hyperboles by using video excerpts of Scoby and me shooting jump shots at practice. Figuring we must be Newtonian geniuses to calculate the required force and proper trajectory to shoot a twenty-ounce sphere through a metal ring only eighteen inches in diameter while running and chewing gum, Mr. Dillard exempted us from homework for the rest of the semester.

To avoid the incessant adulation the day before a game against South Erebus High, we spent the lunch period in Coach Shimimoto's art room. I doodled in India ink and Nicholas sat at the pottery wheel, shaping amorphous clay blobs. Toward the end of the period, Nicholas was pumping the pedal so fast he couldn't get the clay to stay on the spinning disk. "Fuck arts 'n' crafts!" he yelled as wet slabs of clay flew across the room, flattening themselves on the walls and windows.

I'd never seen Scoby mad about anything. I knew he was agitated about the upcoming game, but I didn't know what to say to him. He was always the one who dispensed advice and remained in control. Whenever the crew got stopped for unjustified or justified police shakedowns, it was Scoby whispering, "Maintain, maintain." I looked to Coach Shimimoto, but he was removing clay pancakes from his face and motioning with his eyes for me to say something first. I picked up Scoby's latest masterpiece, a still soggy, pockmarked, nondescript lump of clay, and turned it over tenderly in my hands.

"Nice work. This really captivates the frustrations of the underclass in an abstract yet immediate way. You should send this to the art museum — call it Gog and Magog White House Lawn Defecation."

"It's an ashtray, you moron."

"Yo nigger, why you so upset? We got a game tomorrow, just cool out."

"Man, I'm tired of these fanatics rubbing on me, pulling on my arms, wishing me luck. I can't take it. People have buttons with my face on 'em. They paint their faces and stencil my number on their foreheads. One idiot showed me a tattoo on his chest that said, 'Nick Scoby is God.'"

"Maybe you are God. You'll just have to accept the responsibility and let the clowns pay homage."

"I'm not no fucking Tiki doll, no fucking icon. Don't folks have anything better to do with their lives than pay attention to what I'm doing?"

"They're just trying to say how much they appreciate what you do. It'll get better, man, they'll get used to us winning."

"But they'll never get used to Scoby making every shot he takes," Coach Shimimoto interrupted. He sat down next to us, so overheated that steam rose from his body as if he were a giant humidifier. "Nicholas, you're right, it'll only get worse. You've got to figure out how can you live with it."

"It's not fair. I wasn't born to make them happy. What I look like, motherfucking Charlie Chaplin?"

"So miss once in a while."

"I can't. I can't even try. Something won't let me."

Scoby's eyes reddened and he started to sniffle. He was cracking under the pressure. Watching his hands shake, I realized that sometimes the worst thing a nigger can do is perform well. Because then there is no turning back. We have no place to hide, no Superman

Fortress of Solitude, no reclusive New England hermitages for xenophobic geniuses like Bobby Fischer and J. D. Salinger. Successful niggers can't go back home and blithely disappear into the local populace. American society reels you back to the fold. "Tote that barge, shoot that basketball, lift that bale, nigger ain't you ever heard of Dred Scott?"

I'd never asked Nick Scoby about his gifts. I say gifts because Nicholas had other talents besides shooting a basketball, none of which had any real social value. He could read UPC codes at a glance. He'd look at the series of thin and thick black lines on an unpriced bag of pork rinds or a bottle of seltzer water and immediately call out the price. He also had the power to tell if someone had a drop of Negro blood in his gene pool. Nicholas claimed he could smell a passing octoroon from a block away. Whenever we went on junkets out of the neighborhood to the Beverly Hills Pavilion or the county fair, Scoby loved to approach unsuspecting Negroes living carefree in the white world and blow their consanguine but secret identities. "Say, we missed you at the family reunion! Aunt Tessy wanted to know if you was still passing for Armenian."

Nicholas could never explain any of his talents. If anyone asked about his hardwood perfection, he said that he'd hurt his elbow falling out of a tree when he was little, and that when he cocked his arm he heard a little click telling him when to release the ball. Then he'd snap his arm for effect. His elbow cracked loudly, popping just as he said. But his weak explanation didn't account for distance or the various shots I had seen him make right-handed.

"Nicholas, why don't you just quit?"

"Do what you do best. That's what I've heard my whole life. First it was hopscotch and now it's basketball."

"Hopscotch?" Coach and I asked in unison.

"Yeah, when I first moved out here from Chicago I didn't know nobody, so me and the other outcasts — the ESL kids, the deaf kids — played hopscotch to pass the time. I really liked the game. The sound of your keys sliding into the box, trying to lean from nines to pick up your marker in fours. Jumping from two to eights and clicking over sixes. Shit was a challenge. Anyway, the untraumatized boys chased me home every day. Since I used my house keys as a hopscotch marker, I always had trouble opening the lock. Usually I got the door open moments before the boys hunted me down. One day the key was so worn the lock wouldn't open, and these niggers waxed my shit right on my front porch. When my mother got home she made me wash the dried blood off the stairs and explain what happened. Then she yanked me over to the basketball courts."

"Don't tell me you had to fight every boy who beat you up?" I asked, anticipating a common parental method used to turn squeamish young boys into men.

"No, she made every kid who beat me up play hopscotch with me. They had a good time, too. We was friends after that. Once I was accepted by the cool pack, I started playing basketball and stopped playing hopscotch with the retards."

"What happened to the hopscotch kids?"

"They sit in the stands and scream like everybody else whenever I shoot the basketball."

When the lunch bell rang, Scoby was feeling better. He smiled as if he had had a revelation and told Coach he'd be at practice.

After a light practice, Coach Shimimoto divided the team into two squads for a scrimmage. Usually he divided us using some arbitrary criterion. White sneakers vs. black sneakers, kids who'd never been to the dentist vs. those who had. That day it was dark lips vs. red lips. My upper lip is dark and the bottom one is cranberry red, so I was a bit confused and asked Coach which team I should play for. Coach Shimimoto said that it was a blessing to be able to play for both sides and made me substitute for whoever was tired. It was strange playing for both teams, scoring for one squad, then reversing my jersey and doing the same thing with the other.

I was standing on the sidelines catching my breath when Coach blew a jet of sweat from his brownish upper lip and said, "Gunnar, you know in Japan they play tie baseball games."

"Coach, I could give a fuck if I win or lose as long as both sides have a fair chance to play as hard as they want to play. Do the Japanese have tie basketball games?"

"No. Go in for Adrianna, smartass."

Nicholas didn't shoot much during that scrimmage or for the rest of the year. For us to win basketball games, I had to play like hell. Gradually, I realized that the decision Nicholas had made was to remove the burden of success temporarily from his shoulders and place it solely on mine. The classroom, locker room, and bathroom acclaim fell on me. I'd thrust my hips at a urinal and two cats on either side would glance up from their drippy glans and gleefully let out the interminable catcall, "Guuunnnnnarr Kaaawwwfffmaaaan." When kids discussed the team's prospects in the city playoffs, washing down mouthfuls of doughy burritos with fruit punch, it was "Gunnar has held every all-city ballplayer we've played to fewer than four points. Gunnar is averaging twenty-six points, nine rebounds, and twelve assists a game." When Scoby's name came up, they all said, "Oh yeah, that fool can shoot, but Gunnar has to carry us." Nicholas loved the shift in fame and willingly played his part in the role reversal, calling me "the Deity" and asking me to forgive him for his sins.

There are certain demands on a star athlete that I didn't anticipate or enjoy. The most arduous of which was having to participate in the social scene. Every weekend Scoby and Psycho Loco pressured me to use my star status to get them retinue privileges at the Paradise, the Rojo Cebolla, or the Black Lagoon. When a club manager balked at admitting the volatile Psycho Loco into the establishment, I had to agree to take complete responsibility for his actions, which was like asking a dog collar to be responsible for a rottweiler. Wringing their hands like mad scientists, he and Scoby'd thank me for my kindness, ignoring the fact that I suffered from what the American Psychiatric Association *Manual of Mental Disorders* lists as social arrhythmia and courtship paralysis, meaning I couldn't dance and was deathly afraid of women.

I wasn't completely lacking in social skills. With practice I learned to serpentine cool as hell through a crowded dance floor with the best of the high school snakes. I could hiss at the young women, but not much else. When the opening strains of the latest jam crescendoed through the house, I would shout a perfunctory "Heeeyyy!" showing the clubgoers that I was up for the downstroke and that at any moment there might be a "partay ovah heah." Scoby and Psycho Loco would soon abandon my hepster front for the chase, melding into the swirling mass of bodies and leaving me to fend for myself. I'd watch Nicholas gyrate with Gwen Cummings or Tyesa Hammonds, sometimes both, their bodies one large ball-and-socket joint floating in the same soul sonic waves. Even Psycho Loco could dance. He did this little gangster jig where he leaned back into the cushy rhythms like he was reclining in an easy chair, kicking one foot into the air, then the other, sipping from a bottle of contraband gin and lemonade during the funky breakdown.

Girls interested in dancing with me propped themselves in front of me, a little closer than necessary, swayed to the music, and tried to catch my eye. I stared off in the opposite direction, pretending to be engrossed in an intricately woven bar napkin and praying the girl wouldn't be bold enough to ask for a dance. As an athlete, I had a ready-made excuse for the nervy women who did ask: "I can't, baby. Twisted my ankle dunking on the Rogers brothers in last night's game." I'd get a funny look in return, and the rebuffed coed would return to her circle of friends. The whispers and over-the-shoulder looks followed by phony smiles set off my social paranoia. My auditory hallucinations cleared their throats. "Something wrong with that nigger, he don't never dance. Maybe he just shy. Maybe he's shy? He ain't shy with Coach Shimimoto. I think he fucking Coach Shimimoto. That's why Coach be sweating so much. Boy got some big ol' feets and hands, that's a waste of some good young nigger dick. Fucking an old man."

Soon Scoby and Psycho Loco would interrupt my neurotic musings. "Why you ain't dancing, homes? Crazy honeys is checking you out."

"I don't feel like dancing."

"Are you crazy? There some fine ladies in here. You just scared of women. Scared of pussy."

On cue, Betty and Veronica would march over and demand the next dance, their tresses interlocked in a geodesic dome hairstyle that roofed their heads like an I. M. Pei nightmare. I would mumble yes and they'd lead me onto the crowded dance floor. I'd stand still for a few seconds, vainly snapping my fingers with as much hope of catching the beat as a quadriplegic hobo latching on to a moving boxcar. "Do what we do," Betty and Veronica would say reassuringly. I'd try to mirror my partners' undulating moves, but my body would fail to respond. I was stiffer than a mummified Gumby left out in the sun too long. Instead of bones, my skeletal structure was high-tension wire, and I plodded from side to side with all the mobility of a rusted tin man.

Seeing my distress, Psycho Loco would bebop over to my rescue, force a couple of swigs of his liquid rhythm down my throat, then cruise the floors barking like the Alpine St. Bernard he was. Even with the lubrication of my joints and the steadying of my nerves, the quest for the beat wasn't over. Now I had to fight the urge to be too loose-limbed, prevent my arms from flaying about my body uncontrollably in an epileptic paroxysm. After a few moments I'd relax and settle into a barely acceptable, simple side-to-side step, dubbed by the locals the white boy shuffle. I wasn't funky, but I was no longer disrupting the groove.

As the evening wound down, the house lights dimmed to a deep red haze and the DJ began to play the latest slow jams. Boys and girls floated across the floor superglued at the crotch, grinding each other's privates into powder in a mortar-and-pestle figure-eight motion. Unattached boys tried to look as if they had something better to do, and unattached women looked longingly in my direction, wiggling their hips in the vain hope of tantalizing me into action. I'd pray that Psycho Loco would start a fight so I could leave without having to support someone's head on my shoulder and listen to them warble inane love lyrics in my ear. Invariably, Psycho Loco came through, slugging some fool for stepping on his shadow or some equally petty infraction.

As the bouncers escorted us out, Psycho Loco and Scoby compared the night's harvest.

"I got three phone numbers and Kenyana Huff pinched my butt twice."

"I only got one phone number."

"One number?"

"Ah, but it was Natalie Nuñez's number."

"Oh, you was talking to that? Damn, what did you say to get over?"

"I told her that I'd get her a date with Gunnar if she let me take her to the UCLA Mardi Gras this Saturday. So Gunnar, how'd you do?"

"Do people be staring at me when I'm out there dancing? It feels like everybody is looking at me."

"First off, you ain't you out there dancing. You out there having a brain aneurysm. You move so crazy it looks like you caught the Holy Ghost. Second off, nobody is paying any attention to your rhythmless behind 'cause they trying they own mack on."

"Gunnar, do you even like girls?"

"Yes." Which was true. I just had yet to meet one who didn't intimidate me into a state of catatonia.

"When you gonna get a girlfriend?"

"I had one once in Santa Monica."

"What, some pasty white girl named Eileen, please? That don't count. Nigger, have you ever seen any parts of the pussy?"

"Of course, man. I've fucked . . . er, been fucked . . . um, been fucking . . . I is fucking."

"Does the line go up and down or from side to side?"

During the ride home Psycho Loco would leaf through a copy of *Bow and Arrow Outdoorsman,* passing over pictures of grizzled white men snuggling with dead animals and articles entitled "Ancient Hunting Tricks of the Mighty Neanderthal" or "101 Tick Repellents that Don't Smell like Grandma" and heading straight to the classified ads in the back.

"Gunnar, we're gonna find you a wife. Here we go. Listen to this:

> Hot Mama-Sans of the Orient
> Seeking Dates or Seoulmates
> Inscrutable, Demure. and Pure by Day
> Insatiable, Mature, and Impure by Night
> For Color Brochure send 50¢ to:
> Mail Order Asian Geishas and Dragon Ladies
> Box 900, Sacramento, CA 16504."

"You're sick, you know that, right?"

"Dude, I've never seen you voluntarily speak to a girl. This is the only way. Tried and true, in defunct monarchies the world over. I'm serious now, say I won't."

"You won't."

"Two more years, bro. Soon as you turn eighteen I'm marrying your frigid ass off."

Somehow I knew that Psycho Loco was right, I'd never start a romance of my own accord. But it was difficult to accept sexual counsel from a pugnacious male who had to be drunk to fuck and whose first rule of courtship was "Always make sure your dick is out. That way, no matter what happens you can say, 'Well, I had my dick out.'" Maybe there was an advantage to arranged romance — no dates consisting of gauche attempts to be unceasingly clever and sensitive. Never having to deal with the living-room interrogations from incestuously overprotective brothers and fathers. And I'd never have to put down the evening paper and say, "Listen, honey, they're playing our song." Still,

I stuck to the Judeo-Christian ethics I'd picked up from American television and the English romantics, Ozzie and Harriet, Wordsworth and Coleridge.

"You crazy? How could anyone do that shit? Don't even think about it. It's like slavery or something." Changing the subject, I snatched the magazine from Psycho Loco's hands and said, "My pops said Rodney King deserved that ass-kicking for resisting arrest and having a Jheri curl. He said some curl activator got into Officer Koon's eyes and he thought he'd been maced, so he had to defend himself."

The rest of the way home we talked about our experiences with police harassment: being frisked in front of our parents, forced to pull our pants down near the day-care center, made to wait face down in the street with our hands interlocked behind our heads and feet crossed at the ankles, gritty footprints on the nape of our necks. Scoby said in county jail the guards call the cells Skinner boxes and have nicknames like the Neuterer, Babe Ruth, and Curtains written on their batons and riot helmets. Psycho Loco theorized that the guards beat on the inmates because they were afraid of them. He talked about how he once ran into a prison guard and his family at a Hamburger Haven. The guard was so nervous he pulled his off-duty revolver on Psycho Loco and accidentally shot Hamburger Harry, the mascot. The bullet passed through the lettuce, ricocheted off the pickle, and came to a stop in the mascot's brain.

I asked Psycho Loco if the rumors about a gangland truce if the jury found the cops innocent was true. He said that there already had been a big armistice at the Tryst 'n' Shout Motel. Bangers who had killed each other's best friends shook hands and hugged with unspoken apologies in their watery eyes.

"Damn, I hope they find those motherfuckers guilty," I said with surprising conviction.

"Not me," said Psycho Loco. "I hope those boys get off scot-free. One, it'll be good to have a little peace in the streets, and besides, me and the fellas planning a huge job. Going to take advantage of the civic unrest, know what I'm saying?"

I pictured Rodney King staggering in the Foothill Freeway's break-down lane like a black Frankenstein, two Taser wires running 50,000 volts of electric democracy through his body. I wondered if the battery of the American nigger was being recharged or drained.

five-finger discounts

seven

FOR SOME REASON Coach Shimimoto was reluctant to end practice. Usually these postseason workouts were light affairs, mostly intrasquad scrimmages followed by a dunking contest. This one he kept prolonging with wind sprints and full-court defensive drills. He finally blew his whistle and motioned for the team to gather around him. Exhausted, we flopped to the floor, sucking wind and hoping Coach Shimimoto would take pity on our fatigued bodies.

"What does 'concatenate' mean? Tell me, and you can go."

Harriet Montoya, the only person with strength enough to speak, raised her hand. I didn't have much faith she'd know the answer; the day before she had defined "repeal" as putting the skin back on an orange and peeling again, and we had had to run thirty laps backward. "Concatenate means together. Not like all-in-the-same-boat together, but like connected, like a bicycle chain."

"Close enough. Remember that definition, you soon-to-be revolutionaries." With that, Coach dismissed us into a cool late April afternoon.

On the way home I was wondering what Coach meant by "soon-to-be revolutionaries" when I noticed a distant column of black smoke billowing into the dusk like a tornado too tired to move. "What's that?" I asked Scoby. "Eric Dolphy," he replied, referring to the stop-and-go shrieking that was escaping from his boom box. "No, I mean that," I said, pointing to the noxious-looking cloud. Scoby didn't know, but he was more than willing to make up for his ignorance in smoke formations by lecturing me on the relevance of Dolphy's sonic turmoil to teenage Negromites like ourselves.

Midway through the seminar in music appreciation another silo of smoke twisted into the dusk, this one closer to us. The driver of a rundown Nova sped down Sawyer Drive, leaning on her high-pitched horn for no apparent reason. Scoby turned up the volume on the tape deck just a bit. Another car flew through a stop sign, then reversed its direction. When the car drew parallel to us, the driver flashed a gap-toothed smile, then shot a raised fist out the window and raced away. Soon every driver that passed was joyriding through the streets, honking the horn and violating the traffic laws like a Hollywood stunt driver in the big chase scene. The driver of a Wonder Bread delivery truck pulled a B-movie U-turn, hopped on the sidewalk, then peeled out down an alley. Dolphy's horn matched the curbside cacophony flutter for flutter, screech for screech.

"How does the music make you feel, man?"

"I feel like I'm dry heaving while free-falling from fifteen thousand feet."

"That's it, man, you getting it. Feel, Gunnar, feel. Let the jazz seep into your pores."

People began spilling from their homes. They paced up and down the sidewalks, looking tense and unaware they'd left their front doors wide open. Something was wrong; no Angeleno ever leaves the door open. I caught the eye of a middle-aged man wearing white patent leather shoes, ochre-colored polyester pants, and a Panama hat and standing on his front porch looking desperate for someone to talk to. "What's happening?" I asked.

"Them cracker motherfuckers did it again." The Rodney King verdict; I'd completely forgotten. "They let them racists go. I'm surprised the judge didn't reprimand the peckerwood so-called peace officers for not finishing the job."

Let go? What did that mean? The officers had to be found guilty of something — obstruction of traffic, at least. I doubted the man in the patent leather shoes' version. I could hear the TV in his living room, and I peeped through his doorway. The smirk on the reporter's face told me the man was right, even before I heard her say, "Not guilty on all charges."

I never felt so worthless in my life. Uninvited, Scoby and I walked into the man's living room, set our bookbags on his coffee table, and sat on the couch. I looked out the window and saw a store owner spray-paint BLACK OWNED across her boarded-up beauty salon. I wanted to dig out my heart and have her do the same to it, certifying my identity in big block letters across both ventricles. I suddenly

I wanted to taste immediate vindication, experience the rush of spitting in somebody's, anybody's, face. The day of the L.A. riots I learned that it meant nothing to be a poet. One had to be a poet and a farmer, a poet and a roustabout, a poet and a soon-to-be revolutionary.

I looked at Scoby and said, "Let's break." We gathered our things, thanked the man for his kindness, and prepared to leave. We spent an awkward moment in silence till the man asked, "Is that Dolphy?" Scoby nodded, and we made our way toward the commotion, listening to Dolphy play his horn like he was wringing a washrag. I couldn't decide whether the music sounded like a death knell or the cavalry charge for a ragtag army. We turned the corner onto Hoover and Alvarado and walked into *Carnaval*, poor people's style. The niggers and spics had decided to secede from the union, armed with rifles, slingshots, bottles, camcorders, and songs of freedom. Problem was, nobody knew where Fort Sumter was.

In the middle of the intersection, the Wonder Bread truck we'd seen before was careening in circles, trying to find a path through the labyrinth of flaming dumpsters and rioters. Another stranded teamster in a beer truck crashed into a barrier and broadsided the Wonder Bread man, sending both vehicles sprawling on their sides. The Wonder Bread truck slid to a stop ten feet in front of Scoby and me like a huge shuffleboard disk, its engine sputtering and wheels spinning. The driver scrambled out of the cab. Before he could bolt into the street, I slammed him against the side of the truck. Bug-eyed with fear, he babbled something about having "never done nothing to nobody." I'd never seen anyone afraid of me. I wondered what my face looked like. Were my nostrils flaring, my eyes pulsing red? I was about to shout "Ooga-booga" and give the guy a heart attack when Scoby clambered from the rear of the truck, chewing on a cupcake and holding loaves of bread. Our captive dropped to his knees, begging for mercy. He took out his wallet and showed us pictures of his kids, as if they were for sale. I took a doughy satchel and swung it at his face, striking him solidly in the cheek. I know it didn't hurt, but the man whimpered in shame and resigned himself to the beating. Nicholas and I pummeled him silly with pillows of white bread until it snowed breadcrumbs.

Hillside was surprisingly quiet. There were no roving bands of understood why my father wore his badge so proudly. The badge protected him; in uniform he was safe.

Sitting on that couch watching the announcer gloat, my pacifist Negro chrysalis peeled away, and a glistening anger began to test its wings. A rage that couldn't be dealt with in a poem or soothed with the glass of milk and glazed doughnut offered by our kind host.

"There's a poem in there somewhere," the man said. He and Scoby must have been talking about me. I wanted to slap Scoby; he sat there giggling, egging the man on with a fling of his hand. "What do you write about?" the man asked.

"I write about whatever." I envied Psycho Loco. Strangers never asked him, "What kind of people do you kill? Could you do a little killing right now, just for me?" Psycho Loco dealt with his rage by blaming and lashing out; there was no pretense of fairness and justice, due process was whatever mood he was in, clemency was his running out of bullets while shooting at you.

"Have you ever published anything?"

"Yeah, back in Hillside he writes his poems on the wall."

"I been published in a few magazines too. There's a company in New York that wants to publish a book of my shit."

Even at its most reflective or its angriest, my poetry was little more than an opiate devoted to pacifying my cynicism. Poetry was a sixteen-year-old's Valium: *write a couple of haikus and stay away from fatty foods.* I now know that Psycho Loco's violence was no less a psychological placebo than my poetry, but watching the acquitted officers shake hands with their attorneys and stroll triumphantly into the April sun, I saw his brutality as a powerful vitriolic stimulant. I wanted to sip this effervescent bromo that cleared one's head and numbed the aches and pains of oppression. Psycho Loco had the satisfaction of standing up to his enemies and listening to them scream, watching them close their eyes for the last time. Psycho Loco had a semblance of closure and accomplishment. He was threat. The American poet was a tattletale, a whiner, at best an instigator. You write about blowing up the White House and they tap your phone, but only when you buy some dynamite will they tap you on the shoulder and say, "Come with me."

"Nigger, you ain't never said nothing about no book."

"Nigger, you ain't never asked."

looters, no brushfires. Hillside seemed to be biding its time till morning. Manny Montoya and his wife Sally opened the Barbershop and
Chiropractic Offices and turned it into a way station for weary rioters
coming back from the festivities on the other side of the wall. Handing
out free tamales and steaming bowls of ponchi soup, Sally proudly
told stories about how Hillsiders had historically acquitted themselves
well in Los Angeles' riots. Beating back an armada of drunken sailors
in the zoot-suit riots in the summer of '43, blowing up four police cars
and poisoning six police dogs with cyanide-laced chitterlings and
chorizo in the Watts riots of '65, torturing and killing an entire squad
of National Guardsmen from Pacoima in the infamous Hillside death
march during the I'm-Tired-of-the-White-Man-Fucking-with-Us-and-
Whatnot riots of '68. Manny smiled at his wife's recounting and pre-
dicted that La Insurrección de '92 would be the biggest of them all.

The tamales made me thirsty and I headed over to Ms. Kim's store
to buy something to drink. When I got there, she was yelling in Korean
and pressing Molotov cocktails into the hands of a small group of
bystanders, pleading with them to burn down her store.

"Loot, goddamn it. You saw video. Remember Latasha Harlins.
Burn my fucking store down. I feel better. Rod-ney King! Rod-ney
King! Rod-ney King!"

The crowd refused. Ms. Kim was too well liked. Maybe if she had
been one hundred percent Korean they'd have busted a few windows
just for appearance's sake.

Holding one of her makeshift grenades, Ms. Kim lit the oil-rag
fuse and strode to the front of the store. The crowd surged to stop
her, and she held them at bay by waving the torch in their stunned
faces. Then she wheeled and sent the bomb hurling through the glass
doors. The flames slowly crawled across the floor, whipping through
the aisles, then scaling the counter. Ms. Kim silently hook-shot another
cocktail onto the roof and watched her store burn with a satisfied
smile. A few folks tried to douse the flames with garden hoses, but
Ms. Kim cut their hoses in half with a Swiss Army knife, then went
looking for the police to place herself under arrest.

The next afternoon Scoby and I sat in his basement watching the
rest of the city burn on television. A parade of relatives marched
through his house hawking their wares. "Look what I came up on."

Holding up sweaters and jackets that smelled like smoke for our perusal. "Gunnar, you'd look good in this. Got a lamé collar. Bill Cosby would wear this jammie. You Nick's man, two dollars."

"Nigger, move, you in front of the TV."

It was hard not to be envious of somebody who had some free shit and a little crumb of the California dream. I too wanted to "come up," but I didn't think I was a thief. The television stations were airing live feeds from hot spots around the city, showing looters entering stores empty-handed and exiting carrying furniture on their backs like worker ants carrying ten times their weight.

"Hey, isn't that the Montgomery Ward Plaza?" The mall was about ten minutes away, just outside the wall.

"Yeah, there go Technology Town."

"Oh shit, fools coming up on free computers and shit."

Scoby and I looked each other in the eye for about a nanosecond, then stormed out of the house. Running down the streets, we argued over the merits of an IBM-compatible versus an Apple.

"Dude, I'm looking for a Wizard Protean."

"What? You can't carry out a desktop. Go for a laptop. You get all the qualities of a Protean, plus mobility. Your dumb ass is trying to steal a whole mainframe."

Coach Shimimoto's arduous workouts had served their purpose. We reached Technology Town fresh and ready to celebrate Christmas in April. Leaping through the broken windows, we tumbled over a stack of plastic shopping baskets and landed in a snowbank of Styrofoam package filler. We were too late. All the presents had been opened. The showroom was stripped bare. Broken shelving dangled from the walls; overturned showcases spilled over onto the floor, serving as caskets for dead batteries and the shells of broken stereo equipment. Unraveled cassette tape hung from the overhead pipes like brown riot tinsel. Even the ceiling fans and service phones were gone.

"What happens to a dream deferred?" I said in my best classical recitation voice. Scoby cursed and threw a nine-volt battery at my head.

"Fuck Langston Hughes. I bet when they rioted in Harlem, Langston got his."

"Does it dry up like a wino in rehab? Or gesture like a whore, reeling from the pimp's left jab?"

Paul Beatty

Kicking our way through the piles of cardboard, we left the store and stood in the parking lot thinking of our next target. People were still ransacking Cribs 'n' Bibs, the toddler shop, but rattles, powdered milk, and designer diapers didn't interest us. Scoby snapped his fingers, shouted, "What Did You Say?" and sprinted toward the alley that ran behind the mall.

What Did You Say? was a car accessory emporium that specialized in deafeningly loud car stereos and equally loud seat covers. I couldn't figure out how Scoby planned to get in the place. What Did You Say? was known to be impenetrable. A solid metal garage door that had foiled the attempts of a Who's Who of burglary specialists sealed the front entrance. The famed barrier had withstood ramming from hijacked semitrucks, dynamite, and every solvent from hot sauce for Lucy's Burritos to 150-proof rum mixed with corrosive black hair products.

When we got to What Did You Say?, the steel door was still in place. Scoby and I put our ears against the door and heard what sounded like mice scurrying around inside. We zipped around the back and found a small opening smashed into the cinder-block wall, a guilty-looking sledgehammer lying atop a pile of rubble. Every ten seconds or so a contortionist would squeeze through the hole, bearing some sort of electronic gadgetry. Standing nearby in tears was fat Reece Clinksdale. Reece was bemoaning his girth, because he was too big to fit in the hole and was missing out on the rebellion. He wiped his eyes and stopped blubbering for a bit.

"You guys going in?"

"I guess so," we answered.

"Well, you better hurry up. I think most of the good stuff is gone."

Reece was right. The crawlspace was starting to give birth to zoo animals. Guys were popping headfirst through the hole wrapped in sheepskin and leopard-skin seat covers and looking like cuddly animals at the petting zoo. I helped deliver a breech baby alligator seat cover who'd decided to exit feet first and had to be pulled through the cement birth canal.

When the traffic was light enough to make an entrance, Scoby and I slid through the hole. The absolute lack of chaos was amazing. Instead of a horde of one-eyed brigands pillaging and setting fires, the looters were very courteous and the plundering was orderly. Everyone waited patiently in a line that wound through the aisles and into the storeroom. Once you were in the storeroom, a philanthropic soul handed you a box off the shelf. You didn't get your choice of goods, but no one complained. If you wanted something else, you just got in line again.

Looting wasn't as exciting as Scoby and I had hoped it would be. Nicholas came up on a car alarm and I on a box of pine-tree-shaped air fresheners.

On the way back to the neighborhood, we saw Pookie Hamilton drive by in his convertible bug. I whistled and Pookie pulled over to the curb, waving for us to get in the back seat.

"Where you headed, Pook?"

"I just got a page from Psycho Loco. He needs some help."

I hadn't forgotten about Psycho Loco's planned big score, but the greedy look in his eyes whenever he talked about "the heist" told me that I didn't want to be involved.

"Drop me and Scoby off at my house."

"No time, G."

"Well, where we going?"

"Montgomery Ward's."

When we pulled into the Montgomery Ward parking lot, there were Psycho Loco, No M.O. Clark, and Joe Shenanigans standing behind Psycho Loco's van next to a huge iron safe. Grimy, covered with sweat, the boys were overjoyed to see us. So this was "the heist."

"What the fuck? Are you motherfuckers crazy?"

"Chill, homes. We just want help lifting this thing into the van."

"How did you get it out?"

"Look," Scoby said, pointing to a set of rubber wheels attached to the bottom of the strongbox. Only Montgomery Ward would build a mobile safe. I had two thoughts. Why are all safes painted beige, and would my mother come visit me in prison?

"Dude, I can't be wearing no stone-washed prison outfit for the rest of my life. That shit makes me itch."

Scoby tried to comfort me. "You can wear any kind of shirt you want, just no rhinestones or metal buttons. Besides, I haven't seen one police car the whole day."

He was right. I hadn't even noticed. The entire day had been an undeclared national holiday. Los Angeles was a theme park and we were spending the day in Anarchyland. *All stores and banks remain open, but unstaffed. From this point, waiting time for this attraction is zero minutes.* I calmed down.

The safe was unbelievably heavy, which everyone but me took as a positive sign. I thought the thing could just as easily be empty or filled with employee timecards as stuffed with valuables.

On our third try we almost had the safe inside the back of the van when we all heard an extremely disheartening sound. "What's that?" everyone asked.

"Uh, the Doppler effect," I said.

"Shit, it's the cops."

With a final strain we edged the safe onto the bumper of the van, but our knees buckled under the weight and the safe dropped to the ground with a heavy thud. The sirens were getting closer. No one had the energy for another lift, but we couldn't leave the safe in the middle of the parking lot, not with visions of Spanish gold doubloons dancing in our heads. I looked in the van and saw a length of rope. How stupid we'd been. All we needed to do was tie one end to the safe's handle and the other end to the van's bumper and we could drive away, pulling the safe along behind us.

I heard the cop car pull into the parking lot. My back tightened in anticipation of hearing a gunshot or a threatening "Get your hands up and step away from the vehicle." What I did hear was something I hadn't heard in years: my father's voice. I told the boys to keep going and I'd distract him. I turned around to see my father step out of the car, gripping a shotgun in one hand.

"Dad. Long time no see. Things must really be hectic if you're out on the streets."

I heard the van slowly pull off, and I looked back to see the safe trailing behind it like a tin can tied to the car of newlyweds headed for their honeymoon. When I turned to face my father, the hard rubber butt of the shotgun crashed into my jaw. I saw a flash of white and dropped to the pavement. My father's partner stepped on my ear, muffling his words.

"You are not a Kaufman. I refuse to let you embarrass me. You can't embarrass me with poetry and your niggerish ways. And where did you get all these damn air fresheners?"

Something hard smacked the side of my neck, sending my tongue rolling out of my mouth like a party favor. I could taste the salty ash on the pavement. Ash that had drifted from fires set in anger around the city. I remembered learning in third grade that snakes "see" and "hear" with their sensitive tongues. I imagined my tongue almost bitten through, hearing the polyrhythms of my father's nightstick on my body. Through my tongue I saw my father transform into a master Senegalese drummer beating a surrender code on a hollow log on the banks of the muddy Gambia River. A flash of white — the night of my conception, my father twisting Mama's arm behind her back and ordering her to "assume the position." A flash of white — my father potty-training me by slapping me across the face and sticking my hand in my mushy excrement. Soon my body stopped bucking with every blow. There was only white — no memories, no visions, only the sound of voices.

"Gunnar, my young revolutionary, while you were in a coma, you got a letter from the Nike Basketball Camp. You've been chosen as one of the hundred best ballplayers in the nation. Actually, you're number one hundred." — Coach Shimimoto

"Son, your father and I both think it's best for you to transfer to another school. We're sending you to El Campesino Real in the Valley." — Mom

"Dude, you got fucked up." — Nicholas Scoby

"You gots to get better, cuz. We can't figure out how to open the safe." — Psycho Loco

※

The safe sat in the middle of Psycho Loco's den, a three-dimensional puzzle daring to be solved. Old Abuela Gloria, reportedly an expert safecracker in Havana during Batista's glory days, was wearing a stethoscope and listening to the tumblers click as she spun the combination dial back and forth.

"Isn't Abuela Gloria deaf?" I asked Ms. Sanchez.

"Yeah, but she insisted on trying."

Abuela Gloria removed the stethoscope from her ears and pulled on the latch. Nothing happened. "Fucking goddamn box."

Scoby was calculating possible permutations of a combination lock numbered from zero to one hundred. He'd already tried thirty-two-thousand different combinations while I was in the hospital. Psycho Loco came in from the kitchen and tossed me a cold Carta Blanca. The beer sailed over my head and I had to stretch my aching arms to catch the tumbling bottle.

"Damn, you did that on purpose. That shit hurt."

"Just a little physical therapy to speed up your convalescence."

"Thanks."

"When you flying to Portland to the basketball camp?"

"August sixth, end of the summer. I should be healed by then."

Scoby knelt beside the safe, flipping the dial from number to number and shaking his cramping hands in frustration as his magic failed him.

"Gunnar, look at the safe. Maybe you can figure out a way to open it."

"What I know about opening a safe? That thing almost got me killed. I don't give a fuck if you never get it open."

I was lying and Psycho Loco knew it. I hadn't taken my eyes off the box since I'd been there. I couldn't shake the word "treasure" from my head: rubies, gold lanterns, and ancient scrolls. I wanted to free the genie and fuck up my three wishes.

I wish I knew how a bill changer can tell the difference between a one, a five, and a ten-dollar bill.

I wish I could dance like Bert Williams.

I wish I had a lifetime supply of superballs, so I could bounce them as high and as hard as I pleased without worrying about losing them.

I ran my hands over the safe's tapered edges, then stood back, waved my fingers, and said in a slow, spooky voice, "Open sesame."

"We did that shit already. Ala-kazam, hocus-pocus — we even paid that voodoo lady on Normandie fifty dollars to open it with some of that ol'-time Yoruba religion."

"What happened?"

"She got chicken blood and pixie dust all over the fucking place. Damn near burned the house down with all the candles."

I turned the safe so the door faced me. The wheels creaked under its weight. "I wish we could open this thing right now. I can't take the suspense. Psycho Loco, how did you know where to find the safe?"

Psycho Loco laughed. His mother groaned. "I feel like Ma Barker," she said, and left the room.

"Gunnar, you got to have patience. I've been planning to steal this thing ever since I was ten. You remember how the toy department in Montgomery Ward's was like twenty-five feet from the door?"

"Yeah, that was stupid. Fools used to run through there, grab a G.I. Joe doll or a Hot Wheel car and break."

"Well, there was this race-car set that I wanted, the Tommy Thunder 5000. It came with a racing helmet, the headlights on the cars worked, the whole nine. But it was too big and heavy to pick up and walk out with — I had to get it closer to the door. So every day after school I moved the box one inch closer. I did this for the entire fifth grade."

"Straight genius."

"Little by little, my Tommy Thunder 5000 was steadily easing toward that front door. Finally I had the box close enough to the door. On the day I was going to take it, I was so happy, I invited every kid I knew over to my house to race them cars. I get to the store and my Tommy Thunder 5000 is gone. In its place is a potted plant. In one day Montgomery Ward's turned the toy department into gardening supplies. Where the electric trains used to be were mounds of fertilizer. The video game cartridges were transformed into seed packets. I went berserk and started yelling for the manager. 'Where's my goddamn Tommy Thunder 5000? Who moved my race-car set? I demand to speak to the manager.' Security tried to get me to leave, but I wouldn't leave. I started pissing on rosebushes, demanding to see the manager. The manager comes down and escorts me to his office on the second floor in the back, near the linens. He asks me why I'm so upset and I explain to him how I'd been slowly stealing the Tommy Thunder 5000 and by moving the toy section near the escalator he fucked up my summer. So to cool me out he says, 'Sorry about the Tommy Thunder 5000, but to make up for your troubles you can have anything you see in my office.' I look around. He got lollipops, candy canes, and stuffed animals in there. I see the safe sitting in the corner. I go, 'I want that,' pointing to the safe. He goes, 'You can't have that, young man. That's valuable property,' and hands me a candy cane. I'm like, 'Motherfucker, you said *anything*. That safe

Paul Beatty

is mine, you watch.' And ta-da, nine years later, look where the safe sits, in my living room."

"You are patient, yeesh. Must be that Apache blood. I hope you ain't waiting for the white man to disappear too."

I looked closely at the safe. The tag dangling from the handle flapped in the current of a household draft. The tag read, "Montgomery Ward Duro-Safe. This safe is solid tungsten. Airtight, fireproof, and guaranteed to withstand pressure up to 3500 pounds per square inch." I knew there had to be a way to open it; this was a Montgomery Ward product. Nothing they made worked. Their television sets came with wire hangers and a pair of pliers to turn the channel after the knobs fell off.

I had an idea. I asked Abuela Gloria for her safecracking kit. I set the small metal box about three feet behind the safe, asked Scoby, Ms. Sanchez, and Psycho Loco to help tip the safe onto its back. There on the bottom of the safe was the combination, written on a dirty white label.

4 turns to the right to 67
3 turns to the left to 23
2 turns to the right to 55
1 turn to the left to 63

The best thing about treasure is the assortment. I didn't think gold bars really existed. I thought they were a movie prop used to speed up the plot. Yet there was a shoebox full of domino-size ingots stamped MONTGOMERY WARD 24K. Stacks of dusty paper money sat in the back, looking afraid to come out from their hiding place. Silver and platinum rings, brooches, and tiaras inlaid with rubies, emeralds, and diamonds glittered under the lamplight.

It was surreal to watch Psycho Loco divide the bounty, tossing stacks of money and gold bars around the room like so many paperweights. We played *The Price Is Right* for the jewelry. Whoever was closest to guessing the stickered price won the bauble.

For a while living in Hillside was like living in the Old West in a thriving goldmining town's bubble economy. Psycho Loco customized his van. Scoby bought a car and every jazz CD on his extensive list. Joe Shenanigans, who let out a hearty "Mama mia" upon receiving his share, moved to Brooklyn and tried to join the Mafia. Ms. Sanchez went door to door selling jewelry at discount prices. No M.O. Clark got plastic surgery to remove his fingerprints. His hands looked like they'd been steamrolled, sanded down, then varnished. He got a kick out of harassing the palm readers on Hollywood Boulevard. Those soothsayers who didn't pass out after looking at his glassy palms usually had the temerity to bullshit about No M.O.'s clearheadedness and his smooth future.

I refused any payment for my part in the heist. I only wanted to satisfy my curiosity, not fence gold bars and pray that the money I was spending was untraceable. Psycho Loco overlooked my morality but said he would make sure I profited. He began to take a strange interest in my personal life. What did I plan to do with my future, what size family did I want, did I believe in corporal punishment for kids. When Psycho Loco asked, "What would you do to instill respect for human rights throughout the world?" I realized that I was filling out an application of some sort by proxy. I didn't know what I was applying for, but at the time I thought maybe Psycho Loco was entering me in a beauty pageant.

✿

I spent the last two weeks of my sixteenth summer away at camp, not shooting rapids and learning Indian folk songs but shooting baskets and learning when to double-down and give weak-side help.

E-mail from Camp

Dear Ma,

How you? I know Christina and Nicole are a little chubby but I can't believe you couldn't tell they were pregnant until they were eight months gone. I guess when you work at a free clinic sometimes "you can't see the forest for the . . ." Never mind, I never understood that proverb anyway. I'm sorry to hear that you all aren't getting along, but why don't they stay at the unwed mothers' home rather than live with Dad? Sorry for the third degree, the thought of my sisters having babies at the same time is a little unsettling. Maybe things will be better when I leave the house. I know I haven't been the ideal son.

Paul Beatty

Thanks for the Nabokov, it's appropriate in this place with these bossy white men slobbering over skinny kids. Ma, I swear they look at you like they want to fuck you, using every and any excuse to slap your butt. "Gunnar, your shoes are laced properly." Butt slap. "Kaufman, you ate all your lima beans." Butt slap.

Life as the one hundredth best high school basketball player in America is a trip. As numero ciento I'm the last in line to do everything. Last to eat. Last to use the shower. Last to get issued the camp sweats and practice uniforms with 100 emblazoned on the back. In the "college prep" class, I have to sit way in the back. Not that I'm missing anything. College prep amounts to an etiquette lesson on how to behave once we get there. "Don't get involved with any student groups, and uphold your professionalism and the school's honor on and off the court." Then they pass out a crib sheet with the definitions to twenty words *guaranteed* to be on the SAT.

The best part about camp is you get to meet people from other places. I'm living in a dorm room with Khalil Ibrahim and Zane Cropsy, campers ninety-nine and ninety-eight, respectively. Khalil is from Miami. He's always complaining that he should be rated higher than ninety-nine but the coaches discriminate against him 'cause he's gay. He's right. I overheard one counselor telling a scout that the reason Khalil's court sense is so good is because his "homosexualness gives him a heightened awareness of where other boys are on the court, but his presence may be detrimental to a team of normal kids." Khalil's sexuality gives him one advantage, though: no one slaps his butt.

Zane is from New York City, Manhattan. Or as he says, "Maa-hat-ehn." It's hard to talk to Zane because his speech consists entirely of rhetorical filler. He responds to everything with "Word up, know what I'm sayin', on the strength," like he's having the deepest conversations in the history of speech.

Don't worry about me, Ma, I'm fine. I've been deloused and the condescending white people are feeding me. Word up, on the strength.

Love, your son,
Gunnar

✿

Dear Christina and Nicole,

I'm sorry to hear you all and Ma aren't getting along because of the pregnancy thing, but I can't believe you'd rather live with Dad than stay at the hippo house. You know my motto: fuck that nigger. If you have boys, make sure you don't leave them alone with him. The photos of your bloated bellies are hilarious. When I told you to talk to Coach Shimimoto if you needed anything, I didn't know he'd use your stomachs for artistic canvases. The tattoos make you look like African yakuza, and the swelling gives them a kind of 3-D effect. Christina, *View #36 of the Hollywood Sign from Pete's Bar at Sunset* is cool. I like how Coach used your bellybutton as the focal point, turning it into an ashtray and going from there. Nicole, *Beer Bottle and Butterfly* is absolutely amazing. *Its bold yet welcoming color scheme captures the transformation of inorganic societal byproduct into a state of synthetic beatitude barely distinguishable from the natural order.* Did that make sense? No? Good, I'll be an art critic when I grow up. I told you Shimimoto was a good guy. Did he give you the bullshit rap that his style is derivative of the ancient *ukiyo-e* school as practiced by Hokusai and Ando Hiroshige? Don't believe it — same madness he said in art class. His stuff is a straight rip-off of the Aztec/Diego Rivera/lowrider murals on the freeway underpasses. Shimimoto been in the 'hood too long and don't want to admit it. Wouldn't it be funny if the ink seeped through your pores and the babies came out green and peach? Anyway, judging from his letter, it sounds like he's enjoying the Lamaze classes. See you when I get back.

> Take care and
> puuussshhhh!
> Gunnar

✿

Scobe,

What's happenin', nukka? Coolin'? Niggers out here have heard of you. You're an underground legend. They be asking me is it true you never miss and why don't you shoot more. The coaches are asking about you too. How tall are you? What's your quickness-to-speed ratio? Shit like that. As you can see, they really want to get to know you as a person. Anyway, expect to get much attention next year. I may not be around to watch, though; tomorrow I go into battle. I have to play camper number one, Leon "Housequake" Tremundo. The boy is fucking gigantic. He's 6' 6" and about 245 lbs. from Washington DC. We play dominoes at night and this fool can hold nine bones in one hand so you know, cuz, is like big as fuck. He can dunk from anywhere on the court. He got names for every one, too: the Girls at St. Ignatius Swoon Boom, the Buff Rough Motherfucker Stuff, the Anti-Gravity Levitation Mid-Air Hesitation Crazy Elevation Stupid Escalation Geronimo Look Out Below Cold Crush Two-Hand Flush. I heard during practice the kids on his team have to wear padded helmets 'cause Leon Tremundo killed one of his teammates who was stupid enough to take a charging foul against him. The guy doesn't move that fast, just keeps moving. It's like he plays in slow motion, just flows up and down the court like lava. You can't stop him, he kind of just overwhelms you and you get swamped trying to guard him. If I survive, I'll let you know. His girlfriend is Missy Gibson, the actress from that sitcom *Talented Tenth*. You know, the show where a bunch of seddity motherfuckers be saving the community by rewarding exemplary African-American citizenship with a piece of fried chicken. "By deciding to wait until marriage to have sex, Leroy and Martha are celebrating traditional African values. Here go a thigh, a wing, and a biscuit." Notice they don't never say nothing like "Lucinda decided to have a clitoridectomy. Wow, that's African, have some chicken gizzards, mmmmm." Anyway, back to this behemoth, Leon Tremundo. Every time he dunks on a nigger, he runs into the stands to kiss Missy Gibson. Then she looks at whoever it was he served and blows that nigger a kiss. Sounds like true love.

Remember the pamphlet the camp sent me with pictures of Jacuzzis, the horseback riding, and shit? Well, it's all true. The place is sweet as hell. Me and this white boy from Topeka are the only ones who ride the horses. I eat lunch real fast, then run to the stables. My favorite horse is Chuckles. He's really gentle. You hop on his back and he takes off down the trail at a leisurely pace. I don't have to steer or nothing, just prod him to go faster every now and then. The horse knows each trail like ten-year-olds know the alphabet; they've repeated it a million times but haven't tired of the sounds and twists and turns. I imagine Chuckles's whinnies and snorts are equine for "H, I, J, K, Elemenopee, Q, R, S, T." I sympathize with these animals 'cause this place makes me feel like a racehorse. Every morning I get up at six o'clock to get weighed, fed, and put through my paces.

The only good thing about the place is it's fun to see the whities having to earn they propers for a change. We be disrespecting these peckerwoods something terrible. We have one play called "Milk-shake," which is whoever has a white kid guarding 'em takes that clown to hole.

I'm rooming with these two fools, Touch from Miami and Z-Groove from Brooklyn. They're cool, but all they do is talk about basketball, 24–7. We come back to the crib after eight hours of playing and analyzing basketball and the first thing they do is stick a highlight reel of their hero, Cleotis Jacobin, into the VCR. (We have a big-screen television set in our room.) Cleotis Jacobin plays for Crawdad A & M, a small Division XI school in southern Alabama. The man can literally fly. He shoots a three-point lay-up where he comes flying down the court and takes off from behind the arc and swoops to the basket like he's riding a magic carpet or something. Whenever he jumps, you can hear the crowd in the background chanting "One Mississippi! Two Mississippi!" until he lands. On one move he goes baseline against Tallahassee School of Cosmetology, jumps in the air, stops, hovers, then spins right, sails for a bit, then changes direction and starts floating left. I swear to God, Allah, Jehovah, Buddha, James Brown, nigger's in the air so long the crowd gets to three Mississippi. It was Ham Hock Night, so when he finally touched down the fans threw fatty pieces of pork and bottles of hot sauce onto the floor in appreciation. The reason Cleotis is playing in obscurity is because he cannot shoot. He has absolutely no touch. Jacobin goes to the glass like Peter Pan but finishes like a Kennedy. It's like he's playing basketball with a shot put. In one game he launched a jumper that hit the rim so hard the net fell to the floor. In another he shot the ball and it sailed through the backboard like a rock through glass.

So between Touch and Z-Groove and the adventures of Cleotis Jacobin, I'm going stir-crazy in this hole. I even brought up sex just to talk about something other than basketball. You know I rarely talk about sex. So I say, in my best macho baritone, "Hey, Missy Gibson got it going on justa bit, don't she?" But wouldn't you know it, these guys use basketball as a metaphor for everything. Touch is like, "Yeah, she cute, but she don't make my starting five." Starting five? "I got

Lena 'Methuselah' Horne at the point guard, seventy years old, running the show like a vet. Fredi Washington at the two spot, dead but still full of shake 'n' bake. My big fella in the middle is Iman: statuesque, smooth, good hands. Dorothy Dandridge at a small forward, and Lark McCarthy, the nightly news anchor, at the power spot. Halle Berry is my sixth man off the bench, instant offense." Z-Groove has all dark-skinned lineup: Denzel Washington and Lightning Hopkins at the guards, the forwards Richard Roundtree and Michael Jordan; his center was Woody Strode.

Cuz, I been having nightmares in this hole. Woke up last night sweating and shit, screaming, shaking. Scared the piss out of Z-Groove and Touch. Z-Groove tried to play it off by saying, "What you dreaming about, having a threesome with Gary Coleman and Emmanuel Lewis?" Very funny, right? I didn't know what the hell I was carrying on about. All I knew was that it had something to do with death. Like I was running through different scenarios of how I'd like to die. So we got into a conversation about death or more specifically our demises, from which I concluded that niggers aren't afraid to die but are worried about how to die. We was up till five in the morning talking shit.

Me: Touch, how you wanna go out?

Touch: Definitely on the floor dunking, hang. (Raises his hands in the air simulating a dunking motion.) And you know that. Word up. Have a mad large funeral. Big-ass tomb and shit. Mausoleum with eternal candles, and I'd hire some out-of-work actors to cry at my grave twenty-four hours a day.

Z-Groove: I hear you, kid. Not a bad way to die, but everybody goes out dunking, word up.

Me: What you mean?

Z-Groove: Did you ever see *Come Back Charleston Blue?*

Me: No, I read the book.

Z-Groove: Figures. I don't know about the book, but in the movie there's this hit-man, bodyguard-type nigger named Stretch or some shit, and he playing ball in the park at night. He goes up to stuff this two-hander and gets machine-gunned in the chest and dies hanging on the rim with his 'fro still perfectly combed.

Touch. That's make-believe. Any real motherfuckers die dunking?

Z-Groove: You ever hear of this disease called Marfan's? I did a book report on it last year. It affects tall, elongated motherfuckers.

They're born with a thin aorta, and if they overexert themselves it tears and they die. A while back *Sports Illustrated* did a story on Marfan's, talking about this gangly-type brother who had the disease but didn't know it and died dunking in a pick-up game.

Touch: What about Hank Gathers? That baller with the weak heart who died a few years back after finishing an alley-oop in front of a house full of folks.

Z-Groove: That's awright, only thing is I don't want white people saying I went out happy like a good b-ball-playing nigger. Know what I'm saying?

Touch: What I want to know is, how come none of these overweight, hysterical coaches never bust a gut on the sideline and collapse in the middle of a big game? That shit never happen to white folks.

Me: All I know is I want to die, but I don't want to die alone.

Scoby, this death thing is for real. I can't avoid it so I might as well embrace it. Right? Dude, am I going crazy? Have you finished with Ella Fitzgerald yet?

Later,

Gunnar

P.S. I know, I know, you're saying what was my starting five? Midnight movies at shooting guard, Joan Miró at point guard, thunderstorms at small forward, the beach at power forward, and metamorphic rocks at center.

✿

Dear Psycho Loco,

Enclosed are the photograph and medical records you requested. Why won't you tell me what this is for? The photo is a bit mug shot-ish, but the best I can do. I been thinking about death out here, something about being surrounded by rickety old ex-athletes trying to relive their youths. I'll talk to you more about it when I get back. Thanks for the money, Robin Hood, I hope you kept your promise not to lend me any ducats from the heist. I snuck out and went downtown to buy some books. Here are the answers to the questionnaire you sent me.

Height — 6' 4"

Weight — 187 lbs.

Paul Beatty

Favorite authors — Zora Neale Hurston, G. K. Chesterton, Richard Pryor, and Charles Chesnutt

Favorite foods — Fish tacos and grape juice

Greatest inventions — Right on red, multiball pinball machines, and the ballpoint pen

I should have the results of the sperm count by the end of the week. Incredible medical care at this mug, they got to keep they niggers physically fit.

> Miss ya and stay up,
> Gunnar

✿

Scoby,

Since I'm writing you this letter, it means I played against Leon Tremundo and survived. Leon didn't kiss Missy Gibson once, and after the game she refused to let him touch her. "How you let that black white boy dog you!" The coaches tried to offer me jersey number eight (apparently I don't penetrate enough), but I turned them down.

> Easy,

✿

Mama,

You can do something with my part of the college money, I don't think I'll need it. I was sitting in the bleachers when a white man wearing a Raleigh State shirt sat next to me. He didn't say anything, but he took out his wallet and opened it so I could get a good look at what was inside, a brick of hundred-dollar bills. I thought about taking it and sending it to Christina and Nicole, but unfortunately, you raised me better than that.

> Your still poor
> ghetto child,
> running wild,
> Gunnar

✿

Dear Motome Shimimoto,

I want to thank you for never screaming at me, but I'm not sure if I should. I threw the ball cross-court yesterday and this coach from Wyoming Tech, whose name I don't even know, started yelling at me. As if it were an honor for the greatest coach within spitting distance of the Grand Tetons to shout at me. The other kids put their heads down for a moment, then kept playing. I took one step up-court, then beelined straight for Coach Crude. When I got over there, he tried to stare me down. I put my nose on his forehead and told him if he ever raised his voice in my direction again I'd kill him. Did I overreact? Coach, as soon as I said it, I knew I didn't mean it. So did he. But the fucker still crumpled to his knees and started pleading for forgiveness. Afraid I'd never consider attending his powerhouse program. Guess I'll never be one of those black role models who "transcends race," will I? Thanks for never yelling at me, but maybe if you had I'd be used to it and wouldn't take these assholes so seriously. I think you should tell the coach over at El Campesino not to yell at me. I'd appreciate it, thanks. Can you ask Christina and Nicole not to do anything gross like saving the afterbirth in a jar?

Sincerely,
Gunnar

Paul Beatty

"study long, study wrong"

eight

In RETURN for my father's not pressing charges against me and my friends for stealing the safe, I agreed to go quietly to El Campesino Real High, an elite public high school in the San Fernando Valley. It was hoped that the reinfusion of white upper-class values would decrease the likelihood of my committing another felony, but the two miserable years I spent at El Campesino had the opposite effect. If you want to raise the consciousness of an inner-city colored child, send him to an all-white high school. Five days a week I woke at 5:30 A.M. for the hour-and-a-half bus ride from our shtetl to the pristine San Fernando Valley. The migrant student-workers and I trudged off the bus like a weary chain gang, fighting to stay awake and trying not to be intimidated by the luxury cars in the student parking lot, the self-assurance of everyone from the students to the cafeteria workers. I often found myself short of breath from the change in economic and cultural altitude. Gasping for air, I almost took the remedial schedule and the weeks' worth of lunch money my counselor, Ms. Baumgarten, offered me, but my pride got the better of me.

"Ms. Baumgarten, I appreciate your eleemosynary concern, but have you checked my records?"

"My elemen . . . elmo . . . my what?"

"Just stop patronizing me and do your job. Treat me as an individual, not like some stray cat that you feed once a day."

It had been a long time since I'd communicated with white people who weren't athletes or police officers, and here were goo-gobs of them yammering in the halls and blowing wispy bangs off their foreheads. I meshed in well. It was like swimming; you never forget how to raise your voice a couple of octaves, harden your r's, and diphthong the vowels: "Deeeewwuuuude. Maaaaiin. No waaaaaeeey." Whether they slouched or walked upright like proud *Homo erectus* cutouts from the encyclopedia, these kids were so casual. Most of them never had to look over their shoulders a day in their lives until they saw us get off the bus. I was envious. When no one was looking, I found myself trying to blow puffs of air past my wrinkled brow or emulating that quivering headshake, freeing imaginary blond locks from my eyes.

It was sad to watch us troll through the halls, a conga line of burlesque self-parody, all of us affecting our white-society persona of the day. Most days we morphed into waxen African-Americans. Perpetually smiling scholastic lawn jockeys, repeating verbatim the prosaic commandments of domesticity:

Thou shalt worship no god other than whiteness.

Thou shalt not disagree with anything a white person says.

When traveling in the company of a white person, thou shalt always maintain a respectful distance of two paces to the rear.

If traveling by car for lunch at McDonald's with three or more white human deities, thou shalt never ride in the front seat nor request to change the radio station.

Those niggers most afflicted by white supremacyosis changed their names from Raymond to Kelly or Winifred to Megan. They walked around campus shunning the uncivilized niggers and talking in bad Cockney accents. Listening to teens who've been no closer to England than the Monty Python show saying, "Blimey, Oy-ive gowht a blooming 'edache" will bring any Negro with a shred of self-respect to tears.

Some situations called not for ethnic obfuscation but for rubbing burnt cork over our already dusky features and taking the stage as the blackest niggers in captivity. We pleaded for academic leniency: "Mistah Boss, sir. I'z couldenst dues my homework 'cause welfare came and took my baby brudder to the home and he had all the crayons." We performed with vaudevillian panache, like adolescent interlocutors entertaining the troops back from the Rhine. We gave goofy white kids the soul shake, caught footballs, and sang in the hallways.

On weekends Mom forced me to pal around with the Valley bon vivants. "Gunnar, I want you to hang out with those nice boys from school today."

I bristled. "Ma, make up your mind. You moved us out here. Later for those peckerwoods."

"What's the statute of limitations for safecracking, seven years?"

Paul Beatty

"That's fucked up, Ma."

I'd go into my "Hey, guy" mode and meet my Caucasian crew in neutral areas like Venice Beach or Melrose Avenue and hang out on the strip, eating cheeseburgers and window shopping.

"Stay black, nigger," Scoby would call out as I boarded the bus. Scoby had a standing invitation to come along, but he always declined. Psycho Loco also refused, unless I agreed to set the white boys up for a robbery.

"And what exactly does 'stay black' mean, Nick?"

"It means be yourself, what else could it possibly mean?"

The arrogance of the white kids was enervating and I soon tired of their unspoken noblesse oblige, the subtle one-upsmanship. For instance, Danny Kraft was always bragging that he could name the capital of any country in the world.

"Test me, Gunnar, test me."

"Portugal?"

"Lisbon."

"Poland?"

"Warsaw."

"Luxembourg?"

"Luxembourg, ha."

"Djibouti?"

"What?"

"Djibouti? Little spot near Ethiopia and Somalia."

"Isn't the capital Abu Dhabi?"

"Nope. How about Kiribati?"

"That one's Abu Dhabi."

"You're a dumb fuck. I thought white people were supposed to be smart."

"Well, ask me some real countries."

"What are 'real countries'? Places where real people live? White people? What's the capital of the Maldives? Guinea? Burkina Faso? Laos? Well, motherfucker, what are the capitals? Goddamn jingoistic jerk."

The most important lesson I learned at El Campesino was that I wasn't in arrears to the white race. No matter how much I felt indebted to white folks, I owed them nothing. My attitude changed. I began treating the bus ride out to the Valley as a daily vacation. The school's library rivaled most college libraries and I turned it into my personal athenaeum. I buried myself in Senghor, Céline, Baraka, Dos Passos, decompressing and reacclimating myself to myself, like a diver just returned from a deep-sea sojourn. In the library I could avoid white boys asking me if I thought blacks were closer to gorillas while tufts of unruly chest hair crept past their collars like weeds starving for sunlight. I could hide from smarmy college basketball recruiters who'd never think to look for a black athlete in the library. Ditch classes where the teachers talked past me, saying things like "It's not hard to be a millionaire. What are your parents' houses worth, five hundred thousand dollars? See, that's a half mill right there."

I couldn't escape basketball practice. At two o'clock every afternoon Coach Logan's assistant, Mr. Wurlitz, went around to all the classes I missed and gathered my assignments. At two-thirty he kowtowed and politely asked if I would like to join the rest of the team for practice.

I wasn't the basketball team's only hired gun. In hopes of dominating Valley basketball, the El Campesino Real Conquistadores brought in Anthony Price from Gardena, Anita Appleby from Torrance, and Tommy Mendoza from Echo Park. A few white players would get giddy on bus rides to games, confiding in me that playing with black players was a dream come true. Singing in the shower and jiving in the gym — what more could there be to life?

✤

Early in my senior year I sat down for my weekly career-planning session with Ms. Baumgarten. This time she didn't pester me about applying to the DeVry School of Technology but looked up from her desk, shaking her head as if I'd done something wrong. "I think they might have made a mistake," she said, handing me an opened envelope. My SAT scores had arrived. According to the tables, my verbal score was in the ninety-eighth percentile and my math score in the eighty-seventh.

"What you mean, mistake?"

"Gunnar, you haven't been to calculus once in the past two months, and Mr. Kissio says you wrote an English Lit. composition called 'Machisma Hermeneutics — Hemingway and the Hacienda Gringolust,

An Obsession with the Latino Male.' There's no way you could get these kinds of scores."

Soon letters from colleges addressed "Dear Scholar" instead of "Waddup to the best guard in the nation" began arriving. Now academic recruiters from various schools across the nation called me at home or visited me at school during lunch. The armed forces academies, Harvard, and Boston University were the most aggressive pursuers. I had a good time with the stuffy admirals and majors. After giving me the standard make-the-world-safe-for-democracy spiel, they'd ask what interested me. Removing a picture of Oliver North from my wallet, I'd say in a hushed tone, "Covert ops. Not your average banana republic puppet government stuff — I want to form a rebel army of Laplanders and overthrow all those neutral Scandinavian wussy socialists." I soon stopped getting letters and visits from West Point and Annapolis.

The Harvard recruiter was a marginally known bespectacled public intellectual who had moved west to Los Angeles to set up a think tank of mulatto social scientists called High Yellow Fever. We had dinner at a chic Hawaiian restaurant in Marina del Rey. The regality of the Harvard man's pinkies was hypnotic. Encased in gold rings, these majestic fingers never touched any part of the pu-pu platter, coolly avoided the stem of the wineglass, and punctuated his points on affirmative action with a bombastic vigor unseen since Frederick Douglass. He popped open his pocket watch and suggested we drive to his house for a nightcap. I was mesmerized; this was the first nigger I'd ever seen who owned a pocket watch and the only one I've heard say "nightcap." On the drive over I held his timepiece to my ear, listening to its spring works as if I were an eighteenth-century Pacific islander hoping to trade beads for a metal cricket.

The ersatz egghead lived in Cheviot Heights, in what I swore was the same house I'd stolen the security sign from a couple of years before. Over dessert he gave me a copy of his latest book, *Antebellum Cerebellums: A History of Negro Super-Genius,* and showed me his prized collection of Peggy Lee records. After one listen to "Surrey with the Fringe on Top" I'd pretty much decided I wasn't going to Harvard, but I didn't say anything, because the French pastry was humming.

"Gunnar, why do you want to attend Harvard?"

"It seems like Harvard wants me to attend Harvard. I could give a shit. Harvard, Princeton, Howard, Cornell, Fisk — I'm just determined to get out of Los Angeles. My mom keeps saying Ivy League, Ivy League, Ivy League."

"Look, Gunnar, I understand your reticence, but you're being offered a rare opportunity to sit in the lap of academe and suckle from the teat of wisdom."

"Yeah, yeah. I prefer formula milk, your shit doesn't stink as much."

Sensing he was losing me, he called to his wife. "Honey, come and meet this fine young man I was telling you about."

A white woman in a see-through chiffon gown sashayed into the dining room like a fashion model.

"Baby, this is Gunnar Kaufman. The boy genius projected to do wonderful things with his life. Gunnar, this is my wife, Mindy. You may recognize her — she was the down clue girl on *Crosswords for Cash.*"

"Glad to meet you, Gunnar." She grabbed my hand and kissed me lightly on the knuckles, then locked her hazel eyes on my crotch. "You're bigger, I mean different from the other boys. No tie, no tweed jacket. Muscles. I like you. What's a four-letter word for a Russian mountain range?"

"Ural."

"Smart, too." She touched the tip of my nose with her finger and skipped back to wherever she had come from, rubbing her rear end as if it pained her.

"Gunnar, there are fringe benefits to going to Harvard. Corporeal hors d'oeuvres, if you will."

I snickered as the recruiter's sales pitch grew more desperate.

"I'm going to be frank with you. If I get you to attend Harvard, I get seventy-five thousand dollars, exactly enough to buy a new motor home."

"Motor home?" I asked.

"Couple of years back, some demonic rowdies from down there" — he jabbed his finger angrily toward the ground — "destroyed the old one. They smashed the windows, slashed the tires, urinated on the engine, set fire to the interior. We haven't gone rappelling in the sierras since Lord knows when."

I couldn't believe it was this cat's house me and Psycho Loco had rampaged the night Pumpkin died. "From down where?" I asked.

"Down there!" he repeated, pointing over the stone slope of the San Borrachos Mountains and apparently growing agitated from having to recall the memory.

"Hell, you mean?"

"No, I mean Hillside. The entire community is a Petri dish for criminal vermin."

"So I should go to Harvard and learn to become a gentrified robber baron instead?"

"Yes, you should. I got mine, you get yours. Those poor people are beyond help, you must know that. The only reason I and others of my illustrious ilk pretend to help those folks is to reinforce the difference between them and us. There's a psychological advantage to being the helper and not the helpee. You know the phrase 'Each one, teach one'?"

"Yup."

"Well my motto is 'Each one, leech one.'"

I stopped listening and went out by the pool. The view of Los Angeles, including Hillside, was magnificent. The web of amber streetlights looked like a constellation fallen to earth, awaiting some astronomer to connect the glowing dots to give form to its oracularity. From the sundecks of Cheviot Heights I imagined dimes falling from a stumblebum's Styrofoam cup as shooting stars streaking the night. I heard the nervous laughter of the Seven Sisters standing in doorways, deciding whether to study or hang out. I felt sorry for the night laborers on the moons, selling roses from a bucket and bags of oranges to the comets.

The public intellectual excused himself and then returned with a bundle of black nylon rope and rappelling equipment. "When you go to Harvard, we'll go mountain climbing on your weekends. Let me show you how." He wrapped a belt around my waist, then threaded the rope through its metal loop. Anchoring one end around the pool's stepladder, he pulled the rope tight to make sure it was secure. "Hold the rope loosely with your left hand and use your right to control your speed. When you want to brake, pull back. That's it — now lean back, get your butt down. There you go."

I stepped over the pile of rope and tossed the coil over the fence. It tumbled down the wall until the knotted end was dangling about ten feet from the streets of Hillside.

"What in the hell are you doing? Now you have to recoil the goddamn thing."

Ignoring his admonitions, I scaled the fence, planted my feet firmly against the wall, lowered my butt, and leaned into space.

"Gunnar, where do you think you're going?"

"Home."

"Don't you live in the Valley?"

"Nope, I live in Hillside, the depths of hell."

"You're no Sir Edmund Hillary. Get back here."

"And you're no Lionel Trilling. Later."

I lowered myself into the night.

Mom was disappointed that I wasn't going to Harvard; she thought the public intellectual sounded like a decent man.

"There's a note on the table for you. The recruiter from Boston University stopped by the house."

"He came by the house?"

"*She* came by the house, and she said she'll be back tomorrow."

✿

Ms. Jenkins sat at the kitchen table playing spades with me, Scoby, and Psycho Loco and fielding our questions, my mother hovering over us like a pit boss.

"Would you like another brew, Ms. Jenkins?" I asked.

"Sure, I likes these Carta Blancas — smoother than a mother-fucker. Boston doesn't have nothing like this."

I fetched her another beer, making sure Scoby and Psycho Loco didn't peek at my cards. Ms. Jenkins and I were trying to set those fools.

"What *does* Boston have?" Scoby asked, spinning a king of hearts across the table. "Not much. No black radio. No black clubs. No black political power base. No drive-thru fast food."

"So why would I want to go there?" I asked, trying to emphasize to Nick that this was my interview.

Paul Beatty

"You told me that you wanted to get as far out of L.A. as possible. That's either Orono, Maine, or Boston, Massachusetts, and I know you not no goddamn moose lover. Besides, Gunnar, I've seen your poetry in all the literary journals. I didn't make the connection until I saw the same poems scrawled on the walls in the neighborhood. You probably don't know it, but you already have a following on the East Coast." Ms. Jenkins covered Nicholas's king with a six of hearts.

"This our trick, nigger poet with a bourgeois following on the East Coast," Scoby crowed.

"Nicholas, be quiet," my mother broke in. She liked Ms. Jenkins, but she wasn't about to sell me down the river to any second-rate institution. "Now you said Boston University is Ivy League, but I don't recall its being an Ivy school."

"Well, BU is not an original member, but we recently paid to join the Ivy League."

"What?" said Psycho Loco incredulously, laying a three of hearts on the growing stack of cards and staring me in the eye. "You can't buy your way into the Ivy League."

"You know how colleges have endowments that they invest in the stock market and futures, right? A couple of months back, the Massachusetts lottery was up to five hundred million dollars. The trustees of BU decided to buy thirteen million dollars' worth of lottery tickets, figuring if they covered every possible number combination they would win at least their money back, if not more. As luck would have it, BU was the sole winner. A little hush money in the right pockets, a few well-publicized millions to each member school, and Boston University is in the Ivy League. Of course, we had to offer tuition remission to all the students with IQ's under 125 we kicked out, but they'll get into other schools, if they don't snort it all away."

"Oh shit," I said and slapped down a five of spades.

Ms. Jenkins picked up the book. "'Oh shit' is right. So we're looking for some black students who are going to turn shit out. You down, Gunnar?"

My mother broke in. "Sounds good to me."

"Ma!"

"What about me? Can I go?" asked Nicholas, handing Ms. Jenkins a copy of his transcript and SAT scores.

"Scoby!" I whined.

"With grades and test scores like these, Nicholas, you're a shoo-in, full ride and all."

"What about married couples' housing?"

"Psycho Loco, what you talking about? Married housing!" I shouted, throwing down a jack of clubs.

"When you turn eighteen, Gunnar?"

"June twenty-seventh."

"Then you'll be married, nigger." Psycho Loco stood and flung down a queen of spades with such force it landed on the table with a loud pop. "Get up on that, Ms. Jenkins. You know a dirty bastard such as meself is cutting clubs."

Ms. Jenkins laughed. "Fool, you ain't said shit if an ace of spades has yet to be played," and she blanketed Psycho Loco's queen with the ace of spades, followed reluctantly by Scoby's nine of clubs. "We have married housing. Gunnar, you and the missus can live in one of our luxury on-campus condominiums."

"I'm not getting married!"

"Gunnar, I like the sound of your going back to Boston and following in the footsteps of your great-great-great-great-great-great-grandfather Euripides. It's as if the Kaufman legacy has come full circle."

"Ma!"

"So it's settled, Gunnar's going to BU. Mr. Loco, why don't you attend Boston U? I'm sure I could get you admitted under the auspices of our Unique Quality Life Experience Program."

"Naw, I don't think college is for me. I'd get in there and have to shoot the entire history department. 'What you mean, remember the Alamo?' Blam! Blam! Blam! That be some multiculturalism for yo' ass."

"I'm not getting married."

✿

With my immediate future assured, I stopped going to class and steadily began to lose interest in playing basketball. During games, when I wasn't playing I sat on the bench reading. Coach Logan threatened to fail me if I didn't commit myself to basketball. Psycho Loco suggested I take the GED and forget school, which I did. I decided my last day of school at El Campesino would be the playoff game at Phillis Wheatley. The papers tried to create a civil war atmosphere by depicting Nicholas and me as best friends fighting on enemy sides. There were ugly undertones to the whole affair. The headlines read "Kaufman Seeks to Demystify B-ball Prestidigitator."

By now Coach Shimimoto had convinced Scoby not to be ashamed of his talents and to play hard, not to please others but to please himself. In the past two years Scoby had scored over a thousand straight baskets, and a local media usually clamoring for perfection from its athletes couldn't accept the perfect athlete. Instead of appreciating Nicholas's gift, they treated Scoby as an evil spirit, an idiot savant with a bone through his nose who made the basketball sail through the hoop by invoking African gods. Scoby denied that he was a demigod and told his falling-out-of-the-tree story, but the rumors persisted. One report had him drinking chicken blood and kissing shrunken heads before games. Another had him commiserating with a witch doctor and practicing in a grass skirt. In a failed attempt to inject some humor into the situation, Coach Shimimoto told the news services that during a trip to Africa he had found Nicholas throwing coconuts into a hollowed-out tree trunk from seventy-five feet away and that at age four Nicholas could thread a needle in one try every time. I was portrayed as the Golden Child, white society's mercenary come to teach the pagans a lesson. "Starting at guard for El Campesino Real Conquistadores, Hernán Cortés-Kaufman."

On the morning of the big game, the El Campesino cheerleaders rousted all the white players out of bed for a unity breakfast at a diner in the Valley. They called me from the restaurant to say they wished I could be there eating pancakes with the rest of the team but I lived so far away. While the whities pep-rallied over banana pancakes, I planned my first rebellious act.

During the pregame shoot-around, I walked over to the scorer's table and made some changes to the starting lineup sheet. The horn sounded to signal the start of the game, and as the team huddled around Coach Logan for instructions I stood on the outskirts, slipped on a pair of white gloves, smeared my lips with cold cream, and hid my head under my warmup jacket. The crowd quieted as they announced the starting lineups.

"And now the visiting El Campesino Real Conquistadores. At center, Lawrence O'Shaughnessy." Larry, the lone white starter, ran out to center court, nervously clapping his hands and jumping up and down waiting to greet the rest of the starting team. "At a forward, Anthony 'Rastus' Price." A few people in the crowd laughed as Anthony jogged to his spot with a quizzical look on his face. The announcer continued, "At the other forward, Anita 'Aunt Jemima' Appleby. At guard, Tommy 'Nigger T' Mendoza." Anita and Tommy peeled off and ran to their stations, red-faced but chortling with the crowd. The laughter died down as the fans strained to hear what the announcer would say next.

The band went into an extended drumroll as I sat alone on the bench, my head down and hands folded under my armpits. "At guard, first team all-city, second team all-American, Hillside's own Gunnar 'Hambone, Hambone, Have You Heard' Kaufman." I lurched from the sideline, shuffling through the gauntlet of astonished teammates as slowly as I could, my big feet flopping in front of me, my back bent into a drooping question mark. My gloved hands slid along the floor, trailing behind like minstrel landing gear. The gymnasium erupted. People rolled in the aisles with laughter; light bulbs popped. I don't suppose they could hear me whistling "The Ol' Gray Mare" through the powdered doughnut that was my slack-jawed mouth. I stood at center court and gave a hearty "Howdy, y'all."

Coach Logan tried to get me replaced, but it was too late. The scorebook listed me as a starter, and the referees could find nothing in the rulebook about playing with white shit on your face, and I successfully argued that if you could play in a wrist brace, you could play in cotton gloves. Larry won the opening tip-off and out of force of habit passed the ball to me. I streaked past everyone and threw down a thunderous slam-dunk. Someone called a time out and Coach Logan substituted for me. I shuffled off the court in a somnambulant gait and headed straight to the locker room to cheers of "Gunnar! Gunnar!"

When I returned, fresh-faced and dressed in street clothes, Logan ordered me to sit and shut my monkey ass up. Oblivious to his ranting, I threw my uniform in a pile at his feet, set it afire, and sat next to Coach Shimimoto for the rest of game, which Wheatley won by sixty points. My mother didn't seem too displeased; she and Psycho Loco were in the stands making summer wedding plans.

Paul Beatty

nine

MY WEDDING was a small outdoor affair held in my front yard and catered only by the bag of cheese puffs Nicholas Scoby passed around in celebration of his best friend's betrothal. Psycho Loco was spinning in circles singing "Matchmaker, matchmaker, make me a match," like a Mexican understudy for Tevye in *Fiddler on the Roof*. He had fulfilled his promise and repaid his debt by finding me a mail-order bride through the services of Hot Mama-sans of the Orient. I sulked in the driveway, refusing to look at my bride, my back to the stalled nuptials. Psycho Loco approached me with fake trepidation, rattling the bag of cheese puffs at me and asking why I was so upset.

"Oh nothing, just that you've arranged for me to marry a woman I don't even know without my permission."

"What, I fucked up the plans for the rest of your life? Gunnar, you don't even have an alarm clock, so don't give me no bullshit that I've altered your destiny." Twisting my arm behind my back, Psycho Loco marched me toward the wedding party. "Besides, you should feel honored. Yoshiko chose you over hundreds of potential husbands."

"I'm sure that was difficult. I wouldn't want to spend the rest of my life in Olympia, Washington, cleaning rifles, gutting deer, and drinking Coors Light down at the American Legion Post either. Can you remove the gun from my kidneys? I'll go through with it."

The UPS driver conducted the ceremony. Dressed in tree-bark brown from head to toe like a misplaced Yosemite National Park ranger, he looked at my license, then back at me. "Today's your eighteenth birthday, huh, kid?" He tipped his brown baseball cap at the bride. "Nice present."

Yoshiko Katsu stood next to a stack of designer luggage, only slightly rumpled from the transpacific trip and the ride from the repository. Tall and thickly built, she stood stiffly, her arms straight down at her sides, smiling at everything that moved but never really taking her eyes off me. My mother and my baby-laden sisters sidled up to her, skeptical and unimpressed. Christina's baby pulled on the invoice stapled to Yoshiko's blouse. Nicole pinched a silky sleeve. "Dior?" Yoshiko nodded and bowed for no apparent reason.

"Sign here." The delivery man shoved a clipboard in my face.

"What happens if I don't sign?"

"Then she goes back to the warehouse and collects dust for three days till we send her back to Japan fourth class, which probably will mean three weeks in the hot cargo bay of a transport ship."

I penned my name and shoved the yellow copy in my back pocket. "Ain't she got to sign nothing?"

"Nope, she's just like a package. She came with instructions, but it's all in Japanese. Oh I forgot, you may kiss the bride."

"And you can get your maple-syrup-looking ass in that truck now and go, before I kiss you with a foot so far up your ass you'll be spitting toenails for a week."

Christina saucily sucked her teeth and hissed in Yoshiko's direction, "Girl, I know that's my brother, but you got to watch these niggers. After they get married, they change."

"Mmm-hmm, like streetlights and diapers. You seen what happen to Daddy," Nicole echoed, slapping Christina's palm. "That's why I kicked my baby's father to the curb. What I look like, Sigmund Freud?"

"Carl Jung?"

"Erik Erikson?"

Yoshiko bowed in appreciation of their sisterly sagacity. "*So desu ka? Domo arigato gozaimasu.*"

Psycho Loco tossed me two tarnished gold bands. "Ignore these spinsters. Step up, cuz, and be a man."

I ripped off the price tag and boldly approached Yoshiko. There were no jitters. My hands didn't shake. My underarms were TV-commercial dry. Sometimes the inevitable just seems right. "*Kon'ban wa. Ichi, ni, san, chi,*" I said, exhausting my karate school Japanese and handing her a ring. She laughed, shook her head, and corrected my greeting — "*Kon'nichi wa*" — pointing at the hazy midday sun. We slipped the rings on our fingers and kissed each other

Paul Beatty

lightly on the cheek. She smelled like cardboard. As I stepped off, I noticed that some UPS jokester had stamped "Fragile" on her forehead.

"Who dat heifer Gunnar with?" I could hear the china shop's bulls coming around the corner. "Naw, bitch, that's our nigger! Don't even feel it. You think you can come here playing Yokohama Hootchie Mama and steal our man, you got another thought coming."

Yoshiko turned to face her tormenters, Betty and Veronica, crashing the wedding in a vain Dustin Hoffman showdown for my affections. Betty's hair was styled into a gold-flaked gramophone horn with a little hairpin crank just over the right ear. Veronica had so many extensions in her hair that the wavy locks cascaded down her body like a horsehair waterfall. Yoshiko looked confused; I think she was looking for Lady Godiva's white horse.

I stepped in to help, but Scoby held me back. "Hold up a sec. She's going to have to learn to cope. Let's see what happens."

Betty and Veronica squared off and prepared to battle, thumbing their noses and bobbing up and down like amateur boxers looking for an opening. Veronica snapped a jab that stopped an inch from Yoshiko's nose. Yoshiko didn't flinch; she just bowed and said something in a terse Japanese. Veronica froze.

"What she say, Gunnar?"

"She said that if you persist with your puerile inner-city antics, she gonna take out her samurai sword, invoke her ancestral clan of warriors, and chop you into a Negro roll, inside out with salmon roe."

"You don't speak Japanese. How you know that's what she said?"

"Why you ask then, shit? Maybe she said, 'If I act like I know some karate, I can scare these stupid niggers senseless. They sure don't act like they do on television.' Or maybe she was admiring your hair."

"Think so? Can she show us some of those crazy Japanese hairstyles? We could be the first ones on the block to wear topknots and shit. Maybe I'll dye my teeth black. I seen that on the late-night kabuki plays. That shit would be fresh, nobody got a black teeth thing happening."

Betty and Veronica lowered their fists and returned Yoshiko's bow and then clamored over her wedding ring. Mom, beaming like a lottery winner, wrapped a proud arm around Yoshiko and demanded that Scoby take a photograph of her and her new daughter-in-law.

"Gunnar, I like Yoshiko. I believe she'll make an excellent Kaufman. She got spirit, escaping from a repressive society to seek her fortune in a strange world."

"Ma, Japan ain't some feudalistic country. I mean, they got travel agents."

"Don't matter, I approve."

"I can't believe it. Thought you'd never approve of me marrying a woman who isn't black."

"Yes, but Yoshiko is black at heart. You can tell. She got soul like . . . who's that actor I like always play the Japanese nigger in them shogun movies?"

"Toshiro Mifune."

Hearing a familiar name, Yoshiko nudged my mother in the ribs, put a bewildered look on her face, and started scratching the back of her head and her underarms, impersonating the famous actor.

"That's exactly who I'm talking about. Yoshiko, did you know Mifune was born in China? True, true. His first big part was the bandit in *Rashomon*. Then . . ." Mom ushered Yoshiko into the house, lecturing her on Mifune's oeuvre and smoothly seguing from his role as a doctor suffering from syphilis in *The Quiet Duel* to the types of birth control available in the United States.

Scoby, the do-nothing best man, admonished me for not carrying my bride over the threshold. I kicked him in the shin and told him the only thing I was carrying was a grudge against him for not buying any wedding presents. "What, no blender, some bath towels, nothing? Cheap bastard. C'mon, help me with these bags."

We held the reception in the back yard. Psycho Loco played chef and showed impressive culinary skills: barbecued spareribs, deviled eggs, and to make Yoshiko feel at home, he even threw together a jamming udon noodle soup.

"So, man, how you like your wife?" Nicholas asked from across the table, sucking on a bone and sizing up Yoshiko, who was sitting next to me.

"She all right, I guess. She bow too goddamn much."

"That shit throws you off, don't it. I got leery and put my hand on my wallet, then I started bowing with my eyes closed, and when I opened them she was long gone, grubbing on corn on the cob. And

Paul Beatty

your wife is looking fine picking that shit out her teeth, if I do say so myself."

How did I like Yoshiko? I watched her loudly slurp her udon soup with such powerful suction a noodle bounced off her forehead, slithered down the bridge of her nose, and slunk into her mouth with a loud pop. I could see why my mom liked her; they had the same table manners — none. I remembered how when I showed Yoshiko our room she had carefully unpacked her books, put the titles in my face until I nodded and said "hmmm," as if I could read the bold-stroke Japanese. Psycho Loco once told me that in prison when two men fall in love, they have to be careful not to relax and give in to the passion, because just when you let yourself go, your lover slips his finger into your anus and you're punked for life. I squeezed my sphincter shut as Yoshiko lowered the empty plate from her face, wiped her mouth, and let out a healthy belch.

It wasn't difficult to tell that Yoshiko was equally enamored with me. No one had looked at me the way she did since Eileen Litmus back in the third grade, and I knew what that look meant.

"Gunnar, I don't think that Yoshiko trusts you. She staring at you like you General MacArthur."

As we sat around the table eating dessert and drinking beers, everyone took the opportunity to raise glasses and congratulate the newlyweds. Soon the guests demanded that the couple belatedly exchange their vows.

I stood and raised my beer can in Yoshiko's direction, placed my hand over my heart, and said, "Till death do us part."

"That's it, nigger?"

"I can't make no promises other than that."

"What about 'in sickness and in health, for richer or poorer'?"

"Look, all I know is we're going to die. And when we do, we'll be apart."

"What about if you two die at the same time?"

"That's a good point. Okay, I amend my vow. Till death kills us."

"Now Yoshiko's turn."

"Mom, she doesn't even speak English."

"English?" Yoshiko stood up sharply, a little redfaced and wobbly from all the beer she'd drunk. "Me speak English." To wild applause, ko pecked me on the lips, then climbed onto the tabletop, ing her beer until she reached the summit. My bride, literally on a pedestal, was going to pledge her life to me. You couldn't wipe the smile off my face with a blowtorch.

Yoshiko cleared her throat and threw her hands in the air. "Brmmphh boomp ba-boom bip. I'm the king of rock — there is none higher! Sucker MC's must call me sire!"

"Hoooo!"

"Anyone know how to say 'I love you' in Japanese?"

Mom paid for the honeymoon. She lent me the car, and Yoshiko and I drove to Six Pennants Mystic Mount, an amusement park in the Antelope Valley. We listened to the radio and communicated with nods and exaggerated facial expressions, pretending to understand our improvised sign language. As we coasted into the Mystic Mount parking lot, the wooden white lattice of Leviathan Loops, the world's largest roller coaster, loomed in the distance. Yoshiko screamed and hugged me, moving her hand over imaginary hill and dale. We skipped through the entrance, and for the first time in my life I waited in the endless line snuggling with a lover. I wasn't the odd one out, a car to myself, constantly having to crane my neck backward at my friends and their dates to see how much fun I was having.

On the flume ride I sat between Yoshiko's legs in a fiberglass canoe while we sloshed through the dark tunnels, her chin resting on the nape of my neck, her fingertips cupping my chest. Before that first drop after the s-turn through the eucalyptus branches, I didn't even know I had nipples. Now I was hyperventilating, struggling for air, dangerously rocking the canoe, and splashing the German tourists in front of us as Yoshiko continued to tweak my nipples. "Gott im Himmel." *Will the passenger in boat 37 please remain seated!*

After a day filled with centrifugal spins and free-falls, it was hard to tell whether I was dizzy with love or with motion sickness. We drove home in a weary silence punctuated only by Yoshiko calling out the names of familiar places. San Kreyón Rompido Cribrillo, Rio Califas, Zuma Beach. The Pacific Coast Highway's sharp curves dropped off into foggy banks of nothingness. I felt like Columbus teetering on the edge of the world. "Malibu! Malibu!" Yoshiko, doing her Amerigo Vespucci land ho, tugging at my shirtsleeve, and pointing toward a small promontory overlooking the ocean.

Paul Beatty

It had been a long time since I'd been to the beach at night. On Santa Monica nights when I was having trouble sleeping, I would sneak out and play D-Day on the empty beaches, advancing toward the Normandy beachhead with a battalion of waves. "Stay down, man, stay down." Sometimes I would play dead and let the tide spit up my limp body onto the shore. "Tell Mother I love . . . uhh." While I went to get the blankets and the radio from the trunk, Yoshiko sprinted down the bluff, tossing her clothes to the sand and motioning for me to join her. Hand in hand, we walked into the onrushing Pacific in our underwear. The waves breaking around our shins, then slamming against our chests. Like drunken seal pups, we splashed about in the surf, riding the dark waves into the cold sand, young lovers run aground. Using the stuffed elephants we had won pitching dimes at pillows, we pressed our backs against the wind-shorn bluffs and gave each other language lessons beside a fire of driftwood and the remains of a synthetic log.

I tried to teach her useful American phrases such as "consummate the marriage," "nookie," and "Let's get busy." Yoshiko's instruction was more practical. We played a game of phonetic charades in which she would say a Japanese word and I'd have to guess its English homophone.

"*Bii-ru.*"

"That's easy, beer."

"Okay, *se-ro-ri.*"

"Celery. C'mon, I thought Japanese was supposed to be hard."

"*E-bu-ra-ha-mu Ri-n-kaan.*"

"Four score and twenty years ago, our forefathers — Abraham Lincoln."

"*Ro-san-ze-ru-su.*"

"What?"

Yoshiko threw a pile of sand in the air, stamped her feet, and waved her hands across the sky. "*Ro-san-ze-ru-su.*"

"I have no idea what you're talking about."

Frustrated, my sensei jumped me from behind and rubbed my nose into the sand. "*Ro-san-ze-ru-su.*"

"Oh, I get it — Los Angeles. *Ro-san-ze-ru-su.*"

With the stars as chaperones and Al Green as the R & B mariachi, we courted each other with our life stories and dreams. I couldn't understand her, but I listened intently and let the Suntory whiskey Yoshiko pulled from her purse interpret.

After one swig, I surmised that Yoshiko was a poor farmer running away from a lifetime of toil shucking wheat and paying homage to countless Shinto and Buddhist agrarian gods. Her hands, callus-free on my cheeks, dismissed that theory.

After two swigs she was a famous pop star with writer's block, hoping to regain her soulful edge by soaking up the African-American aesthetic. Singing alongside Al Green, Yoshiko sounded like a lisping crow with laryngitis.

> Here I am, baby, come and take me.
> Here I am, baby, come and take me.

After half the bottle I was writing haiku on her bare back with my index finger;

> wife's rib cage expanding
> contracting, fanning virgin fires
>
> carnal bellows, mmmmm.

Somewhere near the backwash end of the bottle, I'd guessed that Yoshiko was a rebellious teen whose parents couldn't afford the cost of an American university, so she decided that marrying an eligible bachelor would be the easiest way to get a free education. The final choice was between me and an Iowa grad student named Stanley. On the day she'd been suspended from school for maiming the kendo teacher, she was in detention passing the time reading an alternative Japanese magazine called *Phlegm* when she came across one of my poems.

> *Your Problem Is*
>
> how can . . .
> the jehovah's witness, the scientologist,
> the political scientist, the social scientist,
> the mad scientist, the editorial page,
> the 11 o'clock news, the talk radio host,
> the urban planner, the school superintendent,
> the special assistant to the president,

Paul Beatty

the psychologist, the televangelist, the homeless crazy,
the pontiff, the sales clerk, the bus driver,
the late-night cable access fuck,

claim to know my problem
when they don't even know my name

Stanley was quickly forgotten. Under the half-moon gangster leaning over the horizon, I fell asleep to Al Green singing on a belly full
of cornbread and fruit punch

I want to settle down and stop fooling around
Let's get married, let's get married today

and Yoshiko's finger tapping on my anus. "*Anaru zeme,*" she whispered.
I dreamed I was a flying, fire-breathing foam stegosaurus starring
in a schlocky Japanese film called *Destroy All Negroes*. I stomped
high-rise projects into rubble, turned out concerts by whipping my
armored tail across the stage, and chewed on slow black folks like
licorice sticks. The world government sent a green-Afroed Godzilla to
defeat me and we agreed to a death match in the Los Angeles
Coliseum. The winner would be crowned Reptile of the Nuclear
Epoch. I was beating Godzilla into the sea with a powerful stream of
radioactive turtle piss when I awoke to find Yoshiko's index finger
worming its way toward my prostate. Punked for life.

"... stay black, and die"

ten

DURING MY STAY at Boston University I went to one class. My one hour of higher education consisted of Professor Oscar Edelstein's poetry workshop, Creative Writing 104. As the next generation of great American poets stood up and introduced themselves with bohemian haughtiness, I drummed my fingers, trying to remember why I was going to college in the first place.

A thin white woman with a badly scarred face was talking. "Ciao bella, ciao bella. My name is Peyote Chandler, of the Greenwich, Connecticut, Chandlers. Let's see, now. I graduated from London-derry Academy with honors. My favorite poet is Sylvia Plath. My mother is the ambassador to Pakistan, and my father now owns a carpet factory in north Asia. The factory employs hundreds of starving children at what I believe is a respectable living wage of seven rupees a week. I believe in Third World mysticism, animism, extraterrestrial life, and —"

"What the fuck happened to your mug?" I interrupted, chin in my hand and bored with her Mayflower pedigree.

Peyote was eager to explain. "When I was twelve, my boyfriend, Skip Pettibone Helmsford, broke up with me, so I tried to kill myself by sticking my head in the oven like Sylvia Plath did. Only I forgot to blow out the pilot light and I stuck my head into a preheated four-hundred-and-fifty-degree inferno."

A chubby bearded boy in khakis a size too small and a rumpled Oxford shirt moved his elephantine mass to the front of the class, licking the edges of his Drum cigarette. "Greetings, my name is Chadwick Osterdorf III. I graduated from Choate with high honors and I think the only true poet ever to walk the earth was Rimbaud." Some parliamentary "hear, hears" rang out from the back of the class. "It was in his footsteps that I spent this past summer selling guns to downtrodden ghetto youth to defend themselves against the oppressive system."

This time I lifted my head off the desk to interrupt. "Come on, Rimbaud wasn't no gun-running revolutionary. What he really wanted to sell was slaves, black African niggers, but he was too stupid to catch any, so he sold weapons to some king who ripped him off. Some dissident. If you was really a Rimbaudite, you'd amputate those two cellulite-filled legs of yours so the downtrodden ghetto youth wouldn't have to worry about you kicking 'em in the ass."

Professor Edelstein pulled the sleeves of his tweed jacket and pressed his wire-rimmed glasses into his tanned forehead, raising the nerve to confront the boisterous black kid. "And who might you be, young man?"

"My name is Gunnar Kaufman."

"Gunnar Kaufman? Gunnar Kaufman from Los Angeles?"

"Yeah."

Edelstein popped out of his seat. "I heard you might be attending BU, but I never dreamed you'd take my class. I saw your poem 'If Niggers Could Fly' in the latest issue of *Locution*. I've been thinking about it all week." Edelstein took a deep breath and looked up at the ceiling. "'If niggers could fly, where would we alight? We orbit a treeless world, nest on eaveless clouds, unable to stop flapping our wings for even a second, in constant migration to nowhere.' If niggers could fly. Brilliant, absolutely brilliant. How old were you when you wrote that?"

"Thirteen. I was attempting to —"

The Rimbaud wannabe removed a copy of *Inkstone* from his knapsack. "Here's a haiku you wrote."

> the full May moon,
> Christopher Walken's forehead
> finally has competition

Sylvia Plath picked at her scars and said, "I have pictures of your poems."

"What you mean, you have pictures of my poems?"

She produced a coffee-table book of photographs entitled *Ghettotopia: An Anthropological Rending of the Ghetto through the Street Poems of an Unknown Street Poet Named Gunnar Kaufman.*

Paul Beatty

"What they mean by 'an unknown street poet named Gunnar Kaufman?' More to the point, what the hell is a street poet?"

"Gunnar, the urban piquancy of your work is so resonant, so resplendent, so resounding . . . you make the destitution of your environs leap off the page. You're my inspiration."

"What about Sylvia Plath?"

"Well, it's really you. I thought that if I mentioned a black poet, I wouldn't be taken seriously by the rest of the class."

A white woman dressed in a tie-dyed sundress, her hair knotted in blond cornrow braids, slid her fleshy rear end onto my desk and announced herself, kicking her thick ankles high in the air. "Hi, my name is Negritude."

"You're shitting me."

"My parents named me that so I would be a reminder of the hagiocratic innocence possessed by black peoples around the world."

"Visceral sainthood — I see. And the braids?"

"I feel more powerful with my hair like this, really Nubian. You must know what I mean. Your scalp pulled so tight you can hear the howls of the jackals, the bellows of the hippopotami. Oh, I could properly welcome home an Ashanti warrior returned from the hunt with a fresh kill. Would you like to hear me ululate?"

"Not really."

"Alilililililililili!"

I panicked and dashed out of the room, with my classmates and Professor Edelstein close behind. "I can't believe it — Gunnar Kaufman, the underground neologist, the poet's poet, right here in my poetry workshop. Only in America." I felt like I'd been outed and exposed by my worst enemies, white kids who were embarrassingly like myself but with whom somehow I had nothing in common. To prove it I walked through the center of campus and slowly began to undress. Near the School of Engineering I released my sweater to the Boston winds. It sailed like a magic carpet past the trolleys and over the heads and outstretched hands of Professor Edelstein and the students of Creative Writing 104. My shirt, shorts, and underwear followed, sucked into a mini-tornado near the College of Liberal Arts. The clothes spiraled at a dizzying speed with dead leaves and crushed milk cartons. Soon the twister died and they fell to the ground, only to be pounced on like piñata candy by the class.

I continued down Commonwealth Avenue, naked save for sneakers and socks. My black lower-middle-class penis fluttered stiffly in the wind like a weather vane, first to the left, then suddenly to the right. When I reached the vestibule of my apartment building, the campus police closed in on me. I heard Professor Edelstein shout, "It's okay, he's a poet. Matter of fact, the best black . . . the best poet writing today." The cops instantly backed off. I was protected by poetic immunity. I had permission to act crazy.

I pulled off an officer's hat and mussed his hair, then skipped up the stairs to my apartment and plopped face down on the couch, my head on Yoshiko's lap. She rested her textbook on my cheek and with her left hand cleaved the crack of my ass like a hacksaw.

"You all right, baby?"

"Fine. What you reading?"

"Macroeconomics."

"You don't mind me here?"

"Nope, just don't move too much. How was your first class?"

There was a timid knock at the door. "Judge for yourself." Edelstein entered, followed by Rimbaud, Plath, Ginsberg, Eliot, and the rest of the poetry canon, bashfully trying to avert their eyes by gazing at Coach Shimimoto's watercolor prints on the walls.

"Yoshiko, this is my creative writing class. Class, this is my wife, Yoshiko." Shy hellos, then whispers all around.

"He's married? Oh, fucking cool. I'm in Gunnar Kaufman's pad and he's naked, intense."

"Gunnar, a few of your classmates want to know if they can keep your clothes as mementos. You know, they might be worth something one day."

"I don't think one sleeve of a torn T-shirt is going to be worth much."

"What we really came by to say was that we feel you have to publish a collection of your work. Why don't you compile a manuscript, and I'll take care of the publishing end? I know some big-wig Yalies in New York, and you should have a decent advance in a week and a book by spring. The people, your people, need to see your work."

Yoshiko tapped her macroeconomics book on my head, which I interpreted to mean "Say yes."

Paul Beatty

"Okay, I'll give you some things."

"What about a title?"

"How about, ummm, *Watermelanin*."

"Gunnar, you know, this is going to change your life."

The door burst open, then quickly slammed shut.

"Damn, nigger, every time I come over, Yoshiko got her hand halfway up your ass. But you know what they say — 'Once you go Asian, there's no other persuasion.'" It was Scoby, not bothering to knock, standing in the middle of the living room oblivious to the other uninvited guests and talking loudly to make himself heard over his stereo headphones. "What this shit about your life going to change?"

"He's going to publish a book of poems."

"I can speak for myself, Yoshiko. She's right, I'm going to publish a book of poems." Yoshiko subtly plucked a hair from my anus. "Ow."

Professor Edelstein motioned for his class to open their notebooks and take notes. My visitors cleared some space, and Scoby sat on the floor Indian-style, playing an imaginary vibraphone. I guessed he was still listening to Lionel Hampton.

"Publishing a book of poems don't change your life as much as it changes everyone else's life. Sad as your shit is, fools going to be jumping off roofs and shit. I heard if you commit suicide your freshman year, your roommate automatically gets a perfect grade-point average. That true?"

"You thinking of committing suicide?"

"I don't know, maybe. Depends on what your poems say."

"What you doing tonight?"

"I don't know. Ain't shit to do in this town."

"What do you mean, Boston's a great party town," Negritude broke in, looking up from her notes and batting her eyelashes in my direction.

Yoshiko threw her macro book at the interloper, hitting her squarely in the jaw. "Get your slothful, fey, hippy behinds out of our apartment, now!"

The class hustled out of the room, a stream of Japanese curse words escorting them to the door.

"Gunnar, don't make me have to hurt one of these stupid white bitches."

"Slothful, fey? Honey, your English is getting really good. What are we going to do tonight?"

✻

There wasn't a whole lot of nigger nightlife in Boston, much less any fun spots for Japanese nationals. When we first arrived, we cruised the local bars, garish nightspots crammed with white people sloshing beer on one another and singing corny white pop hits from the 1980s. Yoshiko must have punched a hundred guys who tried to pick her up with the line from the Vapors' big hit, "I think I'm turning Japanese, I really think so." Looking for a more austere environment, we tried the gay spots in the South End. Our favorite hangout was Club Tribadism, a gay/lesbian bar with the best jazz jukebox in the city. The patrons tolerated us until one night Nicholas and another patron got into a fight over whether Billie Holiday's "Strange Fruit" could be deciphered as a paean to a mentally ill queer. After a little sword fighting with pool cues, we were driven into the street and banished from Club Tribadism forever. Scoby got in the last word when he proclaimed that Mel Torme was the ugliest dyke he'd ever seen.

By October we had finally figured out that the colored folks lived in Roxbury. Roxbury was an old, hilly community practically inaccessible by public transportation. For the most part it was a desolate place, with little to offer except decent basketball competition and a few juke joints. Our regular spot was Oscar's Onyx, a musty blues bar at the top of the hill on Mission Avenue. Friday nights brothers in platform shoes would get into knife fights, slashing the air with their eyes closed like orchestra conductors. Scoby's barbs always roused the crowd, "You stupid hick-ass bean-eating stiletto-carrying Cooley High niggers is still wearing leather jackets and talking about 'Stand back, sucker, fo' I cut cha.' Niggers probably think the Black Panthers is still active." Later on male and female strippers with names like Chocolate and Brutus walked from table to table, soliciting dollar bills in exchange for a feel. Yoshiko and Scoby had a thing for a potbellied she-male stripper named Smattering of Applause. Smattering of Applause rolled his hips and fondled his tits, and when she bent over to claim her hard-earned tips, hairy butt to the audience, Yoshiko and Scoby would pelt her rear end with balled-up dollar bills. I liked the place because the bartenders wrapped napkins around the beer bottles before they handed them to you and could never adequately explain why. "Habit," they said. The problem was that every night wasn't Friday night. On weekdays, while Scoby and Yoshiko did their homework, I had nothing to do. Scoby suggested I join a club.

I called Dexter Waverly, president of the citywide black student union, and asked when the next Ambrosia meeting was. The black student union was originally called Umoja, but the name was changed because of the whites' inability to pronounce the Swahili word for unity. Dexter cleared his throat. "Mhotep, son of Africa. The next meeting is Monday night at eight in the School of Management basement. Come early and we'll fit you for a dashiki. You can play a talking drum, can't you?"

I purposely arrived late at the gathering. Harvard, BU, MIT Negroes were wearing loud African garb over their Oxford shirts and red suspenders, drinking ginger beer, and using their advertising skills to plan how best to package the white man's burden. "No alcohol, brother," someone shouted. I chugged my real beer, burped, and took a seat in the back, picking up a discarded agenda from the floor. At the top of the sheet was the Ambrosia motto, "The happy slave has a right to be a slave, but is still a slave nonetheless." I could hear my mother on the phone: "Join, Gunnar, sounds like an intelligent bunch of young people."

The Ambrosia members outshouting one another about how brave they'd be fighting on the front lines of America's race war reminded me of a small-town volunteer fire department shining an already shiny engine and bragging about how brave they'd be if they ever fought a real fire. "But are you ready to die and kill for your people?" said chief firefighter Dexter Waverly. Dexter wore a red dashiki trimmed with miniature elephant tusks and tightly gripped the sides of the lectern with both hands. Rallymaster, they called him: able to form a coalition at a moment's notice, knows the copy center with the cheapest rates, media friendly, dynamic speaker.

Bored with the racial braggadocio, Dexter raised a hand for quiet, and the muttering stopped. I wanted to dislike Dexter — it was obvious he was a charlatan — but I was awestruck at how such an ugly motherfucker, with an eczema condition so severe that when he furrowed his brow tiny flakes of skin fell to the lectern, could hold an audience spellbound with a single gesture. I could hear his eyeballs crinkle as he looked up from the one-item agenda and scanned his audience. He seemed so angst-ridden I wanted to throw him a dog biscuit.

"Brothers and sisters" — uh-oh — "Comrade Essie Brooks's combination fashion show and literacy program is a wonderful idea. A stroke of genius, of black feminine genius, of rump-rolling, look-at-that-butter, greasy, you-know-how-we-do, big-black-titty genius. Praise due to Sister Essie Brooks and all sisters like her."

The men barked and stamped their feet. The women swooned and said loud amens, raising their hands in the air like castaways trying to flag down an ocean liner. I sat transfixed, trying to figure out how Dexter, a man whom I was seeing for the first time not in the cuddly company of a white woman, was the Emperor Jones of the Ivy League. Usually dating exclusively white was, for a black person, the equivalent of multiplying a lifetime of accomplishments by zero. It didn't matter what your previous accomplishments were; abolitionist, Motown diva, Olympic figure-skater, inventor of the sky hook, you had zilch stature amongst the folks. Dexter managed to be the school Mandingo and maintain his race loyalty.

Sometimes I'd catch him in the back alleys with the white woman of the moment. He'd greet me with a hearty "Hey, black," and place a reverent fist over his heart. If I looked quizzically at his date, he'd flash the "I know it's hard to tell" smile and say, "No cause for alarm, brother. Sister Cindy Zwittledorf is of Brazilian descent. Third World solidarity, my brother." To validate his claim further, Dexter would wave a small parade flag representing the woman's supposed place of origin in tiny circles. "Viva Uruguay! Tres hurras por Argentina! Oyé como va Bolivia!"

I admit I admired his chutzpah and ingenuity. When Yoshiko and I walked the campus, I sometimes wilted under the evil stares, cowering behind Yoshiko's back and covering my face in a fit of fake sneezes or forced yawns.

"Why you always sneeze when black people are around?"

"I'm allergic, baby."

"Go 'head, Dexter," a woman in front shouted. Dexter nodded in appreciation and continued.

"The fashion show–literacy program will use the Afro-chic to uplift the Afro-weak. What we propose is not a marriage — marriage, if

Paul Beatty

you're lucky, only lasts a lifetime. What we propose is an intellectual inheritance, an eternal trust fund for minds yet unborn. Young, black, not-yet-tainted-by-the-toxic-dyes-of-self-hatred minds. We talking *tabula vivé la rasa*. Nowadays, when you talk to the teachers of our youth, they say, 'The young bastards and bastardettes can't learn. They have short attention spans.' Well, then you need to lengthen the attention span. If the river widens, you extend the bridge. When man invented the jet, did they say, 'No, man, you cannot fly these supersonic jets, the runway is too short — you can't take off, and if you manage to get the plane off the ground, you can't land'? No, they lengthened the runway. And we gonna lengthen the fashion runway for our little black jets. Stretch their attention spans with fine black folks modeling black clothes. Each model male and fee-male — I say fee-male 'cause it cost to be a black woman — each model will carry a sign with a grammar lesson on it. I can see the enthusiasm on the children's faces now. Imagine with me, if you will, the fine and sexy premed major light-skinned Linda Rucker, in a little one-piece bathing suit carrying a sign that reads '*i* before *e* except after *c*.' There'll be booty and learning for days. You think when the boys go to the bathroom and start beating off they going to be saying, 'Goddamn, that bitch was fine'? No. They gone be pulling on their growing black manhood saying, "*I* before *e* except after *c*." Now you know we not going to cheat our young African women out of their thrill. We'll have the bronze god and star running back Thor Haverlock in bikini briefs thunder down the runway with a sign reading "A sentence is a complete thought" balanced on his bulge. When the girls get those hot flashes that accompany puberty, you better believe they're gonna be fantasizing in complete sentences. 'Jesus Christ, that boy is fine as hell.' Anybody have any other ideas for grammatical phrases we can use? Gunnar Kaufman, esteemed poet, first-time Ambrosia attendee, what about you, my brother?"

"How about 'In general, singular subjects connected by *or, nor, either/or,* or *neither/nor* take a singular verb if both subjects are singular, a plural verb if subjects are plural'?"

I left to a scattering of *sotto voce* insults: "Nigger crazy, he trying to confuse the youth"; "Smart-alecky fool need to be playing basketball, that's what he need to be doing."

When I reached the door, Jamal Vickers handed me a manila-colored flier and sneered, "Why don't you join Concoction? You think you better than everyone else." Concoction was an organization of mixed-race kids who felt ostracized by both white and colored students.

CONCOCTION — THE HUMAN STUDENT UNION

The primordial soup's on! Tired of being stewed because of your biracial heritage?

The jambalaya of ethnic duplicity too complicated for your "black" friends?

The reality of the American melting pot too hot for your "white" amigos?

Come and be a part of Concoction's goulash and celebrate your ethnic hybridization.

Future Topics of Discussion:

- How to check African-American/Latino/Asian on your job application and rise above your employer's stereotypes by asserting your biraciality in the workplace in a nonethnic manner.
- Why jazz musicians tend to date "white" women.
- How to prove you are *not* a nigger.
- How to explain that you're basically white despite having Lopez as a surname.
- Jane Paleface, renowned Indian rights activist, explains how to claim one sixty-fourth Native American heritage and get your oil and casino kickback checks without having to live on the reservation.
- Plebiscite on admitting full-blooded Puerto Ricans into the Concoction ranks.

Jamal stood there, hands on hips, waiting for a response. I wanted to explain that I'd already tried to join Concoction under the guise that I was a Rwandan exchange student of Hutu and Tutsi descent but was refused admission on the grounds that its bylaws didn't consider African exogamy dual ethnicity. I decided it was pointless to talk to someone who believed a fashion show would save the black

Paul Beatty

race. Folding the flier into an origami turtle, I handed it to Jamal as a symbol of the progress of his struggle.

My next foray into student activism was with SWAPO, Spoiled Whities Against Political Obsequiousness. SWAPO's main concern was the school administration's support of the National Party's forces in the South African civil war. The best thing about the SWAPO meetings was that I was allowed to drink beer while they wrote the latest act of an ongoing guerrilla theater production, an interminable piece called *Black Consciousness Is a Sovereign State of Mind*.

"Okay, here's the part where we hammer home the point of the play, that white liberalism is the bane of black South Africa. Gunnar, will you be the ghost of Steve Biko?"

"Fuck, no."

"How about the pacifist mediocre tennis player who deserts the revolutionary army, marries a white debutante from Nashville, writes a bestseller on how he found true love in the arms of a white woman and true freedom in the American South."

"You must be high."

"But you're our only black member."

"I wonder why that is?"

"Why aren't there more black people at these SWAPO meetings? We've reached out to all the black organizations, the frats and sororities, the track team. We play classic soul music at the parties. Don't they care?"

"Remove your hand from my shoulder and I'll tell you. See, it's like this — no one could possibly care enough to be treated like a baby seal. Colored people aren't mascots for your political attitudes."

"Then why do *you* come to the meetings?"

"Because y'all got the best weed on campus."

"What can I, as a progressive white male, do?"

"If it's at all possible, shed the fucking John Brown vibe. I don't need no crackers kissing me on the forehead like I'm a swaddling infant and leading me out of slavery. Did you know that the first person killed in the raid on Harper's Ferry was the town baggage master, a *free* black man?"

"No."

"There are no John Browns. Thank goodness."

The white boy burst into tears, soaking his shirtsleeves.

"Come on, guy, why are you crying?"

"*My* name is John Brown."

My last SWAPO event was a teach-in on civil disobedience in preparation for Boston University's gala welcoming of the South African politician M'm'mofo Gottobelezi, the Zulu puppet of the National Party rebels. A graying man in a Grateful Dead T-shirt was singing Crosby, Stills, Nash, and Young's "Find the Cost of Freedom" and taking extended bong hits between choruses. I looked around for a young Rosa Parks, a gold-toothed Ralph Abernathy, but as usual I was the only black there. A grungy imitation Abbie Hoffman offered me a Che Guevara LSD tab: "Power to the people, my brother." When the radical hippie stopped staring at all the braless coeds, he taught us how to form human chains by linking our arms and ankles, how to double our body weight by exhaling and letting our bodies go limp as the fascist pigs carted us off the paddy wagon, and how our parents could use the bail money as a small tax shelter.

As the session wound down, someone asked about the specter of police brutality. The glassy-eyed facilitator ground his joint into an ashtray and for the first time looked me in the eye. "When things get rough, I've found that the police treat us longhairs much more violently than they do our black and Hispanic hermanos y hermanas." I passed my hand over my lumpy scalp and heard my father tapping his billy club on the cement. "So, mis compadres, when things get bleak, remember to sing and sing loud."

A stale version of "We Shall Overcome" chased my shivering body through the snowy streets of Boston, catching me near a statue of Abraham Lincoln lightly touching the head of a kneeling slave. The slave's pleading expression seemed to say, "Free me, boss. You ain't got to free nobody else, just me." I leaned into the slave's brass ear and whispered, "Tag, you're it."

The next night Yoshiko and I woke up with soggy pillows and tear-stained cheeks.

"What was your dream about?"

"What was your dream about?"

"I asked you first."

"I dreamed me, Nat Turner, Gabriel Prosser, Cinque, and Didi Lancaster were fighting alongside the Irish Republican Army, driving through the streets of Belfast in a station wagon, shooting at the British troops, and singing 'Find the Cost of Freedom.' 'F-i-ind the c-o-o-st o-of fr-e-e-e-dom buried in the gr-ound.' After a while we got tired of the British machine-gunning us, so we tied a baby to the back of the station wagon. We'd buzz the Brits and they'd turn to shoot but wouldn't fire when they saw a wailing kid lashed to the rear door. But one day they said fuck it and shot back, killed Nat, Gabriel, Didi, and the baby. I ended up teaching at a hearse-driving school."

"Who's Didi Lancaster?"

"This girl I knew in the eighth grade. One day in front of the whole class, Ms. Hanger, the social studies teacher, said she was stupid and would never amount to anything. Didi beat Ms. Hanger to a pulp and threw her out a window. Broke her jaw and cracked three ribs. The whole time she was kicking her ass, Didi was screaming, "Just because you a teacher don't make you innocent." What's funny is Didi's grades improved after that."

"Whose baby did you tie to the car?"

"Ours."

"Good."

"What was your dream about, Yoshiko?"

"We had a kid and we were tucking her into bed, telling her bedtime stories."

"What's so bad about that?"

"The stories went like this. 'This story is called "The Little Fuck Who Cried Wolf." Once upon a time there was this shepherd boy who always screaming wolf like a little bitch . . .'"

"Oh shit, you got to stop hanging out with them Onyx niggers." I put my head back on the pillow. "Yoshiko, you pregnant?"

"I think so."

"Good."

*

Having failed to find a stimulating extracurricular activity, I soon found myself in familiar surroundings: the basketball gym, my sneakers squeaking, yelling "help right" and "switch," and watching Coach Slick Palomino shout and throw chairs at the white kids. Despite playing well and enjoying Scoby's company on the court, I became depressed with my purposeless life; sad-eyed, I'd toe the free-throw line in an arena filled with screaming maniacs, pondering the worthlessness of my existence.

"Two shots, gentlemen. Relax on the first." The referee would hand me the ball with a stern look, trying to talk with the whistle in his mouth. "Kaufman, you look glum. What's wrong — having a poetic moment?"

"I don't know. Been reading Schopenhauer and I can't figure out my raison d'etre."

"Your purpose in life is to make these free throws, then run back and play defense."

"Fuck that."

Scoby, his chest heaving up and down, would chime in. "Your purpose is to take care of your pregnant wife and raise your kid."

"That ain't no purpose, that's a responsibility. If I had the money, I could pay someone to do that."

"Kaufman, shoot the ball."

"Yassuh, massa."

Swish. Swish.

My only comforts were the boxes of Japanese literature Yoshiko would send me on the road trips. Returning to the hotel exhausted from another game, I'd find carefully wrapped copies of the love-suicide plays of Chikamatsu, the biographies of Yukio Mishima and Sakai Saburo, the diaries of Heian ladies-in-waiting on the bed. My favorites were the autobiographical tales of Osamu Dazai, the heavy-hearted writer who wandered the back roads of Japan struggling to raise the nerve to commit suicide in the Tamagawa River. In return I would send Yoshiko rocks, seashells, and fossils from riverbeds and oceans across America. Sparkling checkered periwinkles and smooth pismo clams from tidepools in Monterey, California. Hideous skeletons of trilobites and dalmanites embedded in sandstone from the Black Hills in the Dakotas. Purple fluorite cubes, emerald-green malachite, sharp clear spears of gypsum from the Utah flats, toast-black slabs of slate from Vermont, tenderly wrapped in love letters.

✿

Dear Yoshiko,

I'm writing this letter during halftime of the Cornell game. Coach Palomino is foaming at the mouth, kicking lockers and shit, screaming like Fay Wray. "This is a must-win game! I know you boys — excuse me, Gunnar, my apologies — I know you men are trying to be winners . . ." Every game is a "must win" game. The *shinos* and the other *coco-jin* (not including Nicholas, of course) are looking shameful and nodding at every word Coach says, like they've done something wrong. Most of these stupid clowns don't even play. I can't understand why they give a fuck. Oh shit, Coach just slapped Isaac Gottlieb for missing a lay-up during the pregame warmup.

Yoshiko, I miss you so much it hurts. *Sabishi kunaru-yo.* I really don't have anyone to talk to. Scoby is losing his mind. Hold on a moment, Coach Palomino is going into the teamwork speech, I don't want to miss this. Two days ago against Dartmouth he pulled down his pants and stroked his penis. "Now I'm going to shoot my wad. Then we'll be on equal terms." Tonight's exhortation looks more conventional — it's the hackneyed "There is no 'I' in team!" speech. There's no 'U' either, but I guess that's immaterial when you're getting paid thousands of dollars to teach young athletes how to navigate the perils of life and hundreds of thousands of dollars to ensure that these same athletes wear a certain brand of sneaker. I still won't wear the shoes. Slick offered me a thousand dollars a game, but I told him to get fucked. He realizes that if he wins, it doesn't matter what shoes I wear. Did I tell you I refuse to stand for the national anthem? Pissed off everybody. I guess Coach has been telling the media I'm a Jehovah's Witness, because during a postgame interview a reporter asked me did I think the United States was in cahoots with Satan. I went into some diatribe on how America is Satan. Some shit about how the United States of America anagrammed was "Foes in death tear. I cum. Taste." The media pretty much leaves me alone now.

All this talk about teamwork and self-sacrifice is making me think about the books you sent me. Mishima said that to reach a level of consciousness that permits one to peek at the divine, one must sacrifice individual idealism. I'm like "Nigger, please." What in hell is the divine? Some bright light with a walking cane and a beard? A state of being so enlightened that you know everything worth knowing? I can pay a drug dealer ten bucks and achieve that level of consciousness, at least for an hour or so. Mishima goes on to say that "only bodies placed under the same circumstance can experience a common suffering . . . Through the suffering of the group the body can reach the height of existence that the individual alone can never attain." I agree, but this "height of existence" trip doesn't have much value on the open market. I think that 6 million gassed Jews, 15 million dead Africans, their lungs filled with saltwater, 436 Champawat Indians eaten by a single tiger in 1907, might agree with me. And what is "the group"? You can't put numbered uniforms on people and say this is "the group" or say everyone born on this side of the fence is "the group." And not everyone experiences pain and suffering in the same way. I can see some masochistic slave fucking up on purpose just for a few precious licks of rawhide.

Speaking of suffering, I think Scoby is going insane. The scrutiny he is undergoing is unbelievable, ten times worse than in high school. What seems like every sportswriter in America, the entire Boston University Philosophy, African-American Studies, Religion, Biology, Mathematics, and Physics Departments, and a horde of German and Japanese scientists are following him twenty-four hours a day. Keeping track of his meals, sleeping habits, shit like that. Once a day some Nobel Prize–winning professor has a press conference to announce a new asinine theory on Nicholas's uncanny ability to put a ball in a basket. The philosophers are easily the most despicable of the lot. I suppose they have the most to lose. Every other scientist can say, "Well, it is at least possible" (they haven't really accepted that he is never, ever going to miss), but Socrates never said nothing about a motherfucker like Scoby. Nick's thrown every theory, every formula, every philosophical dogma out of whack; he's like a living disclaimer. "I am perfection; everything else is bullshit. Your life is meaningless." So the philosophers show up at the games, full of anticipatory schaden-freude, armed with computer printouts calculating the odds of Scoby's missing his next shot. Praying that Nick's next attempt will roll in and out of the rim and the universe will return to normal. Invariably, Scoby goes six for six and leaves them in tears, ripping their papers to shreds and cursing epistemology. They would be a lot better off if they simply called Scoby a god and left it at that, but no way they'll proclaim a skinny black man God.

The scariest part is the team introduction. Silence for everybody except me and Scoby. I'm the preliminary booee — I run out to a smattering of boos, dodge a few paper cups, and try to ignore the catcalls. "Communist sonofabitch. Love it or leave it, you black bastard." Scoby's introduction is communal catharsis. Within moments the court is covered with bananas, coconuts, nooses, headless dolls, and shit. I'm into it, but Scoby gets shook. The few black fans in the house, mostly boosters from the Onyx and the black kids from whatever campus we're at, stand and applaud, but they're quickly shouted down by whites. After Scoby hits his first basket, fights break out; it's sick, there's so much scorn in the world. Usually when you dive into the crowd for a loose ball, the fans try to catch you, help break your fall. When Nick goes headlong in the stands, the reporters scatter, picking up their coffee cups and laptops and letting Scoby crash into the table. They don't even help the nigger to his feet. Assholes. Funny thing happened the other day in Michigan, though. Nicholas was running full-tilt toward the basket and did a swan dive into the crowd for absolutely no reason. His form was perfect; chest out, arms spread, feet together, toes pointed. The fans flew out of harm's way like parking-lot pigeons. In the center of the vacated section stood a small black girl forming a basket with her spindly arms, poised to catch the airborne Scoby. Wouldn't you know it, Scoby landed right on top of her, but she caught his ass. His feet didn't touch down till she lowered him to the ground. The crowd booed her, but it was the first time I'd seen Nick smile in two weeks.

It's not all bad though; sometimes the crowd is on our side. "Our" meaning down with me and Scoby. When we played Columbia, I swear, all of Harlem was in the gym. They were quiet except when one of us scored; they could give less than a care who won. Remember at the Harvard game, black folk from as far away as Peabody and Scituite were in the house. I bet the Harvard kids didn't even know so many niggers existed. It was good to see you in the stands, and hearing you scream, "Take the motherfucker to the hole, Gunnar!" I could feel your eyes on me wherever I went. Did I tell you how mad Coach got when you came to sit next to me on the bench? He thinks it sets a bad example for his best player to hold hands with his wife during the game. Now I pretend you're always there right next to me — Florida, Colorado, wherever. Sometimes if I need to talk to you I'll commit a stupid foul on purpose so Slick will take me out of the game and I'll get a chance to talk to you on the bench. Do you hear me?

Ikaga desu ka? Mai asa nani o shimasu? Asahan ni sakana o tabemasu ka? Senakao sasurishoka? Sometimes I'll be dribbling up-court and I'll hear your voice: "Take that motherfucker to the hole, Gunnar!"

Coach is still rambling on; Scoby is sitting on a stool listening to Sarah Vaughan. That's all he listens to now. I hear you, last time you saw him he was all Bud fucking Powell this, Bud Powell that, what happened to *q* through *u?* I asked him the same thing and he goes, "I ain't missed shit — Quinichette, Rollins, Sanders, Shepp, Silver, Simone, Taylor, and any fools whose names start with *u;* niggers is too sappy. I ain't got time for that free love 'we're all human beings' saccharine jazz." So I ask what's so special about Sarah. "Sarah's not one those tragic niggers white folks like so much. Sarah a nigger's nigger, she be black coffee. Not no mocha peppermint kissy-kissy butter rum do-you-have-any-heroin caffè latte." The boy's crazy. "She be black coffee" — what the fuck does that mean?

Scoby's into the stuff you sent me; at the hotel or on the plane we'll be listening to Sarah and Nicholas will make me read him a Chikamatsu play. Whenever the saké dealer and the loyal courtesan cross the bridge and start looking among the cherry blossoms for a place to kill themselves, Nicholas weeps with the star-crossed lovers. "I know what it feels like to live in a world where you can't live your dreams. I'd rather die too. Why won't they leave us alone? They fuck up your dream. They fuck up your dream." The melodrama goes well with Sarah's sultry-ass voice, though.

I'm beginning to see the sheer casual genius of Chikamatsu writing for the puppet theater. If I blur my eyes I can see the black strings attached to my joints and stretching to the skies. Ah, the freedom of fatalism. Now I can do what the fuck I want and blame it on the puppet-master. *Watakushi wa nodo ga kawakimashita. Biru o ni hon maraimasho.* Nicholas sees the strings, but he spends all his time looking for a pair of scissors. Every now and then the puppet-master hands him a pair of wooden scissors — Charlie Parker, Thelonious Monk, Sarah Vaughan, an open jump shot — and Scoby thinks he's free, thinks he's clipped his strings. The slack string is just a slack string.

I hear the bands starting up — I have to go now. Yoshiko, can you do me a favor? Please make an appointment for Scoby to see someone at the counseling office. I asked the coach to do it, but he thinks if Scoby is averaging nineteen points a game he's fine. We get back next Monday. Thanks. I love you. Here is another handprint in ballpoint-pen ink. Please, rub it over your stomach and give the fetus my love.

The second-best part of the inkprint is that eventually the ink gets all over the basketball and all over everyone else's hands and uniforms. Shit's hilarious. Maybe you should make an appointment for me too. *Aishiteru.* See you soon.

Your husband,
Gunnar

eleven

AFTER THE BASKETBALL season ended, the members of SWAPO and Ambrosia and my publicist from Gatekeeper Press asked me to speak at a rally protesting Boston University's conferment of an honorary degree and a check for one hundred million dollars to M'm'mofo Gottobelezi, the African statesman with all the political foresight of Neville Chamberlain. I was to be the drawing card, the liberal, libertine, and literary nigger stamp of approval. I agreed to speak as long as no one put my grainy mug shot on the fliers.

Things looked different from the dais, behind a microphone, squinting into the spring sun. I was struck by how unaccustomed I was to looking down at people. Growing up in southwest Los Angeles, coming off a season of playing in places known as the Pit and the Hell Hole, I was always at the bottom, the spectacle, the fighting cock looking up. Looking up not out of any sense of great admiration, but because from the bottom there is nowhere else to look. On this earthly stratum we're all dirt; I just happen to be Precambrian dust buried under layers of Cretaceous, Tertiary, and Quaternary snobs. Some things are always on the top shelf, like paper towels in the supermarket.

I stood at the mountaintop, enjoying the view and waiting for my turn to speak. Martin Luther King Jr. Plaza burst with color and protest, an outdoor arboretum where the faces below bloomed like flowers in a meadow. Red and orange revolutionary spring annuals smoked joints, waved signs, and chanted. The yellow and cream-brown daffodils clung stubbornly to their alpaca sweaters and said "Excuse me" when the boisterous Puerto Rican and black townie snapdragons stepped on their Hush Puppies. Communist worker bees with propaganda pollinated minds made penetrable by eighty-degree weather; boom mikes swayed in the breeze like marshland cattails.

"If Boston University persists in lionizing and supporting killers and Uncle Toms like M'm'mofo Gottobelezi, we will not stand idly by and do nothing. This administration's megadollar investment in oligarchical government is . . ." John Brown was trying to fire up the demonstrators. Spittle sprayed from his mouth, his tussled hair hung over one eye, his fist pounded the rostrum. He reminded me so much of Hitler at a Nuremberg party rally that I had to look behind me to check the stage for bunting with swastikas and steamrolled black eagles. "Uncle Toms like Gottobelezi must be . . ." There was that phrase again, "Uncle Tom" — the white liberal euphemism for "nigger." No matter how apropos the label, I always wondered how come there are never any white Uncle Toms. How come the secretary of state is never an Uncle Tom? The director of the CIA is never a traitor to the white race or any other race? Only niggers can be subversives to the cause; everyone else is the "real enemy." As if white folk understand the pressures on the African Bantu, the American nigger, to sell his soul in hopes of being untied from the whipping post.

John Brown said something about unity and looked over at me for confirmation; I spat on the ground, mouthed an obvious "Fuck you," and gazed at the clouds. A silent act of dissension from the keynote speaker not unnoticed by the crowd. John Brown began to falter. He fumbled over his words, and his solidarity rhetoric began to fail him.

The crowd grew edgy and started pushing toward the platform. A middle-aged white man clutching a pen and a copy of my just-published book attempted to scale the platform, grabbing at my ankles: "Mr. Kaufman! Please sign my book — I understand now. I understand." Scoby moved me back, pressed the sole of his shoe against the man's sweaty skull, and booted him off the stage like Walter Slezak kicking the one-legged amputee into the sea in Hitchcock's *Lifeboat*. A white woman protested, exclaiming, "Hey, what about nonviolence?" To which Nicholas replied, "Who said anything about nonviolence?"

John Brown bailed out gracefully with an "I'd like to introduce the next speaker, Dexter Waverly, president of Ambrosia, the black student union." Dexter strode to the podium, pandering to the crowd with stale slogans. "Power to the people!" he said. The crowd snapped back, "Power to the people!" and back and forth they went in a huge game of Simon says.

"Free South Africa!"

"Free South Africa!"

"M'm'mofo Gottobelezi sucks!"

"M'm'mofo Gottobelezi sucks!"

With the crowd roused to a frenzy, Dexter held up my book. "I'd like you to take your copy of Gunnar Kaufman's phenomenal volume of verse, *Watermelanin,* and turn to page 133. Now read aloud with me from 'Dead Niggers Don't Hokum.'"

Every demonstrator from Boston local to university homesteader seemed to have a copy of the book. They read silently to themselves as Dexter read aloud.

> . . . I am the lifelessness of the party,
> the spade who won't put on the lampshade . . .

I couldn't hear the recitation very well because Nicholas was hugging me so tight my vertebrae popped like a string of firecrackers. When he released me, his wet cheek stuck to my face. "I'm proud of you, nigger." I heard my name crackle from the loudspeakers and made my way to the podium. "Now it is with great pride I introduce star athlete, accomplished poet, black man extraordinaire, voice of a nation, Gunnar Kaufman. Remember, America, Boston University, the world is watching."

A camera mounted on a crane swung down and bobbed in my face like a giant metal hummingbird. I looked directly into the lens. "Don't do that," the cameraperson whispered. I continued to look directly into the lens. When I was seven years old, my favorite television personality was Transient Tammy. Sporting patchwork overalls and a floppy hat, Transient Tammy welcomed me home after school with a hearty "Howdy, vagrants." Before introducing the last cartoon, she'd put on a pair of enormous sunglasses. These magic glasses gave Transient Tammy the power to see her bummy friends in television-land. She'd steal toward the camera, dirty knees bursting through her jeans. "I see Suzette in Arcadia, Ingrid in Alhambra, Anthony in Inglewood." I peered into the camera, looking for my mom and Psycho Loco in Hillside, my father, but I didn't see anyone, just my wall-eyed reflection in the lens.

The applause died down, leaving a hum in the air, and I nervously cleared my throat. I wanted to address the crowd like a seasoned revolutionary, open with a smooth activist adage, "There's an old Chinese saying . . . ," but I didn't know any Chinese sayings, old or new. My hesitancy grew embarrassing. Yoshiko waddled over and ran my hand over the circumference of her bloated belly. I rubbed and smiled but still said nothing. I thought, *If I were down there down among the mob, what would I want to hear?*

Scoby broke the silence, shouting, "Thus do I ever make my fool my purse." I laughed. The gathering laughed because I laughed. I decided I'd want to hear candor.

In the middle of the throng stood a commemorative sculpture. A slightly abstract cast-iron flock of birds in memory of Martin Luther King, Jr., who received his doctorate in theology from Boston University. "Do you see that sculpture?" I asked, pointing to this commissioned piece of artwork, which did not dedicate a small piece of the earth and time to Reverend King so much as it took partial credit for his success. "Notice them steel birds are migrating south — that's BU's way of telling you they don't want you here." The black people began to elbow their way to the front. I was speaking to the Negroes, but the white folks were listening in, their ears pressed to my breast, listening to my heart. "Who knows what it says on the plaque at the base of the sculpture?" No one spoke. "You motherfuckers pass by that ugly-ass sculpture every day. You hang your coats on it, open beer bottles on it, meet your hot Friday night dates there, now here you are talking about freedom this and whitey putting-shit-in-the-game that and you don't even know what the plaque says? Shit could say *'Sieg Heil! Kill All Niggers! Auslander Raus!'* for all you know, stupid motherfuckers. African-Americans, my ass. Middle minorities caught between racial polarities, please. Caring, class-conscious progressive crackers, shit. Selfish apathetic humans like everybody else."

The crowd gave a resounding roar of approval. Here I was denigrating them and the people urged me forward. Candor, I reminded myself, candor.

"Now I'm not going to front, act like the first thing I did when I got to Boston University was proceed directly to the Martin Luther King Memorial and see what the goddamn plaque says. Only reason I know what it says is that I was coming out of Taco Bell on my way to basketball practice when I dropped my burrito deluxe at the base of the monument. When I bent down to wipe the three zesty cheeses, refried beans, and secret hot sauce off my sneakers, I saw what the plaque said. It says, 'If a man hasn't discovered something he will dic for, he isn't fit to live. Martin Luther King, Jr.' How many of you motherfuckers are ready to die for black rule in South Africa — and I mean black rule, not black superintendence?"

Yells and whistles shot through the air.

"You lying motherfuckers. I talked to Harriet Velakazi, the ANC lieutenant you heard speak earlier, and *she's* willing to die for South Africa. She don't give a fuck about King's sexist language, she ready to kill her daddy and if need be kill her mama for South Africa. Now don't get me wrong, I want them niggers to get theirs, but I am not willing to die for South Africa, and you ain't either."

The audience hushed, their Good Samaritan opportunism checkmated. There was nothing they could say. "I'm willing to die for South Africa, where do I sign"?

I rubbed my tired eyes, licked my lips, and leaned into the microphone. "So I asked myself, what am I willing to die for? The day when white people treat me with respect and see my life as equally valuable to theirs? No, I ain't willing to die for that, because if they don't know that by now, then they ain't never going to know it. Matter of fact, I ain't ready to die for anything, so I guess I'm just not fit to live. In other words, I'm just ready to die. I'm just ready to die."

I realized I'd made a public suicide pact with myself and stole a glance toward Scoby and Yoshiko. Scoby was nodding his head in agreement, while Yoshiko was pointing to her stomach and yelling, "What the fuck are you talking about?"

I swallowed and continued. "That's why today's black leadership isn't worth shit, these telegenic niggers not willing to die. Back in the old days, if someone spoke up against the white man, he or she was willing to die. Today's housebroken niggers travel the country talking themselves hoarse about barbarous white devils, knowing that those devils aren't going to send them to a black hell. And if Uncle Sam even lights a fire under their asses, they backtrack in front of the media — 'What I meant to say was . . . The quote was taken out of context . . .' What we need is some new leaders. Leaders who won't apostatize like cowards. Some niggers who are ready to die!"

The crowd's response startled me. "You! You! You!" they chanted, pointing their fingers in the air, proclaiming me king of the blacks.

Seizing the moment, Dexter Waverly snatched the microphone, put a warm arm around my shoulder. "Our new black leader, Gunnar

Kaufman." All I could think was *What, no scepter? Don't I at least get a scepter?*

The next morning the annoyingly perky hosts of *Good Morning, America* and its sister shows around the globe — *Buenas Dias, Venezuela, Guten Morgen, Deutschland,* among others — took over my living room, asking questions from leather swivel chairs.

"Buon giorno, Italia. Signore Kaufman, did you know that during last night's reception for M'm'mofo Gottobelezi, Dexter Waverly killed himself in the college president's office?"

"No."

"Si, si, he held a knife to his throat and demanded that President Filbey rip up the hundred-million-dollar check and spit in Gottobelezi's champagne or he'd slash his throat."

"And what happened?"

"Filbey ripped up the check and spit in the Zulu's champagne. Signore Waverly apologized for the interruption, read a death poem dedicated to you, then plunged the knife into his throat."

"Wow."

"Don't you feel responsible, Signore Kaufman? After all, it was your speech that inspired Signore Waverly."

"I don't know. What did the poem say?"

> *Death Poem for Gunnar Kaufman*
>
> Abandoning all concern
> my larynx bobs,
> enlightenment is a bitch.

"That's not a bad poem. But I don't feel responsible for anything anyone else does. I have enough trouble being responsible for myself. Besides, it looks like Dexter's death prevented one hundred million dollars from being deposited in the National Party's coffers."

"Bonjour, France. Monsieur Kaufman, but what about your endorsement of freedom through suicide?"

"My suicide, no one else's."

"Yes, but people are following your example. There are reports of black people killing themselves indiscriminately across the United States. Don't you have anything to say?"

"Yes, send me your death poems."

"*Hyuää huomenta, Finland.* Mr. Kaufman, isn't suicide a way of saying that you've — that black people have given up? Surrendered unconditionally to the racial status quo?"

"That's the Western idea of suicide — the sense of the defeated self. 'Oh, the dysfunctional people couldn't adjust to our great system, so they killed themselves.' Now when a patriotic American — a soldier, for example — jumps on a grenade to save his buddies, that's the ultimate sacrifice. They drape a flag on your coffin, play taps, and your mama gets a Congressional Medal of Honor to put on the mantelpiece."

"So you see yourself as a hero?"

"No. It is as Mishima once said: 'Sometimes hara-kiri makes you win.' I just want to win one time."

"Last laugh?"

"I don't see anyone laughing."

"This is *Namasté, India.* And when do you plan to commit suicide, Mr. Kaufman?"

"When I'm good and goddamn ready."

twelve

DURING THE READING PERIOD before finals, Scoby's behavior became increasingly bizarre. The school psychologist's diagnosis was acute homesickness, and she recommended that Nick move in with Yoshiko and me. At first I too thought he missed the old neighborhood. Scoby tried to recreate Los Angeles in Boston. He plastered most of the walls at school with poems torn from my book. He planted palm trees along Commonwealth Avenue, got run out of Roxbury when he tried to pay some Puerto Ricans to act Mexican for a day. He brought home exhaust from the public buses, which he'd bottled in five-gallon water containers, and released the noxious gases in the apartment. We took day trips to gloomy Revere Beach, sitting under the concrete veranda, complaining about the sun's setting behind us. "Gunnar, I hate this place. Everything is ass-backward out here, man. Here we are in May, fully clothed at a beach with no waves. The best pro basketball player in the city's history is white. The women like meek niggers. People eat thick soup, drink green beer. The cops are fat. The fire trucks are green. If I see one more fucking shamrock . . . It's getting so bad I thought I saw a leprechaun near the river the other day."

The obvious solution was for Nicholas to go home, but there was no home for him to go to; the man in the mauve suit had returned and convinced his mother to sell the house and travel the country, skating in an old-timer roller derby league. My mom offered to put him up, but he was too proud.

He often called himself the forty-eighth ronin. Nicholas Scoby was a masterless samurai who missed out on the revenge at Kira's castle in the winter of 1702 and the mass seppuku two weeks later. "Gunnar, what would the forty-eighth ronin do if he was stuck out here in

Boston, Massachusetts, home of the frappe and the grinder, masterless and alone?"

"He would kneel at the end of the Freedom Trail and stick a sword in his belly."

"Exactly. Gunnar?"

"Yeah."

"You serious about this whole death trip, winning by straight taking yourself out?"

"I guess so. I meant everything I said, but that don't mean shit, you know. Don't mean I'm right, wrong. The poems, the magazine interviews are just words, man. I'm just saying, Look, I'm outta here, all you motherfuckers who act like you give a shit — stop me, you care so much."

"To kill yourself you don't need a permit or anything like that, do you?"

"Naw, I don't think so."

Nick stared past the coastline, and my eyes followed his. The only thing barely visible in the foggy night was Boston's pathetic skyline. The top of the glassy Hancock Building poked through a cloudbank that covered its lower floors in a vapory trenchcoat.

"Tallest building in Boston, right?"

"Fifty some-odd stories, the Sunday brunch from the top supposed to be the move. You can see to Newfoundland or some shit."

"They don't have no nighttime dinner thing?"

"Nope. Closed up."

"What's the second tallest building?"

"The Prudential Building, but I think BU's law school is the third."

"Can you get in there at night?"

"Yeah, during finals week the law library is open all night."

We finished our beers, arguing over the finiteness of music. I rationalized that there are only so many notes and therefore only so many combinations of notes, so it stood to reason that there are only so many songs.

Scoby stood up, preparing to leave, wrapping his belongings in a towel. "Look, cuz, you not accounting for time. Time is what makes music infinite. *Bip, bip, bap, tid, dit, tap* is different from *bipbip baaaaaap . . . tid daaat tap.* See, if Charlie Parker had played Dixie, it would be like colorizing *Birth of a Nation*. It'd be a different tune but the same tune. You dig? You'd be hearing it differently and its meaning would change. Because a musician has they own sense of time and experience of time. For Parker, time was a bitch. He wouldn't play Dixie as no happy-go-lucky darkie anthem. He'd play it as a 'I'm mad and I *know* them cotton-picking niggers was mad,' piss-on-their-graves dirge. You follow? That's why your poems can never be no more than descriptions of life. The page is finite. Once you put the words down on paper, you've fossilized your thought. Bugs in amber, nigger. But music is life itself. Music is time. Played live, played at seventy-eight rpms, thirty-three and a third, backwards, looped, whatever. There's no need for translation. You understand or you don't."

Scoby gave me a shake and a hug and left the beach, leaving his cassette player on my towel. I put the headphones on and drank beer, listening to Sarah Vaughan until the batteries started dying. Her voice slowed and garbled, deepened and faltered. I took a sip of beer and gurgled it in my throat. The sound was inside out, between my ears instead of outside them. Nothing was making sense. On the train home I wrote a reminder to myself to return the cassette player in the morning, then jotted down notes for a poem.

Dixie/"I wish I was in the land o' cotton,
old time dar am not forgotten —
look away, look away, look away, Dixieland."

Is this song/tune/anthem inherently racist?
How in the hell do I know the words to this shit?

If "Dixie" is racist, what makes it so? The title, the lyrics, the historical context, the fact the South lost the war? If the lyrics were outlawed, banned forever, would the music, that gnawing fucking refrain, the sequence of notes themselves, be racist instrumental? Is opera classist? Does the letter *r* discriminate against Bostonians?

Haaaymaahket Square next stap. Chainge heah fa de Ahhbor-way. The Bahston Transit Authawity thanks you for yourah patronage.

Early the next morning Coach Palomino woke me up and handed me a rubber camping flashlight. He told me that Nicholas had jumped off the roof of the law school. A custodian found him in the courtyard; he'd landed on his side, curled in a fetal position, one arm twisted behind him so violently the tips of his fingers touched the crown of his head. The rubber flashlight was in the bushes nearby. The suicide note was on the roof, taped to a case of Carta Blanca.

✻

To my dearest nigger Gunnar Kaufman,

I've just climbed nineteen flights of stairs lugging a case of beers and whistling "Dixie." I shouldn't, but I blame you. Sitting on this ledge, my feet dangling in midair, two hundred feet off the ground, I find my thoughts going back to Tokubei, the soy sauce dealer, and the unbelievably codependent courtesan Ohatsu in Chikamatsu's *Love Suicides at Sonezaki,* the doomed lovers under the fronds of a palm tree binding their wrists, preparing for noble deaths.

I'm on my feet now, looking down into the cloudy quadrangle, my toes hanging ten into the void. I can feel hands on my back, gently pushing. It's funny I want to write a poem.

i step into the void
bravely,
aaa
  aa
   a
   a
  ahhhhh

Not bad for an amateur. Before I go, I forgot to tell you the reason the bartenders wrap napkins around the beer bottles is so clumsy fools like yourself won't drop them. You know the glass gets slippery, the condensation — never mind. These brews are for you. I asked your mom to send them from home so we could celebrate the publication of your book. Cheers. Think of me.

G.K., tell Yoshiko and Psycho Loco I'll miss them. If there's a great beyond, I'll see you all when you get there. Homes, there's a cloudbank floating this way. Dude, I can see the halo around my head, but I'm no angel. I'm ghost, the afterlife is just a lay-up away.

Late,
Nicholas Scoby

✻

That night I leaned out over the ledge of the law school's roof and poured off the top of my beer. The liquid splattering on the ground made me wonder what Scoby's body had sounded like when it hit the pavement. It was a hazy night, just like the previous one. A thick cloud of fog surrounded the building. I placed the flashlight on the ventilator behind me and stood on the edge. I could see my silhouette on the surface of the cloud below. I looked like gray smoke; it was a low-budget Brocken specter, and without the halo, the glory. I folded the note into a paper airplane and watched it spiral into the fog like a weightless kamikaze diving out of the sun. The next morning the letter was on the front page of the late edition of every paper in the country.

When Yoshiko and I landed in Los Angeles the following week, an army of reporters besieged us outside the terminal. Psycho Loco sped up to the curb, stretched out over the front seat of his car, one hand on the steering wheel, the other popping open the passenger door. I didn't know Toyota made a Dunkirk rescue dinghy.

"Psycho Loco, like a motherfucker."

"Where to, my liege?"

"Home."

"Can't go home. LAPD wants to speak to your ass. You like Hannibal in this hole."

"Beach, then — it'll be like closure."

Psycho Loco and Yoshiko sat in the front seat. I sat in the back and put my hand on the dent in the upholstery where Nicholas should have been. I caught Psycho Loco's eye in the rearview mirror.

"Shit fucked up, right?"

"Isn't it always. How his mother?"

"She broke up, like everybody else. Went back to Mexico after the funeral though, something about a match against the Jalisco Jaquecas.

You know, in a lot of ways, Scoby was Hillside. Nobody from the neighborhood ain't never come up like y'all. You two the first."

I pressed Psycho Loco to stop, but he waved me off, insisting that I quit with the false modesty. I needed to hear what he had to say.

"We used to watch you and Scobe bust niggers' asses on television every weekend. Cuz, clowns who dropped out of school in the eighth grade sporting Boston University sweatshirts and shit. Then your book came out. Oh man, we went berserk. Nobody would read it at first. Too scared. I just carried it everywhere I went, proud as hell, throwing it in people faces. 'You better buy this book. Compralo, ese. My boy wrote this, so next time I see you, best to have it on you.' Fools bought your shit too, because I was your number-one publicist in the 'hood. Gave your shit street credibility."

"Right."

"Then one day we was kicking it at Reynier Park, lounging, you know how we do. I just pulled the book out and started reading it aloud. Read the shit cover to cover, twice. Who was there? Me, Hi-Life, Pookie of course, Shamu, L'il Annie Borden, buncha heads, everybody crying. Niggers was happy, but upset at the same time, you know. Then the rally. Nicholas. Nobody asked why, we just understood. Peep my new tattoo."

Psycho Loco held out his right arm for me to examine. On his wrist was a tattooed watch. The face of the watch was an exact likeness of a smiling Nick. In cursive letters along the edge of the thick black band was "Nick Scoby, a nigger who always knew what time it was."

I lay down in the back seat and let the car's motion and the who's who of neighborhood gossip rock me to sleep. I dreamed I was in a squad of black kamikaze pilots. We were ambivalent about the kamikaze label because we thought "divine wind" sounded like a fart that smelled like perfume. We flew planes constructed of balsawood and powered by rubber bands that you twisted before takeoff by turning red plastic propellors. I flew thousands of missions, all failures, because I always came back alive. I crashed into the sides of oil tankers toting fifty-gallon drums of nitroglycerine and swam back to shore, unscathed save for a pair of singed eyebrows. I divebombed the Pentagon, a bucket of turpentine and gasoline between my legs, a grenade in each hand, a methane-farting cow strapped to my back, and firework sparklers clenched heroically in my teeth. Nothing. In

Paul Beatty

shame I walked away from the flaming polygon and caught a bus back to headquarters. In disgrace I became the only kamikaze pilot ever to receive a promotion. Every night I sprinted down the tarmac toward my waiting balsawood plane, hoping tonight would be my last mission.

The numbing cold of a beer can pressed against my temple woke me up. A twelve-pack of reminiscing later, night had fallen, and Psycho Loco was ready to get down to the nitty-gritty. "So when you going to die?" he asked. I'd heard that tone in his voice before; it was the same sarcastic timbre he had used when he goaded Buzzard into shooting a rookie Harlem Globetrotter, who in botching the confetti-in-the-water-bucket trick had accidentally doused Buzzard with water. No one can instigate like Psycho Loco. "You know, Gunnar, for all that shit you talk about killing yourself, you really ain't the suicidal type. Masochistic, yes, suicidal no. So when you going to it, suicide-boy?"

I bored the beer can into the sand and stood up ramrod straight. "Sir, right now, sir, I will kill myself now, sir! Right face, huuh!" Calling my own cadence, I goosestepped toward the ocean while Yoshiko beat out a drum march on her skintight belly and Psycho Loco whistled "The Battle Hymn of the Republic." They thought I was kidding, but when I was thirty yards from shore, splitting waves with my forehead, I heard Psycho Loco yelling for help.

It's very hard for a strong swimmer to drown on purpose. Once my feet no longer touched the sea floor, I felt myself instinctively floating toward the surface, thinking about catching one last wave. Palms up, I flapped my arms and forced myself to submerge into the depths. The ocean was very dark. I curled into a tight tuck and let the tide bob and roll me around like an undersea tumbleweed. The muffled roar of the waves rolling overhead was comforting, and I popped my thumb in my mouth, pretending I was an embryo suspended in amniotic fluid. I began to hear Yoshiko in the shower, talking to our child as she scrubbed her stomach. Telling the child how crazy its parents were. How we were waiting for its birth so we could rent a motor home and drive to Brazil and have a baptism in the rushing waters of the Amazon. *What the fuck,* I thought, *it took Osamu Dazai three or four times to get this suicide thing right.* I swam back to shore, surfacing yards south of Psycho Loco and Yoshiko, knee-deep in the water and screaming at the horizon.

"Gunnar, you come back here and be a father to your child, you sonofabitch. My mother warned me. She said, 'If you marry a Negro hoodlum, he'll impregnate you and leave you for a white girl.' You better not be out there fucking no mermaid."

Psycho Loco dropped to his knees, pounding the surf with his fists. "I loved him. I loved him."

I crept up behind the distraught mourners. "Boo."

They jumped out of their skins, happy to see me alive and pissed off that I wasn't dead.

"Motherfucker! I knew you couldn't do it."

"You didn't know shit. You thought I was in Atlantis by now. Wipe your face, you big baby."

Yoshiko crossed her arms and grudgingly brushed the sand off my face. "You okay?"

"Yeah, except for the mermaid scales on my dick."

Yoshiko hit me in the stomach so hard she scraped her knuckles on my spine. They made me drive home.

It was two in the morning when we arrived in Hillside, and I looked for my mother on every corner, examining every liquor store clique for her tight-lipped smile. Glanced at every passing car looking for a gray-haired woman hunched over the steering wheel, wiping the windshield with her forearm and cursing the defogger. On Robertson Boulevard, near the car wash, the outline of what looked to be an old Bonneville came sailing down the hill with its headlights off. Always the courteous driver, I flicked our lights off and on. In a panic, Psycho Loco drew his gun, opened his door, and leapt out of the car. The Bonneville turned on its headlights and sailed past with a honk of appreciation. Psycho Loco climbed back into the front seat and put a relieved hand to his still rapidly beating heart.

"Shit. Motherfucker, are you crazy?"

"What? I just flashed the headlights. You the one flying through streets with the greatest of ease."

"Ghost Town been driving around the 'hood with their head-lights off."

"So?"

"It's an initiation. They creep around with no lights and some gangbanger apprentice in the back seat has to shoot the first fool who flashes their headlights."

It was good to be home.

Because of the police stakeout at my house, Yoshiko and I checked in at the La Cienega Motor Lodge and Laundromat. Toting our luggage, we elbowed our way through the passel of giggly prom couples tossing their room keys to the night clerk as they headed for the parking lot, smoothing their dresses and spit-cleaning the stains on their tuxedos. We liked the cheap American coziness of our new home, Suite 206. I swept insect carcasses, chicken bones, and dust balls into neat piles while Yoshiko sat at the rickety kitchen table shellacking the backs of live roaches with nail polish and giving them color-coded names: a coat of Sea Urchin Hyacinth for Walter, Sugar-Cone Browntium for Abigail, and Lullaby Lilac for Tatsuo. There was a scream from the room next door. Moments later a radio ad for the La Cienega Motor Lodge and Laundromat came on the combination TV/radio — "We'll leave the light on for ya" — to which Yoshiko added, "So the burglars think you're home."

We were under constant surveillance, so we didn't go out much except to buy beer and TV dinners. During the day we'd open the creaky windows and eavesdrop on the rehab meetings in the community center next door. The crackheads and heroin addicts engaged in acrimonious debate over who constituted the lowest life form. "Ah nigger, don't lie. I seen you lick a dog's dick for five dollars, then when the niggers only gave you three, you offered to fuck the telephone pole. So what I share needles with pus-covered faggots. I am a pus-covered faggot, motherfucker. Or hadn't you noticed?"

Yoshiko and I engaged in our own great debates. I was Du Bois arguing vociferously for a continuation of our comprehensive over-priced Ivy League educations. I suggested that we attend each Ivy League school for one semester, gleaning the best bullshit from the best bullshitters, and emerge as learned scholars prepared to unravel the intricacies of the world or at least work as Wall Street market analysts. Yoshiko was Booker T. Washington fighting passionately for a more proletarian edification, one involving a practicum in the crafts and technical vocations. And what better tutelage than that offered by America's renowned correspondence colleges? Waving our grades from Boston University, four-point-ohs for each of us on account of Scoby's suicide, Yoshiko asked, "Don't you want to earn your way? Aren't you tired of having things handed to you on a silver platter, black man?"

"You're kidding, right?"

"Of course. Look, it'll be fun. Besides, fuck all that snow."

So we enrolled at Redwood State, a college located in a post office box in the hinterlands of Chicago, Illinois. In two months' time I received a bachelor's degree in earth auguries with an emphasis in meteorology, star-gazing, and horse-race analysis. Yoshiko quadruple-majored in jet engine mechanics, urban forestry, auctioneering for fun and profit, and three-card monte.

Between exams we read the stacks of death poems and obituaries that arrived in the afternoon mail.

CARLTON MALTHUS

Carlton Malthus, thirty-one-year-old brewmeister at the Cascades Malts microbrewery, located in Klamath Falls, Oregon, drank himself to death yesterday in Piss Shivers, a tavern in downtown Klamath Falls. Malthus entered the bar and ordered a Crater Lake Blue, the popular sparkling blue pilsner that he developed. He was refused service and then forcibly removed from the establishment for what one bar patron characterized as being "too black to appreciate 'the Blue.'" Returning with a keg of Crater Lake Blue, Malthus vowed to drink until his eyes turned blue or he was given a stool at the bar. Sticking the tap spout in his mouth, he drank continuously for five hours, emptying the ten-gallon keg. Removing the tap, he wrote a short poem, loudly eructated, and died. Malthus is survived by his wife Julie, son Barley, and daughter Ethanol. The poem he wrote moments before his death is below.

> This drunken belch
> leaves the last bitter
> taste of life in my mouth.

CAROL YANCY

Ms. Yancy died when she impaled herself with a turkey thermometer after the checkout clerk at Buy 'n' Buy Supermarket refused to place the change in her hand. After a lengthy argument with store management, Ms. Yancy, ignor-

ing the store's no-smoking policy, lit a cigarette, then stabbed
herself in the frozen foods section. Age ninety-four years.

> Both cheeks caved in with age,
> I pull on a Newport menthol
> one last time.

FALASHA NOONAN

Ms. Noonan, distinguished pianist and leader of the world-fa-
mous free jazz big band Infernal Racket, gathered her band
members for one last rehearsal. During a piano solo, she
scribbled this poem on her sheet music, then leaned into the
strings and smashed the piano lid on her head. Age fifty-five
years.

> Having annotated the sunset
> I double-time to heaven,
> talking whiskey and waltz with Monk.

MERVA KILGORE

Ms. Kilgore, a prolific writer from Philadelphia, published
seventeen volumes of poetry, including her most highly re-
garded work, *Ancestral Hogwash: Songs and Slurs for My
No-Account Daddy.* Ms. Kilgore was giving a poetry reading
at an elementary school in the Philadelphia suburbs when the
school's white principal asked if she'd mind singing "one of
those old Negro spirituals." Hearing this, Ms. Kilgore recited
the poem below, then, with her hand in the water pitcher, bit
through the microphone cord, electrocuting herself. She was
sixty-nine years old.

> Imagine this poem
> is cluttered with references to obscure
> figures of Greek mythology,
> antique birchwood bureaus,
> and a quaint New England bed-and-breakfast;
> then send it to *The New Yorker*

✤

At night Yoshiko and I made soapsud sculptures in the heart-shaped Jacuzzi or wrote critiques of the free porno movies. Sometimes we'd have Psycho Loco drive us to cafés in the Venice and Wilshire districts for the multicultural poetry scene. Packed with mostly white poetry devotees fawning over poets of color, the readings were ribald contests where the audience judged the poetry for political correctness, the amount of white guilt evoked, and sexual bawdiness. All the poets received belittling introductions equating them to canonical bards: "Next up is UFO, the Unbelievable Funky One, or as we like to call him, the Flying Chaucer."

One night a poet known as Kwasi Moto, the Hunch in the Back of Your Mind, read a poem entitled "Uncle Sam I Am." The Dr. Seussesque ballad was an account of how the poet's rough upbringing was responsible for transmogrifying him into a red, white, and blue animal that raped white women and hunted down "nigras and Messicans."

> Uncle Sam I am,
> do you like black niggers and white chicks named Pam?
>
> Yes, I could beat a nigger in the park,
> and eat a pussy in the dark.
>
> Would you stab a Mexican in a tree
> and blame the ghetto on TV?

Psycho Loco looked on in amazement and loudly remarked, "I know they ain't paying this motherfucker for this phony bullshit," then unabashedly placed his silvery nine-millimeter on the table with a heavy thunk. The poet, visibly shaken, began to rush his lines and rattle his text.

> Because of the Anglo-Saxon
> I've no time for relaxin'
> shooting jigaboos and honkies named Sue
> for satisfaction.

Unable to take any more cutthroat drivel, Psycho Loco snatched his gun, walked up to the poet, and stuck the barrel into his ear canal. "You so bad, *read*, you buster-ass mark!"

Paul Beatty

In a sobbing fit, the poor bard continued.

Uncle Sam I am,
scared of no man,
white, black, Klan, or tan.

By the end of the poem, Kwasi Moto had shriveled to the floor, groveling and begging Psycho Loco not to shoot him. Freeing himself from the poet's clutches with a jackbooted kick to the head, Psycho Loco leaned into the poet's bloodied face. "You know what's wrong with you? Your line breaks are all fucked up." With a self-satisfied smirk, Psycho Loco returned to his seat and scanned the stunned crowd. "Well, who's next? On with the goddamn show. Gunnar, you want a beer?"

"Yeah."

"And somebody get my nigger another beer."

Yoshiko laughed for two days straight, but mostly she and I stayed at home listening to the real L.A. street soldiers receive radio therapy.

Station KQBK Sidewalk Talk recognize caller . . . This is Wilfredo from Pacoima . . . I want to say . . . I want to say . . . I've killed, and been killed, entiendes? But leaving mis vatos, it's hard, ese . . . Kamila Parks aka K-Down . . . I'm tired of these triflin' niggers . . . These mens today don't respect theyselves, much less anyone else . . . Hey, yo Lace Love the Mad Body Slammer on the check-in . . . I'm calling to defend myself against the false accusations and prefabrications of the previous caller . . . I respect all womens of the world . . . So I hit the ho once or twice, y' know, no big deal . . . Waddup, I'm Flip-out the Filipino Str-8 Player Baller from Artesia . . . I wanna say more attention needs to be paid to Asian gangsterism . . . The missionary school system be fronting on a yellow brother . . . They ain't out to teach nobody nothing . . . Thanks to our guests . . . Father Glenn Fernandez, Dr. Stacy Ortiz, and ex-banger now community activist Chino "Ojo Negro" Aquadilla, this your host, Ras Vroom Vroom Nkrumah, signing off, and remember, all peoples of color need to come together and en español "color no equal dolor" . . .

We chased sleep, our limbs interlocked under the Lysol-scented quilts, our fingertips playfully hiking up and down our bodies, trying to ignore the fold-out bed's pointy prongs and rib cage–jarring metal bars by whispering potential names for the baby: Jessica, Aldo, Althea, Rosie, Hiroko, Marc, Doreen, Dallas, Octavia, Hiroshi, Joaquim, Corinthian, Marpessa, Sunday, Mamadou, Quo Vadis . . .

On a Tuesday night late in her last trimester Yoshiko had her first craving: animal crackers (only giraffes, bears, and tigers), a blueberry slushie, and salted soybeans. Not too bad. I threw on some clothes and went out into the neon-lit night. Wary of being out alone and on foot, I decided to take the back streets to the 7-Eleven, which was a good two miles away. I darted past the ice machine and eased onto Arroyo Drive, hoping Yoshiko wouldn't mind if I substituted pumpkin seeds for the soybeans, which would be impossible to find in the middle of the ghetto at one-thirty in the morning.

Ten minutes into my mission I heard the sound of helicopter blades churning the hot air. *Niggers must be fucking up,* I thought, remembering the fun we used to have outwitting the police copters by crawling underneath parked cars until we reached safety. I turned onto Whitworth Avenue and suddenly found myself engulfed in a blinding waterfall of blue-white light. Instinctively, my hands shot above my head as I waited for the standard drill — "Face down on the ground, hands behind your head, ankles crossed. Move!" But no instructions were forthcoming. I waited a minute or two and looked for a police cruiser; nothing. No beat cops, only the helicopter hovering overhead and me standing in a fifty-foot circle of light, becoming more appreciative of the moon. What the fuck?

I slowly eased down the street, and the tractor beam kept me at its center. If I moved two feet to the left, the spotlight moved two feet to the left, as if I were wearing a luminous Victorian whalebone dress that hula-hooped around my hips. I entered the 7-Eleven bathed in the eerie extraterrestrial light, and the clerk backed off a bit. I further terrorized him with a robotic "Take me to your leader," and he shot out the back door. Gathering what I came for, I poured myself a blueberry slushie, left a five-dollar bill on the counter, and walked back to the motel.

Yoshiko asked why her slushie was so warm and I told her about being followed by the police helicopter. She rolled her eyes. I motioned for her to follow me. Outside, we stood in the middle of Arroyo and waited in the dark. Nothing happened and Yoshiko grew impatient, sipping on her tepid slushie and whining, "What? What?"

Paul Beatty

"Wait a minute. You hear that?"

I cupped my ears and in the distance could hear the rotor blades. Then a loud click and we were standing in the world's biggest spotlight.

"Cool." Yoshiko smiled and handed me the lions and rhinos from the box of animal crackers. We sat at the bus stop, chewing off the ears of shortbread circus animals and enacting an urban version of *Waiting for Godot*.

"You're sure you don't mind the pumpkin seeds?"

"That depends. Do you want to grow carrots?"

"Do we need carrots?"

"Yes, carrots are good."

"Good as gold."

"There's nothing better than a good smoke."

"Phlegm."

"Now there was a professional."

And so on until the helicopter peeled away with the dawn.

✿

Yoshiko and I took midnight strolls through Hillside, our path lit by the huge flashlight in the sky. Yoshiko liked to pretend she was a newly discovered blues musician fresh from the Mississippi Delta cotton fields, on her first major tour. "Newport 1961." She didn't sing; she introduced herself, the band, and the song. "My name is Lipless Citrus Lime, and dese heah boys is the Dickless Wonders. We gonna play a country blues called, 'We Gonna Play a Country Blues.'" She would close her eyes and hum and moan for about a minute, then bow to the invisible crowd, basking in the spotlight, saying, "Thank ye, thank ye" for another ten minutes. Once a week or so she'd march through the neighborhood carrying a sign updating the status of the baby. "When am I due? Five more days. Come to the natural birthing of the child. Reynier Park — free admission if you bring a clean towel."

Sometimes Psycho Loco would join us on our walks, dispensing his opinions with every swallow of his Carta Blanca. "What kind of black man would let his wife give birth in the park?"

"You know, I think she's doing it as a way of replacing Scoby. Giving something back to the community."

At first the light (and maybe Yoshiko's odd behavior and Psycho Loco's presence) scared everyone away. We'd come strolling down the street, lit up like circus clowns under the big top, and the crowd would scatter like kitchen roaches. Eventually, emboldened by our regularity, folks joined us in the circle, and invariably they stared straight into the light source. "Don't look directly into it, you'll go blind."

We induced labor, making love with the purple and gold dusk beaming through the grimy motel windows. I carried Yoshiko down the stairs and propped her in a wheelchair I'd stolen from the hospital and wheeled her through the streets of Hillside. It was like a one-float parade. Yoshiko's sign read "When am I due? Now. Come to Reynier Park. Admission free if you don't say, 'Oh, look at all the blood,'" and she waved weakly at the people who lined the streets, shaking hands with those who came to the wheelchair to bestow flowers. The searchlight seemed especially bright that warm Friday night.

When we arrived at the park, the neighborhood welcomed Yoshiko with a huge ovation. The stoical Gun Totin' Hooligans provided security, Manny and Sally Montoya supplied clean towels and rubber gloves from the barbershop, and Ms. Kim brought refreshments from her new store. My mom was the midwife, and her obstetric skills were in evidence as she led Yoshiko to a small section of grass turned into a birthing theme park. There my mother had constructed an outdoor maternity ward out of tarpaulins, beanbags, and throw pillows. Next to this was a small bathing pool and a table lined with shiny medical supplies: sutures, scissors, a clamp, and a cellular phone in case of emergency.

Yoshiko undressed and slipped into the pool, flopping around with each twinge of labor pain as my mom checked her blood pressure and timed the contractions. The locals filed by, shouting encouragement and wishing Yoshiko luck. After a few hours it was time; Yoshiko clambered onto the cushy mountain and squatted on the ridge of beanbags. My job was to massage her feet, feed her salted soybeans, and wipe her down with cold sponges. When my mother commanded her to push, Yoshiko looked me in the eye and squeezed my biceps to mush. I returned her gaze, trying to think of something reassuring to say, but all that came out was "Beautiful, beautiful."

Yoshiko stopped grimacing, and my mother placed a slimy guck-covered infant on her chest. It laid its teeny head on her breast; the mother smiled, and the baby made a gargoyle face that I called a smile. Naomi Katsu Kaufman was welcomed into the world with kisses.

Paul Beatty

There was cheering, the blasts of car horns, and bottle rockets bursting in the night sky. A box of cigars attached to a small parachute landed next to the newborn. The card read, "Congratulations from the Los Angeles Police Department. Maybe this one will grow up with a respect for authority." I couldn't be sure, but it looked like my father's hand.

I lit a stogie and put an arm around my wife and child. "Ewwww. She looks like the Creature from the Black Lagoon."

"*Gunnar.*"

"I'm just saying."

My mom put a cereal bowl in my hands and shoved me into the hallowed junction of Yoshiko's spread legs.

"Squat."

I did as ordered, hunkered in front of my wife's swollen vulva and gently kissed her bloody perineum, and awaited the afterbirth. "Ma, this is fucked up. You know, this is my favorite cereal bowl." Yoshiko reached between her legs and condescendingly patted my forehead. The placenta dropped into the bowl, a quivering bloody mass of now useless organ. Someone in the crowd asked when we were going to do this again. I answered, "Next week" and lifted the pulpy organ in the direction of the officers in the helicopter. "Thus behold the only thing mightier than yourself."

Yoshiko laughed and said, "*Roots*, right? Come over here and cut the cord, then give me a beer and a kiss."

✿

Every Friday night we held outdoor open mikes, called the Black Bacchanalian MiseryFests, under the LAPD's simple but effective stage lighting. We jerryrigged a sound system using car stereos loud enough to drown out the noise from the helicopter. I was the emcee, Yoshiko the stage manager, and Psycho Loco did everything else. The shows lasted all night, and the neighborhood players read poetry, held car shows, sang, danced, ad-libbed harangues about everything from why there are no Latino baseball umpires to the practicality of sustaining human life on Mars. Sometimes troupes of children simply counted to a hundred for hours at a time.

Every week there was at least one hour of Community Stigmas. Community Stigmas was a loosely run part of the MiseryFest where the neighborhood's stigmatized groups got a chance to *kvetch* and defend their actions to the rest of the neighborhood. I'd call the registered voters to the stage to explain why they bothered, request that all the welfare cheats step forward and share their fraudulent scams, ask the panhandlers to say what they really thought of their spare-change benefactors, offer fifty dollars to any Muslim who'd eat a fatty slab of bacon. The most poignant nights were the ones when the recovered addicts stepped into the light to soak up the warm applause and address the crowd. "I want to thank all my cool outs who stood by me, but mostly I want to thank self for not giving up on self." Then I'd ask all the current users to step up into the ring of light and speak out. The bold users would swagger into the circle, smoking their pipes, needles dangling from their arms, playing up to the boos like villainous wrestlers. The invitations weren't always voluntarily accepted, and a few reluctant baseheads would be forced into the spotlight by disgruntled friends and family. No one could leave until he'd said something, anything from "I promise on my grandmama's grave to stop" to "I don't give a fuck. I'll smoke till white people have feelings." The drug dealers also got their say. Every third Friday we'd have Psycho's Analysis, where Psycho Loco conducted these heartwrenching gangbanger tribunals. Some hoodlums would volunteer to bare their souls. They'd sit on wooden stools, speaking thoughtfully into microphones, unburdening themselves like war criminals, black gunny-sacks stretched over the heads of the wanted ones to prevent the police from using an overhead skycam to identify them.

Soon the Bacchanalian MiseryFests became gala events; colored folks from all over Los Angeles crashed Hillside to take part in the spectacle. To ensure that the Friday nights didn't turn into a trendy happening for whities bold enough to spelunk into the depths of the ghetto, Psycho Loco stationed armed guards at the gate to keep out the blue-eyed soulsters. Questioning anyone who looked to be of Caucasian descent, the sentries showed those of dubious ancestry a photograph of a radial-tire-colored black man, then asked, "What's darker than this man's face?" Anyone who didn't answer "His butt" or "His nipples" didn't get in.

The networks caught wind of the MiseryFest's popularity and

offered a bundle of money for the rights to broadcast weekly installments. We accepted the best offer and divvied it up among all the
households in Hillside, and the television station agreed to the following conditions.

- Build the Reynier Park Amphitheater and pay for its main-
  tenance.
- Build huge video screens throughout the neighborhood.
- Use only colored camerapersons and support staff.
- All broadcasts must be live and unedited.
- Stay the fuck out of the way.

The next scheduled broadcast was on the two-year anniversary of
Scoby's death. There were widespread rumors that I would use the
national forum to immolate myself Buddhist-monk style and skewer
my daughter Naomi on a barbecue spit rotating over my pyre. Niggers
jammed the theater and filled the streets of Hillside to pay their last
respects. Television expected the rest of the bloodthirsty world to tune
in for the first live broadcast of a suicide.

The fest opened with an hour of silence followed by a parade of
local residents declaring their undying love for Nicholas, most of the
tearful reminiscences starting with "I remember when that nigger
wasn't but about yea big . . ." But it was my show — I was his best
friend, obliged to use the belles-lettres to fortify Scoby's status as a
sainted martyr.

I opened with a powerful two-hour raga-ode to Nicholas entitled
"Barrio Bangladesh," throughout which the audience rocked in their
seats, wailing with my rhythmic recitation. When I finished, I looked
into twenty thousand faces in stone silence. The audience was anes-
thetized, unable to move. A review of the night's festivities stated that
the poem brought every listener in the house to "the zenith of com-
prehension. Not since the New Testament has the death of morality
been so eloquently eulogized." I announced my next poem, "Give Me
Liberty or Give Me Crib Death." After I read the last few stanzas —

Remorse lies
not in the consciousness
of a murderous parent

who rocks a child born into slavery
to divine sleep
with jugular lullaby
sung by sharp blade

and suffocating love
applied with pillow and pressure

Remorse lies
in the slave owner's anguished cries
upon discovering
his property permanently damaged;
a bloody hieroglyph carved into flesh
the smiling lips swollen and blue with asphyxiation

after he calculates his losses
forecasts the impact on this year's crop
he will notice the textual eyes of murder/suicide
read "caveat emptor"
let the buyer beware

— Hillside erupted. Niggers lost their fucking minds. When the huz-
zas reached their climax, I prepared for my encore, a small sacrifice
and show of appreciation to Nick Scoby, to any niggers who cared.

I launched into a solemn monologue explaining how through
painstaking research I'd unearthed proof that President Truman's
threat to drop a third atomic bomb on Japan was not, as he later
claimed, merely an idle boast to intimidate the Land of the Rising
Sun into a speedy surrender. Elongated cries of disbelief rang out from
the bleachers: "Noooo." "Yessssss," I replied, holding up photos of
grinning Manhattan Project scientists casually leaning and squatting
around three bombs, Fat Man, Little Boy, and the newly discovered
Svelte Guy, each with cute slogans like "Flatten Japan" and "Sorry for
stepping on your toe, Joe" chalked on the metallic hull. "You may pass
these photographs around. I have the negatives."

As the photos circulated through the audience, I produced a white
handkerchief and a shiny carving knife from my back pocket and
placed them on the rostrum. Carefully smoothing the hanky out
toward the corners, I issued a challenge to the United States govern-

Paul Beatty

ment. "When I was a child, my dad — before he left us, the fuck —
whenever I did something wrong, he used to say, 'I brought you into
this world and I'll take you out.' Well, Big Daddy, Uncle Sam, oh
Great White Father, you brought me here, so I'm asking you to take
me out. Finish the job. Pass the ultimate death penalty. Authorize the
carrying out of directive 1609, 'Kill All Niggers.' Don't let Svelte Guy
lie dormant in the basement of the Smithsonian. Drop the bomb.
Drop the bomb on me! Drop the bomb on Hillside!"

I placed the pinky of my right hand on the handkerchief. With my
left hand I picked up the knife and sterilized it with a couple of passes
over my pants leg. Before someone could ask, "What the hell are you
doing?" I brought the knife down over my finger and hacked it off
with one strike.

I'd prepared myself for the pain, but I wasn't ready for the
amplified sound that pounded out of the monitors. One hundred
thousand crunching watts of stainless steel cleaving through bone
followed by the solid *kachunk* of the knife into the mahogany lectern,
followed by my gasp, the audience's gasp, and my deep inhalation in
shock. The first thing I heard was the familiar voice of Coach Shimimoto yelling from the front row, "Suck it up, Kaufman!"

I reeled for a moment, then meticulously wrapped the speckled
red-and-white handkerchief around the severed finger, exactly as I'd
seen Robert Mitchum do in some American yakuza movie. Staring at
the space where my finger used to be, I held my hand high above my
head. The blood ran down my arm, and what didn't pool in my armpit
puddled next to my sneakers. I lowered my head, then exited stage
left, the soles of my blood-soaked shoes sticking to the floorboards as
if I were walking in yesterday's spilled soda.

❁

That night cemented my status as savior of the blacks. The distraught
minions interpreted my masochistic act as sincerity, the media as
lunacy. The more I tried to deny my ascendency, the more beloved I
became. Spiteful black folk and likeminded others from across the
nation continue to immigrate to Hillside, seeking mass martyrdom.
They refurbish the abandoned houses and erect tent cities on the
vacant lots, transforming the neighborhood into a hospice.

The government's reluctant confirmation of the existence of Svelte

Guy spurred a massive letter-writing campaign asking the government not to waste the uranium and to test the antiquated A-bomb by dropping it on "those ungrateful passive-aggressive L.A. niggers." Ignoring the Japanese claim of dibs to the bomb as a keepsake of war, Congress passed a motion to quell our insurrection by issuing an ultimatum: rejoin the rest of America or celebrate Kwanzaa in hell. The response was to paint white concentric circles on the roofs of the neighborhood, so that from the air Hillside looks like one big target, with La Cienega Motor Lodge and Laundromat as the fifty-point bull's-eye.

epilogue

IT'S BEEN A LOVELY five hundred years, but it's time to go. We're abandoning this sinking ship America, lightening its load by tossing our histories overboard, jettisoning the present, and drydocking our future. Black America has relinquished its needs in a world where expectations are illusion, has refused to develop ideals and mores in a society that applies principles without principle.

Past movements in the black struggle seem to have had the staying power of an asthmatic marathoner with no sense of direction, so I suppose as movements go, this one is better than most. No more pleading for our promised forty acres and a mule only to have some hayseed Dixiecrat respond, "These people wouldn't know a switchback from a switchblade." No futile attempts at organization. No "Help fold, staple, and label" parties. No one asks for donations. You never hear words and phrases such as "grass roots," "mobilize," "subcommittee," "Who has the phone tree?" and "COINTELPRO" bandied about with counterinsurgent smugness. Best of all, in my humble opinion, I'm not the type of leader to promote self-help and self-love with put-downs and vituperation. You'll never hear me say, "Scientology is a gutter religion." I didn't satiate our sweet-tooth cravings for respect and vengeance like a Sunday-school teacher rewarding good behavior with Uncle Tom White Chocolate, Sneaky Hebrew Butterscotch, and Empowerment Peppermints.

> Who can take a rainbow, drop it in a sigh,
> soak it in the sun and make a groovy lemon pie?
> The candy man, the candy man can.

Mostly I stay at home, Suite 206, the La Cienega Motor Lodge and Laundromat, bathing Naomi while Yoshiko and my mother watch Zatoichi movies, the blind swordsman plowing through his unlucky foes like a wheat thresher. Sometimes Psycho Loco comes to visit, wearing his silver radiation suit, just in case the feds decide to annihilate us ahead of schedule. I dip Naomi in the Jacuzzi and rub baby oil into the creases in her arms, and my best friend and I talk, death-row prisoner to visitor.

"You know, Gunnar, with all this suicidal madness, you taking the easy way out. Why don't you fight back? Go out like a hero. Dirt on your face, guns blazing."

"Psycho Loco, everyone who's ever challenged you, what have you done to 'em?"

"I waxed that ass."

"So it's useless for an enemy to challenge you, right?"

"Si, claro."

"Might as well kill myself, right? Why give you the satisfaction. The trippy part is that when you really think about it, me and America aren't even enemies. I'm the horse pulling the stagecoach, the donkey in the levee who's stumbled in the mud and come up lame. You may love me, but I'm tired of thrashing around in the muck and not getting anywhere, so put a nigger out his misery."

I pile the suds high on Naomi's head like a wobbly Ku Klux Klan hood and tell her the Kaufman history. I begin with the end — Rölf Kaufman, her grandfather, my dad, who died last week. The only officer in the history of the Los Angeles Police Department to commit suicide by eating his gun, choking on the firing pin and leaving the following poem in his locker.

> Like the good Reverend King
> I too "have a dream,"
> but when I wake up
> I forget it and
> remember I'm running late for work.

Paul Beatty